PRAISE FOR
The Nest

"Mary Flinn realistically captures the ideals of an empty nest filled with rekindling passions of soon-to-retire Cherie and her rock-and-roll-loving husband Dave – then flips it all over when Hope, the jilted daughter, returns to the nest to heal her broken heart. Between her mother's comical hot flashes that only women of a certain age could appreciate, the loss of her laid-back father's sales job, and the good news-bad news of other family members' lives, can Hope find the courage to spread her wings and leave the nest again? Flinn's deft handling of story-telling through both Cherie and Hope's voices will send readers on a tremendously satisfying and wild flight back to *The Nest.*"

~Laura S. Wharton, author of the award-winning novels
***Leaving Lukens, The Pirate's Bastard,* and others**

"With *The Nest*, author Mary Flinn's fiction borders closely on reality as she explores how a downturn in the economy causes one family to experience crisis. But Flinn also has impeccable comedic timing; just as the crisis looks like it will take a tragic turn, a gut-bursting laugh is in store for the reader. Put together all these elements and ultimately, you have a story that reaffirm the values that are truly important to Flinn's characters—and all of us."

~Tyler R. Tichelaar, Ph.D.
and award-winning author of *The Best Place*

"Mary Flinn's latest novel, *The Nest,* is another must-read. Savor each delicious word of this novel as it will keep you enthralled until the satisfying end."

~Donna Small, author of
Just Between Friends and A Ripple in the Water

"Mary Flinn's *The Nest* is a story about friendships, relationships, and family. The connection Cherie has with her fellow teachers, Hope's journey through breakups and falling in love, and the daily ups, downs, happy, and sad times Cherie's family experiences, will make you both shake with laughter and pause to wipe away a tear as you reminisce about your own past."

~Kimberly B. Pendry , Thomasville, NC

the Nest

A Novel

MARY FLINN

For my family

ACKNOWLEDGMENTS

As always, so many people are helpful whenever I write a story in which I need assistance with the details. I owe my sincere thanks to several people who helped me out, whether it was describing a wedding gown, giving advice on a medical issue, giving details of a particular business, or the timely and involved task of reading my manuscript and giving feedback. Thanks respectively to Margaret Kinlaw of Diva Bridals, to Dr. Robert Ehinger, of Eagle Family Medicine, to Guy Morrison and Landon Wilder of The Shrimp Connection. Thanks to Heather Allen of Capital H. Creative, Inc. for her insightful knowledge of art management, and to Wendi McMillan and Suzanne Carlson for their travel notes. Deep appreciation for their time and advice to Laura Wharton, good friend, sounding board, and author of *The Pirate's Bastard*, and *Leaving Lukens*, to Kim Pendry, my new book club friend and fellow teacher, and to Donna Small, author of *A Ripple In the Water* and *Just Between Friends* for reading my manuscript. Thanks to the High Country Writers and the Watauga County Public Library for their excellent writers' workshop in the spring of 2013, and all of their efforts to promote North Carolina writers. Thank you to photography mentor, longtime friend, and partner-in-crime Mimi Skerett Williams for taking my author photograph, and for helping me with the cover photos. Thanks to Frankie Todt for modeling for us. You are both beautiful women, from either side of the camera!

Thanks to teachers everywhere. I was blessed, having had some of the best. You have the most important job there is, outside of motherhood, and we don't show you nearly the appreciation you deserve.

In each book, many of my favorite songs inspire the themes and ideas from which my characters are developed and my plots are built, creating an instant soundtrack in my head. Without the following songs, *The Nest* would not have taken the road it did: "We Are Never Getting Back Together" by Taylor Swift, "Love Like Crazy" by Tim James and Doug Johnson, and sung by Lee Brice, "No Hurry" by Zac Brown, "Hey Pretty Girl" by Kip Moore, "Bless the Broken Road" by Marcus Hummon, Jeff Hanna, and Bobby Boyd, performed by Rascal Flatts, and the songs mentioned in Dave's backyard band rehearsal. I hope you will listen and enjoy the lyrics.

Thanks also to Shiloh Schroeder of Fusion Creative Works for making another beautiful book. It is always a pleasure and a reassurance to know my dreams are in such competent hands. And to my editor and proofreader, Dr. Tyler R. Tichelaar, you are a prince. Thank you for your endless patience, wit, advice, and indulgence as I continue learning my trade from your marvelous expertise. You are always right. But this time I think I was able to teach you a thing or two, like how often a bathroom should be cleaned!

Thanks to the small independent bookstores everywhere, bloggers, and websites that have graciously taken up the cause of promoting local authors. And to my readers, you are the reason I continue writing. Your encouragement is phenomenal!

Most importantly, I offer deep heart-felt gratitude to my family, Mike, Jessica, and Shelby. You are all wonderful, smart, funny, loving, and goal-driven independent people who continue dreaming with me and tolerate my weird imagination. I love you all more than you will ever know. It's a blessing having each of you in my life!

Chapter 1

CHERIE

It's Valentine's Day, I remembered thinking this morning, fanning my face and walking in my red robe and slippers into the frigid relief of my dark garage. I'm at that age when being a hot woman has "a whole 'nother meaning," as we say in the South. When a woman can have her own private summer on a twenty-degree North Carolina morning in February, she knows the true meaning of a *hot mess*. My husband and my daughters, on the other hand, merely believe I've become prone to exaggeration, and possibly even a bit senile, when I get so distracted by the prickly heat under my blouse that I lose all train of thought. Alas! They'll never know the extent of my malaise. Well, eventually, my girls will get it, but it will be far beyond the point when I will care about their sympathy. It was this heat on this winter morning that led me to the greatest embarrassment of my middle-aged life…so far. I would have no idea that this particular incident on this particular morning would begin the unraveling of my nest.

Rowdy, our four-year-old black lab, greets me at the door, as I knew he would, ready to be let out to use the grass and then eat, or eat and then be let out, as he is such a big pig. He licks the toes of my slippers, forever unable to resist the bunny ears. The girls gave me these years ago for my birthday, which happened to fall on Easter that year, and they've been my wardrobe staple since then.

"Hold on, Rowdy!" I say to him, filling his bowl with the recommended amount of dog food. Dave and I have him on a diet, as duck hunting season is over and Rowdy is no longer in need of excess body fat to keep him warm, swimming to retrieve Dave's ducks, which were mighty scarce this year. Before I can blink, the food is gone and Rowdy is circling at the side door of the garage, so I open it and he is out like a shot.

Can it be normal to sweat *everywhere?* I think to myself, feeling a little rivulet of perspiration run down my chest; I hate to say *exactly* where. I can almost feel the beads appearing around my ribcage where I will eventually have to put clothes on. Right now, I am so hot that I cannot fathom getting dressed, as I swipe the back of my neck under my hair, which has just endured the hairdryer that started all this, I think, removing my robe and hanging it on Rowdy's leash hook on the wall.

I never know what causes my body to heat up the way it does. Was it just the hairdryer, or stressing over all I've got to do today at school? The February cold on my bare skin feels divine. What the hell is an *Edmodo?* I guess I will find out this afternoon. What administrator in his right mind holds a training workshop on Valentine's Day for God's sake? This new curriculum is about to suck the life out of all of us, and for the technologically baffled, it makes me flash just thinking about it. I laugh at myself, wandering around the garage stark naked, well, except for the bunny slippers, but at 6:00 a.m., *who is going to see me?*

Dave is dead to the world, after getting in from the airport later than expected last night, due to flight delays between Chicago and Raleigh. And then there was the hour-and-a-half drive home after that. He didn't even bring his bag in, I notice, peeking through his car window at his golf clubs, boxes upon boxes of athletic shoes, and ah, yes, there is his carry-on bag. The door bangs shut, effectively precluding Rowdy from returning to the garage. I don't want him outside barking at the kids who'll soon be waiting for the school bus, so I turn to walk over to the door, when the mudroom door opens and Dave hits the garage door button. The light comes on, the garage door begins to rise, and before I can make it to the wall to grab my robe, Rowdy has returned under the rising door, wagging his tail furiously, and lodging himself between me and Dave's car, just in time for the newspaper delivery man to drive by our house! I know this because I hear the familiar thud of the paper landing on the end of the driveway, in tandem with my scream and Dave's shout.

It sounds something like this: *Thud!* "*Oh my God, Dave/Cherie!*" I cannot get around the damn dog fast enough to get out of the way, and the newspaperman's car engine can be heard clearly idling at the foot of our driveway. My husband begins to laugh as I squeeze shut my eyes, hoping somehow that it will make me invisible, bending over and shoving my eighty-five-pound dog out of the way so I can retrieve my robe and restore some sense of decency to this bad omen of a morning.

Now clothed, I whirl around to see the car pulling slowly forward, and mutter, "The show's over, *perv!*" under my breath, while Dave is doubled over, his laughter caught before he could even get his breath to let it out. His face is contorted in a ridiculous grimace, and there is no sound coming from his mouth as tears stream down his face. As I push past him in a huff to the safety of my kitchen, he regains his breath.

"Ohhh! Wow! What the hell are you doing, Cherie, parading around the garage in nothing but your personality?"

"Shut up, Dave. Why'd you hit the button if you saw me there?"

"I *didn't* see you, baby! But Harold Snelling sure did!" he laughs again, as the tears and the posture return. "I didn't know where you were. I came to look for you and I remembered that I left my bag in the boot."

I shove past him in a huff to the safety of my kitchen.

"The *boot*? You're *British* now?"

"Aw! Don't be mad. I've been with Andrew McCarty for three days; you know, the sales rep from New Zealand? He says stuff like that all the time and I guess I just picked up on it," he says, going to the fridge for creamer while I remove our coffee cups from the cabinet. It's like a dance, our morning routine, and we rarely step on each other's toes. (I was planning to invent intravenous coffee to drip into one's veins upon waking up, but I hadn't gotten around to that yet. The automatic start is as close as we've been able to come.)

"Oh. Yeah. How was your trade show, by the way?" I ask, fanning myself, wondering whether hot coffee would serve me well at the moment.

Dave hesitates and looks at me, the lewd grin gone momentarily. "Brutal, as I'd expected. Three days on my feet and the flight from hell getting home. I'm getting too old for this shit." But then he says gently, with his usual flirty twinkle, "Oh, Happy Valentine's Day!"

I have to smile then. His black and silver hair is standing up in points all around his head, making him look a little like a porcupine; however, a cute one at that.

"Thank you. And the same to you!" I say, giving him a chaste kiss since he has yet to brush his teeth. He strokes his matching black and silver goatee and grins at me again.

"By the way, you sure looked good out there, you know?"

I groan. I am round and short, and suddenly, I realize the glow of my alabaster skin under the light of our garage would have looked anything but *good*. But my husband has a knack for charming me, and everyone else for that matter, which makes him the successful salesman he is.

"Ha! Ten more pounds to go," I say, running a hand over my chubby hip, "and *good* might be a word I'd consider."

"Me too," he says, grabbing a hunk of his stomach through his T-shirt to commiserate with me. "Make mine a double; I have twenty pounds to go!" More charming. "Who needs a six pack when you can have the whole keg?"

I hand him his coffee, laughing like one of the guys, which I think is why he likes me.

He turns to go to our bedroom.

"Didn't you forget your suitcase?" I ask, my organizational skills bubbling over, and at this early hour, confounding even me.

"Oh, shoot, yeah," he says, snapping his fingers, circling back to the mudroom and out the door to the garage.

Finally, I have cooled down enough to dress and reapply the makeup that has melted off, but the phone rings as I attempt to leave our kitchen. Glancing at the caller ID, I notice it is our twenty-six-year-old daughter, Hope, calling. Unusual; 6:20 a.m. is not an hour she normally sees…

"Hey, Punkin'!" I coo into the phone, trying to convey hope that nothing is wrong, but my heart sinks at the sound of her voice, immediately leading me to believe she's been in an accident.

"Mom," her quavery voice breaks into a sob, leaving her as unable to continue as her father was just moments ago, but this time, it is not from laughter.

"Honey! What *is* it?" I breathe into the phone as Dave bumps back through the door with his suitcase, questions in his eyes at seeing the expression on my face. "Are you okay? Have you had an accident? Where are you?"

Openmouthed, Dave and I stand still as statues while I punch the button for the speaker phone and she tries to collect herself.

"Oh, Mom!" she sobs, "Liam and I broke up!" I try to process this while there is more sobbing from her end.

"Ohhh! Honey, I'm so sorry!" I coo again, sincerity weighing down my voice. I have to turn away since Dave is fist-pumping the air and jumping up and down as if the Braves have just hit a grand slam.

Oh, for God's sake! I mouth back at him before asking her, "What in the world has happened?" and remembering so many conversations with Hope that ended with me saying, *You can always move back home*, knowing this day would come sooner or later, but still!

Dave is hanging on for every word, no doubt ready to rip Liam to shreds at the next opportunity. And I can't blame him. As good as this news is for Hope in the grand scheme of her life, I know Dave wants to kill Liam for hurting her. It's hard parenting adult children who've made unwise decisions. Sometimes you just have to be ready to pick up their pieces.

"He's leaving…" she heaves. "He's going to Italy to paint."

"He told you that?"

"No! I found out from his Facebook page. I'll tell you about it tonight. I want to come home. After work today. Is that okay?"

Dave's eyes grow large as he circles his lips, giving me a wary look.

"Of course, honey. What time will you be here?"

"Around six. I'm packing now. I'm going to my friend Jessica's now to shower, but I'm outta here. I haven't slept all night. I should have left last night, but I didn't want to wake you and Daddy."

"Oh! It's okay. I'll see you this evening."

"Okay."

"Okay," I say to her and look at Dave's conflicted face. "We'll both see you then. Are you okay?"

"Yeah," she heaves again.

"Okay…well, bye, honey. I love you."

"I love you, too, Mama."

I push the button, ending the call as Dave puts his hand on his hip. "Well, shit!" he says.

"Shit," I agree.

"Can't say we didn't see that one coming."

"No, but I hate to see her so hurt like this…again." This, after her broken wedding engagement right after college, must leave her feeling devastated.

"He told her before he wasn't going to be tied down, you know, for his art."

"I know, but still, she's hurting. Damn, I'd go to Italy," I say, crossing my arms over my chest.

"Well, it seems she wasn't invited."

"Hmm. I wonder what the whole story is. I guess we'll hear about it tonight."

"Yeah, well, about tonight. I wanted to surprise you, but I got us reservations at Bimini's."

"Bimini's…" I murmur.

"Yeah, ironic, isn't it?"

Bimini's is our favorite seafood restaurant, and ironically, it is one of the places in town that sports a Liam Ferguson mural of a Caribbean harbor at sunset, a pretty amazing mural for a casual place like that. Anyway, Bimini's does have the best seafood in town, thanks to Dave's best friend, Jeff, the owner. There is always a crowd.

"Huh. I guess she might not feel like going with us."

I twist my mouth. "Maybe not." I run fingers through my mess of curls and shake them to cool me down. It takes so little to get me heated up, but Hope's call has turned on my burners again. "Well, I need to go and get dressed. It's going to be a late day. I hope I get home by six. What time are the reservations?"

"7:30," he says.

"Wow, Dave, you must have planned well in advance!" I say, batting my eyes, honestly surprised and delighted. He isn't usually this prepared! He must have called days in advance to get reservations on Valentine's Day. I wonder whether I'll get flowers. *That* never happens in this house.

"I do love you, you know?" He taps my nose and kisses me before giving my derriere a little squeeze as I turn to go back to the bedroom.

"I love you, too."

My colleagues are hanging on each word as I tell this story at lunch. Since all of us are English teachers at the local high school, we are constantly trying to outdo one another with our storytelling. Their previous tears of laughter from the garage part of the story are dry now, as these wonderful bachelor friends of mine are reacting, solemnly and appropriately, to the part about Hope's breakup with Liam while I lick the last of the yogurt off my spoon with an effective flourish.

"Oh God, that is so sad!" says Taylor Kimbrough, the tenth grade English teacher and debate team advisor. I almost see tears of sadness in his eyes, and his cherubic, from-another-era face is stricken with this news of Hope, whom he has come to love vicariously, having never laid eyes on her. As always, he is riveted to whatever I might say, which is slightly unnerving, but I attribute his rapt attention to the fact that he is such a young first year teacher and I am a last year teacher, retiring after thirty years of service in June. It's not that he holds me in any reverence, I think; instead, he searches for the increasing number of commonalities and insecurities that we both share, which must be highly reassuring for him. I, on the other hand, am too giddy with anticipation to care. If I haven't become a good role model by now, he is shit out of luck!

"I *know!*" I say, watching Walt Hurley smile politely, paying Hope his condolences with a mere nod. He has come to love her, too, although he hasn't seen her in a couple of years. I know that eventually some profound piece of advice or supportive comment will come forth, a moment I truly need and expect from him. That is why he has been my friend for the better part of a decade. At forty, he is sixteen years younger than I am, and neatly, Taylor is sixteen years younger than Walt. We are only missing Audrey Brown today, who is out of town for some mysterious reason. I think her husband has whisked her away for some Valentine's fun. She is between Walt and me in age, with her oldest child, a college freshman, out of her nest, and one of my closest friends as well.

"Do you think he's leaving her for a *man?*" Taylor asks, aghast, as he takes a large and suggestive bite of his banana. He is the only one of us who, according to him, is allowed to eat bananas in his presence; nonetheless, I turn my head at this provocation. Were she present, Audrey would be having a field day with Taylor's choice of fruit, using it as an opportunity to goad him and start a fracas.

I ponder his question for less than a second. "Uh, no. I really don't believe Liam could be gay."

"And that, madam, is a darn shame, from the pictures I've seen of him!" he says with a grin, which prompts an indulgent smile from Walt. The poor man could give a course in restraint and tact, neither of which Taylor exhibits when he is with us back here in the English department office. He does well to conceal his sexual preference, comments, and opinions from his students and their parents, so it is natural that he should let it rip with us at lunch.

"Now, I would hardly think that he's your type!"

"Oh, but opposites do attract!" he says, winking at me. "But seriously, Cher, when you retire, you should write a book. You know, about all of your experiences with your children and that insane man you live with!"

"I know, and don't think I haven't thought about it."

"You should write it and Walt can help you publish it."

"I'd be honored, and relieved," says Walt, taking a bite of his turkey sandwich. The man never sleeps, with teaching by day, and running his editing business from home in his down time. I don't know how he functions.

"What are you working on now, Walt?"

He crosses his eyes. "Another business book. They all say the same thing, just a new spin on the thread-bare clichés on which we've all cut our teeth."

"So you need a good novel to amuse you, don't you, Mr. Hurley?"

"Yes, Ms. Johnson, it would be a vast improvement over my latest fare."

"So what's stopping you, Ms. Johnson?" asks Taylor, egging me on. "You've got the empty nest at home with both of your daughters gone, and your husband traveling all over Christendom. You could start right now. What's holding you up?"

As I think about the story I would write, which would result in my murder by one or all of my family members, because, of course, the book would be all about us, my cell phone mercifully rings and both men roll their eyes. Letting my finger drift upward, as I have seen on TV, I say, "*I have to take this*. It's daughter number two." Walt sniggers; he hates cell phones and all they imply about being indispensable.

"Wesley! God bless her!" Taylor says, throwing his eyes to the ceiling and crossing himself.

"Hey! What's up?"

"Oh, Mama! I just heard about Hope and Liam!" her usually cheery voice is aptly woeful.

"I know! What did she tell *you*?"

"Not much, but she sounded really upset. I'm coming home for the weekend after my last class tomorrow so I can hear the scoop, and you know, be the supportive sister."

"Well, I'm sure she will appreciate your coming. Have you heard from Ren today?" I ask, smiling, knowing full well that Warren Reynolds Henry, Jr. will make her Valentine's Day all that it should be, even from Austin, Texas.

"Yeah…he called earlier and wanted to know where I was. I'm working at the hospital today until 7 p.m. so what else is new, right?" she says, sounding as if stifling a yawn.

"Oh! I'll bet he wants to know where to send your flowers! I guess he's really missing you, huh?"

"Yeah…. It's our first Valentine's Day apart, but it's not a big deal. It was nice to talk to him," she says, making me glad she does not overdramatize her life. Ren had the good fortune to land a job at Apple after graduation last year, so I'd say twenty-two year old Wesley has good reason to be patient. "Anyway, I'll be glad to get home. Since I'm the lowly nursing assistant who's working tonight, I have the weekend off when the other girls are on duty."

"Well, good. We'll all be glad to see you," I say, ready to wrap up the conversation since my friends are looking bored. I want to ask more about her grades and how nursing school is going, but there will be time for that when we talk face to face. "Let us know when you hit the road."

"Mama, Greensboro's just a little more than an hour from Chapel Hill."

"Still…I won't rest until I know you're safely home!"

""kay. Love you! Tell Daddy hey!"

""kay! Love you, too! Bye, Sweetie!"

And then Walt makes the pronouncement I knew would be inevitable.

"It looks as though your flock is returning to the nest for the weekend! And mother bird is back to work again," he says, smiling his patient smile, but something makes me want to smack him.

Chapter 2

HOPE

I am sitting in my parents' driveway…again. *God!* This is the last freaking place on the planet I want to be right now. Anybody want to know what failure looks like? Just look inside this car. I sat here two years ago, after my fiancé and I broke off our engagement due to irreconcilable differences. I was a basket case then, and sat here in a pool of tears that day. Things do change. I'm surprised I'm not crying anymore. There's nothing left after this morning. I've done well to hold it together all day at the boutique. Nothing like immersing myself in gorgeous clothes to make me forget the latest douche bag in my life. Still, it is unbelievably hard to realize that at twenty-six years old, I am starting all over again. Each time, it seems harder and harder to pick myself up again. *What is wrong with me?* Is this torture ever going to stop?

Since the economy crashed four years ago in 2008, I have lost the job I was trained for, teaching art in an elementary school. I am forced to work in retail stores and to bartend to make ends meet. I am in debt up to my eyeballs, and every man to whom I have ever been attracted has been cursed. With what, I'm not sure. Me, maybe?

I close my eyes and lean my head back against the headrest, remembering the ashen look on Liam's face. How caught off-guard he'd been when he walked in and saw me looking at his tablet last night. He'd left his Facebook message open, as if inviting me to look. Was he such a pussy that he had to let me find out that way, not able to tell me himself? That big, 6' 3", hot, hunk of a man who's beguiled me for over a year has turned out to have no balls whatsoever.

Such fabulous news, Liam! Of course you can stay here! Can't wait to have you all to myself in Tuscany! It will be like old times. Let me know when you will arrive. You will be so happy here! Ciao!

Big smiley face.

Some girl named Amelia, (now *my* Facebook friend so I can keep tabs on her) with whom he'd gone to grad school, was already cleaning her bathroom and changing the sheets in joyful anticipation of his arrival. Ironically, she kind of looks like me, too, long dark hair but with brown eyes. Nowhere near as original as I am, but good-looking enough to lure him away from me. Who am I kidding? Anybody who lives in Italy would be lure enough, no matter what she looked like, but she *was* attractive. Whatever history they obviously shared in a previous life is also unknown to me. What can I offer him that could possibly compete with life in Tuscany anyway? Last night, we'd slept together one last time, but this time, there was no amazing sex. Not that either of us slept; he held me all night, out of guilt, probably, but I wanted nothing further from him. My phone is ringing. It's Caitlin from Natty Greene's calling me back.

"Hope?"

"Hey, Caitlin. I wanted to tell you I'm free tonight, after all. Need any help in the bar?"

"Hope, what's wrong? You sound drained."

"It's nothing. But I can come in if you need me."

"We've got a full crew on tonight. I think we've got it covered."

"Okay. Well, if it gets to be more than they can handle, just call me. I'm available."

"You and Liam have a fight?"

"You could say that. Just call me, okay?"

"Okay, hon. Take care. Will we see you tomorrow night?"

"Yeah. You can schedule me as much as you want from now on."

"Okay. I'll see you tomorrow."

"Bye."

I end the call and look up at the window of my house. My nice, warm, sweet house. The front porch looks so inviting, with Mama's dark green striped cushions on the black wrought iron bench and rocking chair. In the spring, her perennials will be in bloom. There is not much landscaping, but it is pleasing and it suits my parents' busy schedules. My mother is looking discreetly out the window. I can see her curly blond ponytail whip around as she darts away so I won't see her watching. I wonder if she knows I've been sitting here for ten minutes. If she says I told you so, I will kill her. But she would be right. Still, I just don't want a lot of drama. My parents aren't like some; they leave you alone. Hovering has never been their style, but when your kids are fuck-ups, you need to take notice at some point. Could they have kept any of this from happening? Nope. Did I listen to them? Hell no. I'm sure she is wondering, *where did we go wrong?* I relish the thought of dissolving unnoticed into my wonderful bed and going to sleep for days. I'm sure my parents are going out; after all, it is Valentine's Day, and even my dad won't forget, I hope. I did remind him, after all. I'm exhausted.

Mama's head appears again, so I sigh and heave my shoulder against the door, making myself emerge from my Civic. We all drive Civics in this family, except for my dad, who has a Honda Pilot that's large enough to carry all his samples and take us on vacation. For my dad, it's all about the gas mileage. We all wear the same brand of athletic shoes too, since he's been Puma's sales rep for over twelve years.

The door swings open and I am in my mother's welcoming arms. She is wearing a red satin shirt and her hair is a mess of curls, caught casually in the back, the way she usually wears it. I am taller and more slender than she. Right now her soft body feels like heaven as she sweeps me into the comfort of our home. She smells like home; a mix of her shampoo and school books. I know she will have tea for me. I hate to have to tell her the saga, and then to drop the news on her that I know she won't want to hear.

Chapter 3

CHERIE

I thought I was done being mama bird. I'm dusting the furniture in Dave's office; actually, it's a small study off the foyer in our house with a window that looks out over the front yard at the neighbor's house across the street. I run my hand across the smooth cherry finish of his desk, one of the many lovely pieces produced in the Johnson Furniture factory before it all went overseas. I'm looking at our family pictures and wondering what it would be like to sit here for hours, crafting stories and clicking away on the keyboard of our desktop computer while Dave is traveling, as I spill the details that comprise the crazy chaos of our lives. Gazing out the window, I laugh at the dead ferns that still hang from Margie Perry's front porch. Really! It's February, for crying out loud! Margie's husband, Todd, has been unemployed for over a year, and they can't find it within their busy schedule to take down their dead ferns? I shouldn't judge. I can imagine that a hefty dose of depression goes along with unemployment. Anyway, what could I possibly have to say that anyone else could relate to?

Everything.

The sound of Hope's car engine is there before I see her swing her white Civic into the driveway. I'll have to talk to her about her speed. In this neighborhood, the mommy patrol is just as present as the police who crouch on the hillsides, waiting to nab the speeders, while the children who play in the streets seemingly dare the rest of us to run them over. I don't get it. What are yards for, anyway?

As I peek discreetly out the window, I see Hope sitting in her car, one hand on the wheel. She has cut the engine but sits staring at a spot on the front steps; not sobbing, texting, or talking on her phone, but just staring. My heart drops to the floor. This is the last place she wants to be, I realize. Defeat is written all over her face as she heaves open the door and climbs out, slipping a purse I haven't seen over her shoulder. I can almost hear her draw in the ragged breath as she sets her mouth and pulls her coat tightly around her. I want to think of something lighthearted to say to her, but seeing her like this, it's just not in me. My daughter is one of the most attractive people I know, with her sleek, almost black hair and steel blue eyes, the spitting image of my Dave, but today, she could blend in with the sidewalk.

I meet her at the door and throw it open, as well as my arms, and she sinks into them immediately, wordlessly, *totally bummed,* as we used to say in the '80s.

"Hey..." I say, giving her a big squeeze and a kiss on her temple. She smells delightful, but there is a sadness about even her smell just now, the smell of tears that's not right about this girl who has always been able to peel herself off the floor and rise valiantly to the occasion. It's the smell of hurt. And I don't like it.

"Hey, Mama. Where's Daddy?"

"Probably out buying my card," I say and we both laugh. The laughter doesn't reach her eyes, but it's okay. At least she can laugh. "I started the water for some tea. Want some?"

"Sure," she says, following me into the kitchen. I turn on a lamp to create a mild sense of cheer. Her dark hair is pulled back into a ponytail, accentuating the fine round shape of her head. Hope wears the latest of fashions, which right now is represented by a short taupe coat over remarkably skinny jeans with low, wedge-heeled boots and a soft colorful scarf, making her look as if she's just stepped off the cover of a magazine. I hadn't even gotten around to wearing the tall boots the girls wear, and now, I notice that there is a new style. Even the coat is different; when did the appearance of the empire waist translate to winter coats? I stopped trying to keep up years ago when college tuition, car insurance, and mortgage payments overtook my sense of style. She must be in debt, but she doesn't tell us. Still, she is stunning, even with the puffy eyes she's tried to conceal with the best makeup.

I pour hot water over tea bags in our favorite mugs and we wander into the family room. Matching comfy sofas face each other with a large, tufted ottoman between them with a bamboo refreshment tray, so I park the cups there, and take a seat beside her on one of the sofas, angling my knee in toward her. She still wears her coat.

"Honey, don't you want to take off your coat?"

"In a minute. I'm still cold."

My eyes fall to the purse again. It's a delicious shade of plum leather, and I assume by the stylized initials on the clasp, it must be expensive. "Nice purse."

"Thanks. It's my Valentine's present from Liam," she says flatly. Then she looks at me as if I don't get it. "It's a Tory Burch," she says without emotion, but her large blue eyes tell me that I should be impressed. A vintage cash register "cha-chings" in my mind with three figures popping into the price display, but I'm sure my wildest guess is not even in the ball park. We do not shop in the same genre, even though I am the one with a salary. And benefits.

"Ah! Take the Tory Burch and run! That's my girl," I say, sipping my tea, suddenly wondering what in the hell is going on here.

Then she stands and removes her coat, tossing it on the opposite couch, and smoothing her loose cream colored blouse. She is so thin; thinner than I remember the last time I saw her. Liam's bohemian lifestyle does not apparently include *food*. Hope gives me the ghost of an eye roll and sits back down, still without emotion, and there is her face—the face that means there is more to know than I will ever find out, and that as much as she loves us, she really hates being here. She reaches for her tea and takes a sip, warming her hands around the cup.

"So tell me everything." My girl, who ten years ago was all giggles, confidence, and exuberance, is a shell of her former self; a quiet storm is forming inside her. I ache to look at her. I can only imagine the hurt, anger, and betrayal she must feel. She is quiet so I proceed. Selfishly, I remember that I have a dinner date in just an hour, and as much as I'd like to open a bottle of wine and commiserate with her endlessly, I'd like to get this discussion moving. "Did you bring clothes with you? I'm assuming you're going to…spend the night?"

She swings her gaze to me, tracing her finger around the rim of the cup. "Can I move back in, Mama? I have a carload of clothes, actually. I won't be in your way. I work three nights at the bar, so you'll hardly see me."

I am prepared for this. All she had at Liam's were clothes and toiletries anyway, and the rest of her belongings and furniture have been in storage for almost two years.

"Oh, honey, of course you can. You know Daddy and I love you and just want you to be happy. What happened?"

As she opens her mouth, Dave clunks in through the mud room, huffing and puffing. As we look around, we see him emerge, managing to carry two large vases, each filled with red roses. "Hellooo!" he says, as if he is saving the day, and maybe he is. He has not sent me flowers in years, but I want to swat him. One sends flowers to women where they work, so that all the other women can see them and feel jealous. Then you take a picture of them and post it on Facebook, telling all your Facebook friends what a romantic guy you were lucky enough to marry and rub their little noses in it. But that's my Dave. Today, however, Dave has done a really sweet thing to bring Hope flowers, too. Matching flowers. "Happy Valentine's Day! For my girls!" he says, beaming proudly.

"Ohhh! Thank you, Honey!" I gush as he comes toward us with his gifts. Maybe if I play it up, he will repeat this performance. Hope and I take our respective vases.

"Thanks, Daddy." Hope grins for a moment, but then her mouth breaks and tears spill over, making her cover her face with her fingers. Dave looks around, setting her vase of roses on the kitchen table before following us into the family room.

"Aw! Sweetie! Come here," he says, and Hope goes to him, letting him envelop her in his arms. A Daddy hug is what she needs. Hope and Dave go together like cops and donuts, with about the same elegance. "Screw what's-his-name. I love you!" he says to her, winking at me over her shoulder. Then his face questions and I shrug, still at a loss for the 411 he wants.

"Want some tea?" I ask him, lifting my cup slightly. Hope is my size and Dave is not much taller, I notice again. Wesley is the only one of us who has garnered any of the family's height. She gets it from Toots, Dave's formidable mother, who in her youth must have been at least 5' 10". Hope wipes her face on the back of her hand and they move back toward the sofas.

"No, I'm good," he says, and I notice he visibly restrains himself from going to the fridge for a beer. Hope has captivated him, as she has me.

"We were just getting to the details," I say, as Dave takes my place beside Hope on the sofa, watching her compose herself, so I sit gingerly on the ottoman beside our tray.

"Liam is leaving to go to Italy in a month," she says, but we know this already.

"Didn't he mention it at all?" I ask for the second time, in disbelief that this could be a fact he'd overlook. *What a prick!*

"No. I mean, he always said he wanted to travel. I knew that. There were indications, but I never let myself take them in. He never planned on getting tied down to anything here…or me. His job at You've Been Framed was just a means to an end, and he'd finished all his commissions here. After the science center reopened last month, and his murals there were finished, he thought this would be the time to peace out and take off. He told me I could come, but it was so lame. I knew he didn't mean it, especially after reading that girl's message to him on Facebook. I'm sure she wasn't including me in her invitation for him to stay with her. He'd been talking to her about it for a few months, and I'm just hearing about it last night. And only because I found her message."

"Well, did he say when he was planning on telling you?" I ask, my mouth agape.

"He said he wanted to wait until after Valentine's Day."

I look at Dave, who shrugs, as if he can understand the logic in Liam's thinking. "Oh, how considerate of him," I say, unable to purge the sarcasm from my voice. It's a slap in the face, and it's easy to support my daughter, but maybe I've spoken too harshly for the moment.

"Really," she agrees. Hope picks at a cuticle on her thumb and stares vacantly. "He said he loves me, but I shouldn't have ever let myself get this attached to him. I knew this would happen. I should never have moved in with him," she says, and Dave and I both nod vigorously, emphasizing our objections to that move from the start. But Hope is a force to be reckoned with, much like a tornado. Once she makes up her mind, there is no reasoning with her, which makes me suddenly angry. I know she is young, but she knew better. We told her. She could certainly have spared herself this drama, this hurt. Will she ever take my word for anything?

I think about our dinner reservations and check my watch discreetly. Should we stay? Should we go? How fragile is she at this moment? I do have a life, even though I am sorry for her latest crisis.

"You have plans. You and Daddy should go," she says, noticing the glance at my watch. Then she surveys my appearance. "Are you going to change?"

I am wearing the same red silk blouse and black pants I wore to school today, thinking I'd wear it to dinner. This kind of fashion faux pas does not sit well with my daughter, whose eyes are just the slightest bit large as she regards me now. Do I look that bad? My hand rises automatically to my hair. Maybe I'll put on my freshwater pearls that Dave gave me for Christmas and add some heels.

"No, I was planning to wear this," I say with confidence as Dave comes to my rescue.

"You look great!" he says, grinning at me. My little porcupine is the sweetest. "I'm going to go like this, too. Do I look okay?" he asks our fashionista offspring.

She considers his question, his khakis and sweater, and his outstretched hands. His clothes match nicely today, without any help from me. But then I have color coded his closet and explained the warm and cool colors system—repeatedly. "Where are y'all going?"

"Bimini's," we say together, and she does an outright roll of the eyes this time, the irony of the place not lost on her, either. But it is a casual place so she does not urge us to change clothes.

"Would you like to go with us? I'm sure they can add another chair. Or, hell, we can all sit at the bar!" Dave says, grinning.

"Uh, no, thank you," Hope says. "Is there mac and cheese in the cabinet?"

What's for dinner? It's starting already, making me panic strangely. I am so used to being on my own, and liking it.

Yoga, feels like my smug answer, empty-nester that I am, but that would be insensitive, considering all that is happening with Hope. Maybe I should break down and make her my homemade and truly *decadent* macaroni and cheese. We can eat on it for a solid week, and she could use some spoiling right now. But I have my own Valentine's Day celebration that I'm really anticipating, with Dave…. *What to do?*

"There are some leftovers in the fridge. There's ham and green beans, and some roasted potatoes with rosemary from last night. Help yourself to whatever you can scrounge up," I offer as she looks uninterested. It wouldn't surprise me if she just slurped down a bowl of cereal and crashed with her laptop in her bed, maybe watching season four of *The Tudors,* what usually happens when either one of my daughters holes up for one of their brief stays. And it will not be the first time she's sought refuge in the nest. I knew this would happen from the very first day that Liam entered Hope's world.

Chapter 4

HOPE

It takes them no time to leave for their date. I'd high-tail it out the door ASAP too, if my brooding daughter came home at an inopportune time like this. At least Daddy had the wherewithal to make dinner reservations. And the flowers, well, Mama's flowers were *my* idea. I'd called to remind him about Valentine's three days ago, with strict instructions to have her red roses delivered to her at school. Maybe it was too much to expect, but at least he came through with them at home. Okay, squealing in on two wheels counts for something, and throwing in a vase of roses for the pathetic jilted daughter was sweet. I love my dad. He's no Prince Charming in my book, but I love him, and he makes Mama…happy? Whatever it is he makes her, I want that someday. Just to be content with a simple grocery store vase of roses, and knowing that the guy you're married to loves you back. For thirty years, he's loved you back. That would be enough.

I set my cereal bowl on the counter, and then think to rinse it, leaving it in the sink, and drag myself upstairs. Kicking off my boots and changing into yoga pants and my favorite Victoria's Secret sweatshirt, I sink gratefully into my bed and open my laptop, which makes the only light in my bedroom. My body moves as if I've aged four or five decades, so hibernation is all I can manage tonight. My suitcases are still in the car, but surely there will be something in my closet I can wear to work tomorrow. At some point, I promise myself I will get situated, but right now, I don't freaking care. I just want to submerge myself in the funk that is my life tonight. A glance at my phone tells me that Liam has not called since 12:30 this afternoon. At that point, I couldn't speak to him without coming unglued, and I'm fairly certain I couldn't do it now, were he to try again. He is probably joyously lost in his painting without me there to distract him. I could run through my photos and look at all the images I've captured of him over the past year, and the feeling is more than tempting, but I don't want to cry anymore tonight. *How does he not love me?* Stop it. Thoughts like that do not help. Wishing to dispel his images, I squeeze my eyes shut and press my fingers to the lids, but again I am unsuccessful. Memories flood back to me, since I am here alone, without the diversions of clothing racks, and idle conversations with customers. *Will that be credit or debit? Would you like your receipt in the bag...?*

"Yes, I think I do have a remittance for you, Hope," he said to me in his strikingly crisp voice on the day we met. Mama and I had stopped in You've Been Framed after someone in the store had called to inform me that one of my photographs had been sold. I'd never seen Liam Ferguson in the store. He was new, a picture framer they'd hired since I'd been exhibiting my work there. Part art store and part frame shop, the deal was that they would frame my photos, and when something sold, I'd get my cut. I watched his hairy forearms while he rifled efficiently through a collection of envelopes he'd pulled out from under the cash register. Not my type at all, he was tall and burly, with that circa 1970s long brown hair and that I-don't-give-a-shit-what-you-think-about-it grunge jeans and hiking boots look, with a dark button up shirt with rolled up sleeves; the quintessential artist and downright freaking hot man. Leaning in briefly to check the envelopes, I was further distracted; he smelled as good as he looked. Even Mama was fanning herself when he glanced across the counter at us. Albeit unaffected, he was breathtakingly virile, something one doesn't encounter every day in this town.

"Actually, there are *three* payments here," he said, suddenly smiling at me, making me go stupid and hoping he didn't notice. So far, he was acting like the professional I needed to be, so I looked down and swallowed, getting up the nerve to look at him again. Why does God make men like this and then society expects us not to respond?

"Oh, thank you," I said, feigning nonchalance, taking the envelope and looking around to see which pictures had sold. As if reading my mind, he looked at the attached sales page and filled me in.

"Two of the baseball pictures sold, and the other was the pumpkin patch one. I liked that one, too," he said, grinning, exposing the dimple in his right cheek under the scruff.

I swallowed again. "Oh!" I was now officially and profoundly stupid, feeling the telltale burn on my face.

"And the pictures of the baseballs are great as well. Lots of people want those, especially when they see that some of them are autographed."

"Those are my dad's baseballs. He has a great collection."

"Kind of an *I Spy* effect with them all piled up like that, like a jar of marbles or something," he said, bringing to mind the picture riddle books I loved. "Do you have more prints? We can frame them and have them ready to display by the end of the week if you can bring them in."

"Uh, yes, sure. I'll bring some more in tomorrow."

He looked pleased, and he glanced at my mother, who was also glowing about my work.

"Do you do other photography as well?" he asked as he rearranged the paperwork in the folder, slipping it back under the counter.

"I'm starting to," I began. "I lost my interim teaching job at the end of the school year, so I'm beginning to do photoshoots of children and families…some couples, that sort of thing. The job market is so bad right now that my art degree is rather meaningless…."

"Tell me about it," he said, trying to catch my eye. His gaze seemed so earnest. I tried to avoid letting mine linger. "That's why I have a master's degree. Hopefully, I'll be able to do more than frame other people's pictures myself one day."

Out of the corner of my eye, I could see my mother exploring the back of the store, pretending to be absorbed in a bin of watercolor bird pictures, and slipping a finger around inside the collar of her shirt.

"What kind of art do you do?" I asked Liam.

"I paint…"

"Oh, what's your style?" I asked, trying to sound casual through the sudden dryness in my voice, but the way he was looking at me made it difficult to talk at all.

He hesitated a moment. "*Big*," he said, with the most lascivious grin I'd ever had thrown my way. I felt my eyes spinning like a hypnotized cartoon character. The dam was breaking somewhere beneath my midsection. Thankfully, he continued so I didn't have to respond. "I'm painting murals mostly, these days. Have you ever been in Bimini's?"

"The restaurant? Yeah, we go in there all the time. Jeff, the owner…I guess you know him, he's my dad's friend. The mural is your work?" I stumbled, feeling ridiculous.

"Yeah," he said, regarding me thoughtfully with those deep set brown eyes, warm as honey. My hand went instinctively to rearrange my hair. He watched me do it and then said, "I used to paint people, but now it's mostly seascapes and landscapes. Maybe it's time to change it up again, I don't know…" he said, his voice drifting off.

"So, I'll come back tomorrow and bring you some more photos."

"Great. I'll look forward to seeing you again, *Hope*," he said, extending his hand for me to shake. The flesh on flesh contact with him made my knees quiver, as if I were thirteen again. I released his hand, turned, and left the shop abruptly, praying to God that my mother was behind me.

My phone is ringing, hurtling me back to reality. It is *him*. God, I can't do this! But I want to hear his voice, so like the addict I am, I answer breathlessly, trying to calm my own.

"Hey."

"Hey....I was worried about you." I am drowning in a sea of unwanted intimacy. I have forgotten, after only a few hours, his pull on me. There is silence on my end. I cannot speak. He continues in that voice, deep and manly, but so edged with care that I am sure I cannot talk. "Are you okay? Say something....Listen, Hope, I'm so sorry I hurt you. You know I never wanted to see you so upset like this." This new voice of his is oddly fragile, unfamiliar, making me want to cry.

I try to speak, but say nothing.

"Are you there?"

"I'm here."

"Good. You sound...good."

"I don't know what to say."

"I know. I'm sorry. My timing sucked. Actually, all of this sucks. I suck."

"Yes, you do suck." I laugh a little, and so does he.

"So...are you really gone?" I imagine him running a hand through his hair and leaning against the kitchen counter in the dark.

"I guess so. If you're leaving in a month, there's really no reason for me to stick around. I just wish you'd told me…earlier."

"I know. I kept trying to figure out how. You can still go with me, Hope."

"Right. You and me and Amelia; that's such a cozy little scene."

"It's not like you think."

"What? She's a lesbian?"

"She might be. I don't know. I don't know her that way."

"She apparently wants to know *you* that way. And she has a room for you…. I doubt that bringing me along would be what she has in mind. Tell me about her. How exactly do you know her, and how long has this plan been in the works?"

I hear him hesitate. Surely he was ready for this question. "We were in grad school together. Amelia is half-Italian. Her parents are divorced and her mother lives here in the States, but her father owns a vineyard in Italy. I went there once with her, and Charlie and Kira back in school. My father knows her dad, actually, being a vintner himself. They have room for me to stay in their caretaker's house in the vineyard, and I can work there for my room and board. The place is big enough for a studio. It was a no brainer, Hope. She's doing marketing with artists, helping them get connected with dealers, and we've been talking for a couple of months. That's all."

Suddenly, the world is much smaller than I ever wanted it to be, but it is obviously working in his favor and not mine. I know this girl has more designs on him than he's willing to admit to me.

"Then there's no place for me in your plans, so don't ask me. And you know I can't afford it."

He sighs. He knows I'm right. He's just trying to pacify me, especially with his other *gift* I've just learned about. "What's keeping you here, Hope? Nothing."

"*Nothing*, Liam. I have absolutely nothing. But if you really wanted me to come along, you would have given me more notice. You would have planned it with me. My passport's probably expired. I can't just up and go."

"Why not, Hope? I didn't know this was all going to work out until just a couple of weeks ago. I didn't tell you because I wasn't sure. Why would I get you all excited about it if it wasn't going to pan out?"

My hand flutters at my face. The man is maddening. Of course he can do this. He has no possessions, and he didn't even think he had me. It's the way he rolls. He's probably already bought his plane ticket…and secured his visa; hmmm.

"I love you," he says, and I think it sounds like he means it, but I know I shouldn't let myself believe it. The sound of it wrecks me, as if I'm being hurled against a tree. If it is true, it doesn't matter anyway. It is not enough.

"But, you told me when we got started that you weren't going to commit to me."

"I know. It doesn't mean I don't care about you. I'm not asking you for commitment."

"What are you asking then? That I just drop my life here and follow you to Italy and just…*hang out?*"

"Yeah, that's pretty much it. It beats hanging around *Greensboro* working in a dress shop and bartending. Isn't it enough?"

"No. I can't be like you. I need more…." *A house, a job, a husband, a family*, everything he doesn't want to hear.

"More what, Hope? You *have* everything I am. You can come with me. We can be happy."

"Until when? Until you decide the gig is up? Or that maybe you do like Amelia better than me? I can't do what you do, Liam. I'm not…*Janis Joplin* or anything. It's not the '70s! I just can't bounce around like that.

I need more stability. I need a plan. I want some say in my life." I want to be responsible.

He is silent. We are too different. But there is something that binds me to him dangerously. I can feel his heat through the phone. If he were in front of me, I know I would lose all my resolve, but it is easier this way, without smelling the musky manliness of him, without his sweet mouth on mine, sucking the independence from my soul, and his beautiful, capable hands on me, kneading the freedom from my flesh. Here, alone in my childhood bed, I can be the grownup I need to be.

"I can't," I say, needing to be the one to speak.

More silence. "When can I see you again?"

"I don't know…I can't see you for a while."

"But you have some things here, and we have something we've got to settle."

"I know. You weren't counting on loose ends, were you? I can't talk about it with you tonight."

"Okay. We'll talk later. After you sleep on it."

"Okay," I manage to whisper.

"Goodnight, Hope."

Chapter 5

CHERIE

My fingernails drum distractedly on the candlelit table, glancing at Liam's remarkable impressionistic mural of boats in a Caribbean harbor at sunset. I'm imagining Hope submerged in her covers, watching TV on her laptop and half-dozing, trying to forget him. *What is she not telling me?* Brown paper covers the table and I watch as Dave scribbles down all the places we can remember spending our Valentine's Day dinners with the pen from my purse.

"Do you remember me taking you to the Jewish Mother in Virginia Beach that first Valentine's Day? Actually, it was the morning after."

He succeeds in drawing me back to the little deli, trying extra hard to entertain me tonight. I throw back my head and laugh. It has been years since I thought about that night…and the following morning! I was such a groupie! Those were the days…I'd drop whatever I was doing to follow his cover band if they were playing in a town within driving distance from East Carolina University.

"Blueberry blintzes," I murmur, resting my chin in my hand and gazing at him, remembering his glossy black hair and those cool blue eyes that would fire up whenever I flirted with him. Thirty-two years ago. I was a looker myself back in those days. Those were the days when I wanted nothing to do with my family's sleepy little summer existence on Sullivan's Island. I was looking for action.

"Yeah...that was what you had. I remember. You didn't go much for the lox and bagels with cream cheese."

"No. That was your thing. You were such a brave young *Southern boy*, trying to branch out and try new things." That was Dave, always pushing the envelope, even if it was just breakfast.

Dave holds my hand. "Sweetheart, don't worry about Hope. She'll be *fine*," he says, thumbing the back of my hand and grinning at me. I haven't fooled him for a minute. "And you know I'm glad she's out of Liam's clutches and back at home with us, but you know what this means, right?"

"No more loud sex and walking around the house naked?"

"Exactly. And I had such high hopes for us later this evening. But however it turns out tonight, let's enjoy our dinner. This is our night."

His silver and black porcupine hair is fingered in place and he smells so good. Something about the way he smiles at me takes me back to the "cheap little seaside cafe" as we used to call the bar where I worked in the summer of 1980; the summer we met and he changed my life....

It was the summer I'd been invited to stay with a college friend at North Carolina's Outer Banks. My mother was saddened that I would pass up a vacation at Sullivan's Island where we always spent the better part of our summers at my grandmother's beach house, but I was ready for action, and a change. I *must* have been taller then. I was surely skinnier, with long curling wheat-colored hair that later earned me the nickname "Curly Fries" when Arby's came out with its yummy little version of French fries that resembled my head. Apparently, the combination of all that was me was enough for Dave Johnson to notice the first time his rock 'n' roll band played at the Mainsail on that hot July night.

My fellow barmaids always had the same discussion when every band came to play at our place on the Outer Banks.

"Which one of them would you sleep with?" one of us would ask.

Usually the response was a binary choice. You had your Nordic camp, which preferred the tall, slender blond men, and then there was the ripped, dark and handsome team, leaving the vote an even split, but when Too Far Gone came to town, the favorite was definitely the strapping, black-haired guitar player Dave Johnson, hands down, every time. And he became *mine*, all because I had a particularly fetching dance move or two that he'd noticed.

He sat at the bar beside the bass player and watched me count the tip money from the jar. The other girls were scrutinizing us from the far end, where they were wiping out dirty ashtrays. The sunburned bass player smoked while Dave watched me over his Heineken.

"You're a good dancer," he said, referring to my little break from the bar, when I'd danced with one of the locals who came in often. "We like it when people get into the music and dance like you did." For an instant, I caught his steel blue eyes, unmistakably, although discreetly trained on my ass, which was not bad in those days and in those shorts.

"So, how did you guys come up with the name Too Far Gone?" I asked, trying to keep the flush from my cheeks.

"All the good names were taken," he said, picking at the label on his bottle. "Arrogance, The Good Humor Band…The Captain and Tennille…."

I smirked, making him grin. "No, really, the name suits us…or at least, it will in a little bit," he added with a twinkle, taking another sip of his beer. Resting his chin on his hand, he watched me arrange the bills so they all faced the same way. "So what's your name, sugar?"

I should have been offended, but the sound of his voice defied offense.

"Sugar," I said, stacking the bills smartly against the bar and replacing the jar for the next night. His eyebrow rose with mine and he started one of those slow grins that began on one side, eventually overtaking his face. I felt my lips beginning to purse in an attempt to hide my enjoyment of his smile, but I got the feeling he saw right through me. His big, bedroom eyes locked onto mine and he became Mr. Serious, making fireworks go off somewhere in my midsection.

"No, seriously, what's your name?"

"Cherie," I said after a brief hesitation.

The grin appeared without warning this time. "Like 'My Cherie Amour'?" He knew the Stevie Wonder song like everybody else did. I rolled my eyes.

"That's the one. I kinda like Sugar better, though."

"Sugar, I'll call you whatever you want, long as you'll let me dance with you."

"But then, who'd be playing the music?"

"I'll just sing to you."

"Cocky, aren't you?"

"Might as well be. If I don't love myself, who's gonna love me? I'm God's masterpiece. That's what my grandma says. She's eighty-nine years old and she's never wrong."

That was one of those explosive moments in life that we remember for the rest of our lives. Boys who admittedly loved their grandmas always got to me. And the sudden openness on his face that smacked of sincerity pulled me under like a rock. My feet might as well have been set in concrete because I knew I was going to want more of this man. Judging by the smile on his face, he knew it too.

Jeff, the owner of Bimini's, brings me out of my dream, setting a plate of almond crusted halibut in front of me. "Happy Valentine's Day, Cher!" he says, bending to kiss my cheek as I'm fingering the string of pearls around my neck. With a side of pureed potatoes and roasted asparagus, I am in heaven. Dave has the salmon with dill sauce, and he looks just as enraptured as I am.

"Oh! Thank you, Jeff! This looks delicious!" I say.

"Oh, man, oh man! There is nothing like fresh fish. Got any in the back I can buy from you to take home?" asks Dave.

Jeff places his hands on his hips and laughs. "If I had a dime for every time someone asked me that, I'd be a rich man. I need to start a business. People ask me that question at least half a dozen times a night."

As he lifts his beer bottle, Dave looks thoughtful. "How about one more of these, and another pinot grigio for my date?"

"You bet," says Jeff with a wink, hurrying off to his next task. The place is hopping tonight.

Dave glances down at his phone, showing a call coming in from another one of his colleagues that he ignores again.

"What's going on? Why are Daniel and Tim calling you on Valentine's Day? Don't they know you're out wining and dining your hot wife?"

"No idea, but they can wait," he says, draining the rest of his beer, and digging into his salmon.

I taste my halibut, groaning with delight. "Taste this. It's amazing! You haven't said much about your business trip. How did it go?"

"That can wait too," Dave says, stroking his mustache down to his goatee with his thumb and forefinger, a habit he has when he's distracted.

"Then what are we going to talk about?" I ask, waving my fork in the air. "Hope will be fine, business is off limits. Want to hear about school…?"

He shrugs, taking the bite of halibut onto his plate and offering me some of his. "This salmon is out of this world! I'm going to make this for you tomorrow night. I'm going to get the recipe from Jeff before we leave and I'm going to do this tomorrow."

"Good!" Dave is known for his good cooking by all of our family and all my jealous girlfriends. We've had many barbeques and parties over the years where he's been the chef. "I guess Hope will be working at Natty's tomorrow night. Oh! And I forgot to tell you; Wesley's coming into town tomorrow after her classes."

"Good. Why?"

"To see Hope, of course. So count on her for dinner too, I guess."

He pondered a moment and gave me a serious look. "Okay. Good. Can you get home early?"

"On a Friday? Hell, yeah!"

We eat in silence for a few moments, savoring the dinner. Like a dam about to break, I can hold my feelings in no longer. "I'm sorry. You might not want to talk about it tonight, but I have this awful feeling that Hope might be pregnant."

Chapter 6

HOPE

Natty Greene's is the medicine I need, I think, drawing a couple of Wildflower brews from the tap and adding an orange wedge to each for the server waiting at the end of the bar. Zac Brown is playing in the background, and he ain't in no hurry today. So, neither am I, I try to believe. It isn't Liam's style to come stalking me, even if he says he loves me; on the contrary, he is all about freedom. I know I'll have all the space I need to detox myself from his hold on me. Plus, I get to wear jeans and a T-shirt to work here, so there's no stressing out about how I look, which is definitely not anything I care about tonight. At least I showered. God, I've never said that, even to *myself!*

"The place is dead," says Jessica, drying glasses beside me, miffed, of course, because she's hoping to score some big bucks since she missed out on last night's crowd.

"Oh, right! How was the date last night?" asks John, one of our cooks, who's sitting at the bar, dragging his feet to get back into the kitchen. He was here last night and hasn't quite recovered from the onslaught.

Jessica presses out her upper lip and gives us some comedic eyes. "I'm giving up, becoming celibate, and moving to Alaska."

"That bad? Why Alaska?" asks John, raking fingers through his hair and glancing over at a young man filling out his job application at a nearby table.

"Because that's where all the *real* men are," she fires back at him, a little too harshly for my liking. I like John; he's twenty-eight and going nowhere fast, but he entertains us, which at the end of the day, means he's all right. And he's really cute.

"But you'd get cold. Stay here. I'll keep you warm. Or you could go to Italy," he says, throwing me a barb, and sipping some iced tea. Well, maybe he is a jerk at times....

"Don't pick on me; you don't know what I might slip into your drink!" I warn him, eyeing his iced tea, and giving him my one-cocked-eyebrow testy face.

"You girls are *so* missing the boat," he says, pointing his hands inwardly at himself. "Here I am, right in front of you, and you look through me like I'm not even here. I could make both of you so happy. At the same time. All of us. Together. A John sandwich. You should try it."

We laugh at his deadpan delivery. He's such a puppy. And it's not like I haven't thought about it. At first I thought he was a loser, but I can't tell. He seems smart, and he has a college degree in something and used to have a big job...but what the hell is he doing cooking in this restaurant? What the hell am I doing bartending in this restaurant?

"Don't you need to be in the kitchen, doing like...your *job* or something?" I ask.

"Yeah, in a minute. I have to take care of some business first," he says, standing, stretching, and smoothing his white apron. Removing his baseball cap from his back pocket, and placing it backward on his head, he saunters over to the young man at the table. "How ya doing? My name's John. I'm one of the managers here," he says as Jessica and I squelch our laughter. He takes the man's application and looks it over, flipping it over to the back. "Frank?" He reaches out to shake Frank's hand, then pulls out a chair and slouches down in it, passing a hand over his chin.

He studies Frank for a moment and then casts his eyes about the room. "So Frank, what are your career goals? Where do you see yourself in five years?"

Poor Frank! Jessica and I remove ourselves to the opposite end of the bar where we can guffaw privately, but then she ruins it for me.

"Have you heard from Liam today?" she asks, bringing my laughter to an abrupt halt. But I'm feeling surprisingly better about the whole fiasco after I have slept on it.

"Nope. Don't care, either."

"Good for you," she says, laying a gentle hand on my shoulder.

"And thanks for letting me change at your place. I didn't think he would be home from work when I got there, but I just couldn't risk seeing him, yet. With where my parents live in Pleasant Ridge, it would take me thirty minutes to drive out there after I left the store, and then thirty minutes to drive back into town to get here. I don't know how I'm going to make this work. That was the whole point in moving in with Liam in the first place. The pool house was close to both places I work."

"No problem. Just keep my key. If I had a two bedroom, you could move in with me." Her hair is perfect, as usual, a longish bob that curves gently downward around her heart-shaped face, making her look like a movie star when she flashes her smile and her huge green eyes at people. "I've been through this so many times it would make your head spin."

"Are you going to tell me I'm better off without him?"

"I will if you want me to. But I know you have unfinished business with him. How are you, really?"

"I'm fine," I lie, and it sounds quite convincing. "I know I'll have to see him again at some point. We have something else to take care of. I'd just like to gather my strength. You know, it would be really amazing to be able to just…chuck it all and run away with him to Italy. He's right; I have nothing to lose, except I'm so afraid that if I went with him, he'd ditch me."

She snorts. "What better place to be ditched?"

"And then there's Amelia. I know there's more to her than he's telling me."

"I don't know, Hope. Maybe Liam is onto something. Love the one you're with. Don't get tied down. He's not feeling any pain, is he?" At my uncertain face, she shrugs and says, "Then do what you want to do. I mean, look at all the people we know who are in their twenties, or thirties for that matter. Half of them don't have real jobs, and most of them are living at home with their parents because they can't make ends meet. I'm barely scraping by on my own, and I don't have a minute to myself, working two jobs. What could you possibly miss by running away with Liam? You sure you don't want to go with him?" Her big green eyes are suddenly too invasive; I can't look at her.

"I don't *know!* If he'd been serious about really taking me along, and I'd planned for it like he apparently has, then yeah, maybe. I just…can't be spontaneous like he is. I mean he's all singing 'Me and Bobby McGee,' but I just can't take the leap, even if I had the money. We're too different. Besides, I don't think I can trust him, or maybe it's that I don't trust myself. *God!* Why am I such a mess? I hate going back to the nest—and starting all over again! My parents are probably freaking out that I'm back again."

"Don't worry about it. Do what you need to do. Screw the rest of it. Now is not the time to worry what other people think. I mean, look at John. He doesn't give a flying flip what anyone else thinks. Things will change. You'll find what you're looking for. And it probably won't come with a penis, either!" she says, laying the palm of her hand on her hip.

A laugh sputters from my lips as we watch Caitlin, our manager, approach the table where John stands and extends his hand toward her.

"Frank, great meeting you! I'll turn this over to our general manager, Caitlin. Good luck to you!" He gives us a little salute as he struts through the swinging door to the kitchen.

Chapter 7

CHERIE

I pull my Civic into the driveway, noticing that Dave's car is there. He's taking a day to work from home, as he usually does on Fridays. Wesley has not arrived, but I see from her text message that she's just left Chapel Hill, so we'll have an hour or so before she gets home. Hope will be going from her job at the trendy boutique to Natty Greene's, so we won't see her until at least midnight. I don't know how she functions. I have papers to grade this weekend, but that's not nearly as tiring as what she's doing. Only the young have that kind of stamina!

Collecting my school bag and my groceries before I attempt to extricate myself from the car, I think about my conversation with Audrey Brown today at lunch. The boys, as we call them, were otherwise occupied, so we had a private chat about Hope and all that was going on at my house.

"It's such a common thing these days, to have your children move back in, Cher," she'd said. "Think of all the people we know who are going through it. My husband just got reemployed after five months. My nephew, who is twenty-five, did an internship in Paris with one of those luxury brand designer companies, and he lives at home. He can't find a job and he has a master's degree! It's a tough economy."

Audrey was right. It was a bad time all over the country. And I did know so many people singing the same song; kids out of college without jobs, returning to the nest. The lot of them was going to create a new demographic; marrying later, if at all, having a child, if at all, much later. The responsible ones would be living life as the older underemployed and possibly giving up on their dreams, not realizing their potential, while at the same time, bearing the burden of care for all the people their age in the same boat, without the sense to refrain from getting married and having children they can't afford. Wow! And they're inheriting the national debt. Good luck. It's depressing. All I can do is encourage my daughter to keep her chin up, and realize that she shouldn't take any of this misfortune personally. We are only a few precious steps ahead of the way it was during the Great Depression. It could be so much worse. But there are things she can do to better herself. At least, she's not running off to Europe with Rasputin!

I bang through the door to the mudroom and into the kitchen, with as many grocery bags as I can loop around my fingers swinging at my sides. I heave the plastic bags onto the counter, grumbling because I've forgotten to take my cloth bags to the store again. Slipping my tote bag off my shoulder, and placing it on the desk in the kitchen, I listen to Dave on the phone in his office. He's begging off now that I'm home, and I hear him say goodbye to whoever it was. When he shuffles into the kitchen, he rallies with a smile, but I can tell he's had a tough day. Still in a sweatshirt and jeans, I wonder if he's been out of the house all day. I notice dishes in the sink, but I pretend not to care.

"Hey! Need any help?" he asks, coming to give me a hug. He kisses me just like every other day. Like the gentleman he is, he holds my coat as I slip out of it, and he hangs it on the hook in the mudroom.

"No, I've got it all in. I went to the store."

"So did I. I stopped by Jeff's earlier and got some fish from the restaurant. It's fresher than anything you can buy in the grocery stores."

"So you're really cooking for me tonight?"

He nods and takes my hand. "Yep. Want to come and sit with me for a minute? I need to talk to you about something before Wesley gets home."

"Sure," I murmur, puzzled. He and Hope must have talked this morning before she left for the boutique. "Is everything okay?" He doesn't even go for beer in the fridge; this must be serious.

He glances at me as we sit together on the sofa, turning into each other. His long fingers stroke my knee as he lets his hand rest there, as if bracing me. *I know Hope is pregnant! And she told him before she told me!*

"I didn't want to ruin our Valentine's Day dinner last night, but I need to tell you this before the girls get here. And before you hear it from anybody else."

"What?"

"My position was eliminated on Wednesday. The company went through another restructure. Our whole division was cut."

My mouth falls open as it takes me a moment to process what he's just told me. I look into his eyes and know that he is not kidding. My fifty-seven-year-old husband is unemployed. I manage to swallow. And I won't be retiring in June.

"What? Tim and Daniel too?"

"Yeah, all of us. Bob and I had an appointment yesterday, first thing. I went in to review my sales prospectus for the second quarter and he dropped the bomb on me."

I am in shock. "*Dave!* No! I thought they always made cuts like that right before the holidays, you know, at the end of the year."

"I know. They would have, but they thought that was too cruel, right at Christmas, so they waited until now. Bob went to the mat for me… and for Daniel and Tim," he says, leaning on his knees and rubbing his hands together. "I thought another cut might have been under consideration, but I didn't realize they were that close to dropping the axe."

"Shit."

"I know. Shit. Shit, shit," he says, raking his hands through his hair.

"We'll be all right, Dave," I say, reaching for his hand.

"I know. I'll find another job. I've been working on my resume all day, and talking to people, looking at the job sites. I called my friend at the Employment Security Commission. I've contacted all of my customers to let them know what's going on."

"Is there any severance?"

"Yes. They gave me a seven-month package with continued health benefits. My pension is still intact. Surely I can put something together in seven months. So my job for the next seven months will be looking for a job. I'm not going to let us down. I'll find something."

"Oh, honey, I know. You could sell manure to a *cattle farmer*. At least I'm working and I can keep at it as long as I need to."

"You can retire, Cherie. I'll find something and you can go ahead with your plans."

"Well. Let's wait and see about that. Maybe this is a blessing in disguise. Are you going to tell your mother?"

He scoffs. "Hell no."

"You'll have to tell her eventually."

"What is she going to do for me? She knows how I'd feel about working for the company again. As you well know, our parting of the ways twelve years ago did not help any business relationship we could ever have again. And I'm not going to China."

I remember it like it was yesterday—*The Cold War*. Dr. Violet Johnson was a powerful woman. She'd been called Toots for most of her life because she was certainly no shrinking Violet. When Dave's father had died, Toots had moved the family's furniture company to China, letting go of the local workforce—all of their friends who ran the manufacturing plant in High Point, except for Dave and his older brother, Eric. Sadly, it was a typical business move in those days, but Dave had been livid, wanting to keep the operations here in the States. Eric didn't seem to mind a bit, and he was happy to stay on as a vice president, but he had to be willing to spend most of his life in China. Considering he was not married and didn't have a family to be concerned with, he was able to make the move seamlessly. Dave, on the other hand, wanted no part of the deal, and seeing as most of his friends who worked for the North Carolina based company got the boot, Dave took the lick as well. He'd held it against Toots for the last twelve years, when the war between the two of them had begun.

Toots had moved on, leaving Eric to run the company. Instead of moping around without her husband, it seemed she'd barely missed him; she continued her career in nutrition and wellness, becoming a pioneer in her field, and at eighty years old, was still a formidable exemplar of what taking care of oneself nutritionally could do for a person. She gave seminars all across the country, and when she was at home, pursued her other passion, ballroom dancing.

That's what I have to compare myself with. In the early days of my courtship with Dave and our marriage, I felt so intimidated by her. But for thirty years, Dave has always put me before her. He wanted normalcy, and I was it. So being the rebel he was, he'd married down, to the family's disdain, or so I thought. Before he met me, his image as the upstart rock 'n' roll musician was a painful thorn in the family's side, until they persuaded him to give it up for a more stable job with their furniture company, a job that didn't suck, and Dave was good at it. Toots had me to thank for bringing him down to reality, but she never acknowledged me.

Toots Johnson is the last person he'd go to for solace or money, but possibly the most able to give financial help if Dave ever needed it. Toots could bankroll an army if she wanted to, rattling around in her Sedgefield mansion, and snow-birding down to Florida, where she is wintering in Long Boat Key as Dave and I speak. She might as well be in China with Eric, for all we see of her. I'm sure she loves Dave, but they've spent their lives alienating each other. How long can they possibly go on this way? I'm afraid he will regret their distance at some point, and by then it might be too late.

"I can do this by myself, Cherie. I don't need her. As if she'd help me in any way, shape, or form," he says, cracking his knuckles, a sign he was brooding.

"Don't let your stubbornness get in the way of an opportunity, Dave. You'd network with anyone else; why not her?"

"Because she'll go out of her way to berate me and refuse to show me even the decency I deserve."

He could be right, and Dave always landed on his feet without her help, but it's hard to watch a mother treat her son that way. But then, Toots has always played hardball. I felt sorry for him. Hell, I felt sorry for me! I'd take Toots' money in a heartbeat!

"Oh Dave," I say to him, pulling his head to my chest and hugging him. Wrapping an arm around my waist, he lets me comfort him. "It will be okay. We can tighten our belts and move along. At least we've paid the last of the college tuition."

"And two of the cars are paid for. Except, now, I have to buy a car, or buy the company car. I have to send back my laptop and printer, and take over my phone service."

"When is your last day?"

"End of February," he says, suddenly looking up at me from our embrace. "Do I look old, babe?"

"No. You've aged much more gracefully than some of your friends," I tell him, and it's true. "You're still hot." To convince him, I kiss his forehead and stroke his hair behind his ear. I still think of us as if we're in our twenties. Every once in awhile, I gasp at what I see in the mirror. Who *is* that woman and what happened to her *neck*? When I bought wine yesterday in the grocery store, the young male clerk was literally checking me out to decide whether to card me. He'd smiled at me and casually glanced at my eyes, thinking I was maybe too old for him, and then when he got a gander at my *neck*, his face told me all bets were off!

"But all this gray hair is going to make me look like an old man when I'm out there competing with all the college grads," Dave says, bringing me back.

"Maybe, but you've got way more experience than they do."

"Well, experience can be expensive, and remember, there are a lot of others who are older than them but younger than me who are all looking at the same job sites. Why would anyone want to hire someone like me with nine or ten more years to retirement when they could snap up a kid who'll do three times what I've been doing for a third of the pay? You know, that's what it's going to boil down to. And when they see this keg of beer I'm carrying around my midsection, they'll look at me as if I'd be a liability."

"If you think that about yourself, they're sure to think it, too. You've got to sell yourself. Nothing's ever stopped you before, Dave. You can work the angles and make them all believe what you want them to believe. You're crafty that way. Start hitting the gym. You're going to need all the endorphins you can get. We'll spiff up your wardrobe." I'm on a roll, now. "We can do this. And…if there's one thing you are, it's persistent," I say, realizing *my* new job in this household—captain of the cheer squad.

"Thank you, baby," he says, stroking the silver and black goatee. "Maybe it's time to shave."

Chapter 8

HOPE

Why is it that when we're down, we always tend to dredge up our past failures, as clear and painful as if they'd just happened yesterday? Well, okay, in my case my other major failure happened two years ago, but the wound still smarts, as if it had just happened last week—before Liam. As I drive home from the bar this evening, the trip gives me thirty minutes to wallow in my past transgressions, despite how loudly I turn up the radio and belt out how *you and I are never getting back together* with Taylor Swift. There is nothing like a good country music song to help blast away the murk. At least it will make you think that there is at least one other person out there who has done something just as stupid as you have; or someone else has been dumped on, just like you. I can't quite get that from listening to the amazing vocal and instrumental music Liam likes when he paints. I am completely unfamiliar with the music that he likes; I just know it intrigues me, even though I can't relate to it, another fundamental factor in our demise, apparently.

Snow begins to swirl against my windshield as I leave the city, and by the time I've reached the small town limits of Pleasant Ridge, there is a dusting on the road, and the white flakes assault my windshield like an invasion of tiny aliens. Deer stand in awe of my headlights on the roadside as I glide carefully along the country highway where I am the only vehicle at this time of night; past midnight. Lee Brice serenades me on my way, the perfect Valentine's ballad called "Love Like Crazy," making me swipe at a tear on my face, and cursing because I have let my guard down without even the presence of alcohol to lure my brain into whatever sappy territory I've wandered. *Why doesn't he love me the way I want to be loved?* Fuck it. Might as well sort through all the skeletons in my closet. It's a long ride.

Okay, I've never had much trouble getting a date, but this is big. I have to skip over all the boyfriends I had in middle school and high school. I'm sure I thought my heart had broken so many times before now, but only the important ones come to mind on a night like this. The public boyfriends are the ones people see when they look at you with those pitying little glances. It all hurts, but I've chosen not to waste time over all the heartbreaks; however, being engaged was a major foray into the public eye of society, and I was certainly there once.

Matt Broadway was my fiancé two years ago. We met in college when we did our internships at the same elementary school. He taught P.E. and I taught art. Three of us carpooled together and were prone to go for beers on Fridays after the long and crazy weeks we'd put in. It was like being on a roller coaster, and none of us knew what we were doing at first. Matt was great with the kids and fun to be around. He was so supportive of me when I'd express how insecure I was with my teaching skills or when I worried about grades, or better yet, when I'd gotten in over my head with the credit cards I'd taken out for *emergencies*. The wardrobe I thought I needed for teaching turned into quite the national disaster after I'd racked up a few thousand dollars on my cards. I consoled myself with all the air miles I was racking up as well.

We quickly became an item. Matt was good-looking and took care of his appearance so that all the women took note of him and his clean-shaven arms and legs. His sandy wavy hair and easy smile always tugged at me in a way I couldn't resist. We went together like models on a catalog page, people said; perfect for each other in all the ways that count. We were engaged by the time we graduated and he'd snapped up a job in Raleigh, where we'd both wanted to live. I was able to get hired on an interim contract for the art teacher, who was going out on maternity leave at a nearby school. When that was over, I got a job at an elementary school in the area. Matt and I set up house in an apartment we rented in a nice, older neighborhood. I thought I had it made.

Matt's meticulous nature was so appealing at first. He didn't mind cleaning up when I forgot to. He paid the bills I'd neglected, and he encouraged me to get out of debt. I soon realized that my untidy ways and financial irresponsibility got under Matt's skin bit by bit. He seemed competitive with me about the smallest things, and he would be irritated if I outdid him. I felt as though my supportive friend had somehow turned against me, and that everything we did was turned into a competition. His fastidiousness began to irritate me as much as my sloth incensed him. All we did was argue. We argued about the bills, the chores, then the wedding arrangements. Neither of us was happy. He'd complained about me to his parents, making me feel like I'd never live up to being what they wanted for their son. And in the end, I didn't. He didn't want to be with me, and I didn't want anything to do with him, either. So one wedding dress and a photographer later, we were both single again. He was lucky enough to keep his job, even though he got moved to a less than desirable school, which was more than I got. My art position was cut so I moved back home and sent out job applications all over the state, but the budget cuts to the arts left me without any hope of employment. Three weeks ago, I heard from friends that he'd gotten married. *I wonder if she has my ring.*

And then after I gave myself eight months to recover and get my feet back on the ground, I met Liam. He was the total opposite of Matt, making me sure that his carefree ways and erudite maturity would paint the backdrop for my blossoming into the person I was meant to be. He loved everything I did. He liked my art, my personal style, and took care of me spiritually without the fuss of material things, letting me do my own thing. I was inspired by his art, wanting to explore my potential with photography. I took endless photographs of him, and he painted me many times, with and without clothes. The way he lived, without any desire for material possessions, challenged me to do the same. He sold or gave away most of his work, and constantly talked of his travels, his desire to see the world, and painting what he saw, creating beauty for others to enjoy. He saw things quite differently than I did, but with Liam, it wasn't a competition. It didn't connect us either, as I came to see in the last months.

I knew there was a restlessness about him that I couldn't figure out. He'd talked about selling his art to a dealer in Italy, one that a friend had used and recommended. We'd even discussed traveling there, but he knew I couldn't afford to go. I'd still been trying to get myself out of debt. Liam had never been anywhere longer than a year so it was not really a shock when I found out he was leaving, but I'd never realized the extent of his plans with Amelia…until two days ago.

Chapter 9

CHERIE

If Hope is the spitting image of Dave, then Wesley is my reincarnation, except thankfully taller. I like seeing a tall, youthful me come swinging through the front door in her pea coat, scarf, and tall brown boots, a style I recognize, and probably paid for last year. Good. We are still getting mileage out of these clothes.

"Mama!" she says, hugging my neck, her ash blond curls softly tickling my cheek. I hold her back to look at her. And to think, she does not believe she is pretty.

"Mama! Have you lost weight? You look great! Hey, Daddy!" she says, and she gives Dave a cheery hug as well. "You're wearing your coat?"

"I'm grilling," he says. He's the only man I know who barbeques in February. My mood is rapidly improving, despite the pile of Honors English tests I know I have to grade after dinner while they watch the Duke vs. Carolina basketball game on TV; it's the hottest rivalry we have going in North Carolina.

Dave is looking better too, with Wesley here, safe at last. I always worry when my girls drive at night. His salmon is resting, just off the grill, and the two of us have just finished concocting the cucumber dill sauce to go on top. The asparagus is roasting in the oven, and a pot of garlic smashed potatoes sits warming on the stove. Is it any wonder we're fat and happy?

"Hey, Wes! Are you hungry? We've got salmon and asparagus for dinner."

"Asparagus?" she asks, wrinkling her nose. Her ivory cheeks have gone pink from the cold, even from her brief dash from the car, and her hazel eyes are sparkling. I know what she is thinking; it will make her pee smell funny, and after years of admonishing that kind of talk, she won't say it, but we all laugh anyway.

"So what's the word, girlfriend? Ready for the big game tonight?" Dave asks, extending a hand to take her coat, coming out of his own.

She grins as she hands over the coat and pulls off her gloves, slowly, one finger at a time. "Yes, I am! And actually, I do have a bit of news. Is Hope here?"

"No, honey, she's working at the bar tonight. Didn't she tell you?"

"Yes, but I wanted to make sure. Mama, you know I told you that Ren wanted to know where I was on Valentine's Day?" she says, pulling off a glove.

"Yes. Did he send flowers to the hospital?" I ask, throwing a chiding glance at Dave, but of course, it is lost on him. Or at least, he pretends not to be rebuked.

"No. He *brought* them to me at the hospital. He flew in from Austin to see me, and he *proposed!*" she squeals, pulling off the left glove and holding her hand up to the light, so we can see the light glinting off of a diamond ring on her finger. A very large diamond.

"Ohhhh!" Dave and I say together. I am totally knocked off my feet, but Dave nods happily.

"I knew it. Good for Ren. Congratulations, baby girl!"

"Oh, my God!" I say, grasping my daughter's hand to examine the lovely ring, set in white gold, or maybe it's platinum, with a princess cut diamond in the center, surrounded by smaller ones spilling down the band as well. "That's *gorgeous*! Did you pick it out?"

"No! He did this all by himself. I had no idea!" she laughs, her face flushed with happiness. "Ren said he'd talked to you about it at Thanksgiving, and that he's asked Hope for her blessing too!" We nod. The young man did it right.

"Tell me all about it! What did he say? How did he propose?" I ask, holding her hands, literally feeling her excitement flow into me.

Wesley giggles, the sound only *she* can make, the same signature giggle that got her in trouble with so many of her teachers back in elementary school. "Mama, calm down!" she laughs. "He…he brought me the flowers just as I was getting off my shift, I guess so all the nurses could see," she began.

"Oh! That is *so sweet*! What a charmer!" I say in full gush so Dave will get a clue, and I see him doing a little eye roll at my dig.

"So then, he asked if I'd stop in the solarium with him for a minute before we got on the elevator to go to my car. He seemed so anxious, you know, like he was about to burst at the seams. Nobody else was in there and it was kind of dark, so he took me over by the fountain and started talking to me about how much he loved me and missed me. He said he wanted to do some things, lots of things, like plant some trees, and find a house together, and ride horses on the beach, and have kids. And that he wanted to do it all with me. Then he held my hand and told me how he missed holding my hand, and that he wanted to hold my hand forever," she says, breaking into an even larger grin. "Then he got down on one knee and pulled out this little velvet box and asked me if I'd hold his hand forever, as his wife…." By now she begins to tear up, and so do we. "And of course I said yes, and I was shaking when he put this gorgeous ring on my finger! A couple of the nurses had followed us down there and they were standing around the corner, squealing and clapping their hands and hugging us! It was so sweet, and of course, I started crying, and Ren was crying. He said he'd wanted to wait until we were somewhere else, but he just couldn't stand it. He'd seen the solarium on the way in and kind of thought, 'Hey, that would be the perfect place.' And it kind of was!"

Shivers are running through me and I am truly excited for my daughter. "Oh, honey! That is so wonderful. I'm so happy for you!" I give Wesley a hug, and Dave joins in, congratulating her again. This new happiness is something I want to dive into myself, but then I think of Dave's news, and what has just happened to Hope, and my heart sinks visibly.

A flicker of recognition passes over Wesley's face and she looks at Dave, who glances back at me.

"Oh, I *know*! This is really bad timing, but Ren didn't know about Hope and Liam. I want to be so happy, but knowing what's happening with her makes me feel bad. I almost didn't come home, but I'd told Hope I'd be here. He went to Cary to visit his parents to tell them the news, and to give me a chance to come here and be with Hope. I'm sorry; I guess this is not what she'll want to hear."

"Well....It's not just that, honey bun; there's something else that's got us a little down tonight. Still we're really happy for you! You shouldn't have anything dampen your spirits," Dave says and draws Wesley into one of his bear hugs.

"So, what's going on, Daddy?"

"Why don't you two sit down and I'll open this bottle of wine," I offer, and they take their usual breakfast places on the island stools, as I slice the foil off the chardonnay with the wine tool and begin to twist the corkscrew into the cork.

Wesley watches Dave's face carefully. "She's not *pregnant*?"

"No!" we say in unison, and I add, "At least we don't think so."

Dave shrugs. "No. I lost my job yesterday, sugar."

"Daddy! Why?"

"It wasn't a performance thing. The company went through another restructure and eliminated our whole division. It was pretty ugly. Daniel, Tim, and I all got cut at the same time."

Her brow is knit with concern; she has never seen her father in a vulnerable position before, so I see she is at a loss for words as I pour the golden wine into three goblets. Dave and I look at each other, wondering how to soften the blow, and he answers all of her questions, which are the same ones I asked an hour ago. Feeling surreal, I drift about the kitchen on automatic pilot, pulling plates from the cabinets as they discuss the ramifications of our new situation. As I seem to float unaffected through the kitchen, doing the wifely, motherly things one does, I feel so many emotions at once, pulling at me from all the angles—shock for Dave, sadness for Hope, exhilaration for Wesley and Ren, and disappointment for myself. At least we are healthy. *At least it's not cancer*, my mother used to say; before she had it, anyway. We have some savings. We have each other. There is the severance, and health insurance, and I am an able bodied person who is blessed to have a job, and much too young to be rocking on the front porch. But I don't want to rock. I want to rock 'n' roll! Dave and I wanted to travel…. But not tonight. All of those feelings will have to wait. Everything is on hold. There are no deadlines and timeframes. Except for one.

"Have you and Ren talked about when you want to get married?" I ask quietly, making Wesley look at her hands which are folded tentatively on the island. She is deflating in front of us. I see a tear glisten at the corner of her eye as Dave rubs her shoulders.

"We thought about the fall; October maybe, but it can wait. There's no hurry. I'll be working then, hopefully, in *Austin*," she says, looking at us for our reaction. I've been steeling myself for the time when she'd leave us, but Texas seems like an entire continent away. "I could live here after graduation and save money for the wedding. I can babysit or wait tables again. And the wedding doesn't have to be big. Neither of us wants a big to-do, you know?"

She has wasted no time in down-playing her plans, but I don't buy it for a second. We know Ren's family is large and well off, and they love to celebrate, which is why we like them so well. And I know my daughter has dreamed of her special day, as all young ladies do when they first fall in love and imagine all the magic that could be in store for them.

"Well…nothing has to be decided right away," I say, smiling, but feeling like the damn pin that just burst my daughter's bubble.

Chapter 10

HOPE

I find myself sitting in my car again, looking at my parents' house, wondering why I am here. My little sister's red Honda is in the driveway and the lights are off inside, except for the blue light from the TV downstairs. I imagine my parents have gone to bed and that she is curled up under our favorite blanket on the couch waiting for me, watching TV and texting Ren until I arrive, to give her the low down of what happened with Liam. So I haul myself out of the car and go inside.

Shaking snow from my hair, and peeling off my coat, I can hear the sports announcers on the TV even before I enter the den. I find not only my sister snuggled under her blanket, but my father as well on the opposite sofa, sprawled, half-covered with a matching blanket, his mouth open, and snoring softly.

Ah, yes, the Carolina basketball fans, asleep after the Duke game that has resulted in double overtimes. I have no clue who has won the contest, as I could care less about any of that tonight, but it was playing on the flat screen when I left Natty's. I should care, with it being my sister's school and all, and had she gotten me tickets, it would be a different story. From the commentary, I quickly surmise that Carolina has squeaked by one more time, and the replays are in full swing as I lift the remote control from my father's hand and flick off the TV, causing his and Wesley's eyelids to flutter in confusion at the interruption in sound. I wonder how long they'd sleep here if the noise were to continue the rest of the night. Rowdy is stretched out in front of the fireplace where the gas logs flicker. He thumps his tail at me but does not move.

"Hey, sugar," my dad's voice is groggy, as he extends a hand to me.

"Hey," I say back. "Were you two waiting up for me?"

"We were trying to," he yawns, stretching. "Carolina won in double overtimes," he says.

"Yeah, I just heard. Good for the Tar Heels. It's snowing."

"Really?" He looks around as if he could see, but gives up. "Here, sit with me a minute," he says, clearing a spot for me as he sits up and sheds his blanket while my sister continues to sleep soundlessly on her opposing sofa.

"How was work tonight?" he asks.

"Slow at first, but then it picked up. I made eighty bucks."

"Then it was worth it. And you made it home okay? Were the roads getting slick?"

"No, not really. I took my time."

"Good…I wanted to wait up so I could tell you what's going on."

"What's…going on?"

Dad looks at me with a harried face, surprising since he's just woken up. "I lost my job yesterday. The company did another restructure and this time they cut my entire division. Tim, Daniel, and me, we're all out of jobs, effective at the end of the month."

I gape at him. Not my dad. He's my rock. I can't imagine him being down on his luck. He's always been on top of his game, even when Toots put the screws to him back when I was in the third grade and she'd canned him for some Chinese people she'd never met. *What the hell?*

"*What?* You didn't say anything about it yesterday."

He shrugs. "I know. There was a lot going on. And it was Valentine's Day," he says, giving me an ironic smile. "It sucks, but we'll get through it. We'll be fine. I'll find something else."

I stare at him, still in disbelief. "*Daddy!* When did you find out?"

"Yesterday. I just told your mom today. It's been quite a shock for both of us."

"I'll bet. Wow…. Maybe you should get the band together again."

He tosses back his head. "Ha! That would be fun, but fairly unproductive. I doubt I could scrounge up the rest of the guys at this point anyway."

"They were gonna play at my wedding."

"Yes, they were. But that was because it was your wedding."

He smiles and I have to smile back; all that seems like decades ago. It was fun planning it to a point, when Matt wasn't involved. Too bad I couldn't have married someone else. I was good at planning, just not good at picking the right groom.

"Oh, well. I'm sorry, Daddy. You'll find something." He's not the first dad I've heard about who has lost his job these days.

"Yeah, a young stud like me shouldn't have any problem."

"You will." I look at him, and suddenly, he seems old to me, something I've never really thought about my father. He's always been cool in my book. But tonight, his hair is more silver than black, and his midsection is chunkier than I remember. And after consuming the beers that are represented on the tray by the three empty bottles, he looks more tired than ever. He knows what I'm thinking, and his eyes fall to the floor for a moment. *Ugh!* It's awful. I know the feeling. I've had five jobs since I graduated from college and look at me, living at home like some lazy-assed freeloader.

"Well…I guess I'll go on to bed. I hope you sleep well, sugar."

I cover his hand a moment with mine. "You too, Daddy. I'll see you in the morning."

"Okay. Pancakes?" he asks, as he collects the empty bottles, the spoils of his celebration with Wesley.

"Sure. I don't have to work until six o'clock in the evening."

He stands, tossing the blanket over the back of the sofa and gives me a hug and a kiss on my forehead. "Will you put Rowdy out in the garage before you all turn out the lights?"

"Sure, Daddy. Goodnight. I love you."

"Night, sugar. I love you, too," he says, going into the kitchen and placing the bottles in the recycling bucket before heading toward his bedroom. My mother is surely out for the count at this time of night, and I appreciate that he's tried to wait up for me. I guess he and I will be holding down the fort while she works. Rowdy pushes his butt up in the air and stretches, then wags his tail and comes to get a lick off my wet shoes. I stroke his ears and I swear he smiles at me.

I turn back to Wesley, who is stretching on her sofa, and as her hands reach above her head, she smiles at me. "Hey," she says groggily.

"Hey." I squint my eyes, noticing the spectacular glimmer of a diamond ring on her left hand in the firelight. "What the hell is *that*?"

"Oh. Shit," she says, collecting herself and coming to a sitting position on the sofa in her sweats and Carolina T-shirt. "Ren flew in from Austin yesterday and proposed," she says sheepishly, as if I'd never figure it out on my own. This is just great. She had the best Valentine's Day ever and I had the worst. Wesley and I are at two completely different places, polar opposites. I'm the South Pole, frozen, desolate and barren, without hope of survival. And she's the North Pole…with Santa Claus. My sister is about to be Mrs. Claus and I'm circling the drain. Of course, I thought I had Santa Claus too, and he turned out to be a big fat lie. Go figure. Life really sucks sometimes.

And two bombs at once; her *and* Dad, and I haven't even had a chance to tell my part of the ever-increasing family saga.

"Huh. Well, congratulations. Ren called me, you know, a while back to get my approval. So I've known about this for a couple of months."

"So…are you happy for me, or what?"

I take a step closer so I can sit beside her on the sofa. "Let me see that thing," I say, picking up her hand to examine the ring; the big, fucking beautiful ring that sits on her finger; the ring that should be mine, considering I'm four years older and should be getting married first. Crap! I just want to wallow in self-pity, especially now. But it wouldn't be nice. And I am happy for her, really I am. "Wow! Ren outdid himself. You know, I saw this before you did."

"Are you trying to make me feel bad?"

"He sent me a picture to see if I thought you'd like it."

"What'd you say?"

"I said, to hell with her if she doesn't; I'll marry you!"

My sister dissolves into laughter and we hug each other on the couch.

"I'm happy for you, Wesley; I really am. Ren is great. You're so lucky. Can I take your engagement pictures?"

"Of course! I was hoping you would. He'll be here Sunday afternoon, before he has to fly out that night. Want to cram in a photoshoot?"

"Sure. Maybe there will still be snow on the ground. We can go over to Mr. Ellis's place and shoot in front of his red barn."

"Ooh, yeah! And…I was hoping you'll be my maid of honor; that is, if we don't elope."

"Oh! Of course I will! So, how did he propose?" I ask, knowing she'll tell this story a hundred times, just like I did, and I listen with due respect to the details as her face lights up, the way it usually does, the way it freaking should when she mentions Ren. After four years together, we all believe he is one solid dude.

"Wow! That's so romantic. I'll bet Daddy's ecstatic."

"Yeah, he is, and thanks. You know how Daddy loves Ren. But I'm sorry. I didn't want this to hurt your feelings. I came here so you can tell me all about Liam."

I blow air between my lips in an attempt to blow it off, but she is not fooled. I'm sure my tears in the car on the way home have left my eyes and my entire face red and puffy. I even feel a little heave as I draw in a breath. But I pull myself together and say, "Screw him. He's leaving in a month, so what else is there to say? I'm moving on. He and Amelia can go fuck each other for all I care. And they probably will."

"Well, I'm glad you're not bitter," she says and we both laugh. My usual potty mouth has become even filthier in my current state of abandonment, and she can tell how upset I am by the number of dirty words that have just come flying out.

"Ohhh! I'm sorry! I'm *awful!* Please, someone put me out of my misery!" I say, wiping my hands across my face and shaking my head. "I'll tell you the whole pathetic story, but it just boils down to this; he wanted to go to Italy and see the Sistine Chapel and all the other masterpieces of the world, and I didn't fit in with his plans. I mean the guy has a bucket list a mile long, and I'm not on it. I never was."

"Yes, you were," Wesley says, taking my hand. "You were his muse."

"Well, if I was, I guess we're both over it now. The only thing that bothers me is that I've got to start all over again, you know? I'm so freaking *old!*"

"Right, twenty-six is *ancient.* I can see your wrinkles from here. Really, though, how *are* you?" she asks, and I know she wants me to pour out all my feelings, but I can't just now. The last thing I feel like doing is crying again, so I'll just continue to blow it off. Besides, she's so happy....

"I'll really miss the sex," I say, making her snort, but I mean it. Matt had nothing compared to Liam in that department. Just thinking about sex with Liam makes me shudder, and heave again. Oh, the things we did to each other on a regular basis! But I won't say this, even to my sister. What has this guy done to me? I'm ruined. There will never be another man who will beguile me and intrigue me as Liam has. I knew we would end, but it sucks all the same.

"You won't have to wait long, I wouldn't think. You've never had trouble getting a date. Think of it as a new adventure. Who are you going to meet next? There's someone even better than Liam out there for you, Hope." Her eyes catch my purple purse. "Oh, wow, look at that purse! Where did you get that?"

"Liam's parting gift to me, my Valentine's Day present."

"He must feel really guilty."

"I guess, but it *is* just what I wanted."

"Surprising, though, as material things mean so little to him. That was pretty thoughtful of him, knowing it would mean so much to you."

"I know, right? It was just a guilty payoff."

I watch Wesley fold her blanket as I rub Rowdy's head. He rests his chin on my knee and closes his eyes, resettling his tongue as if he's dreaming. "Are you bummed about Dad's job? I mean, it can't bode well for a wedding if he and Mama don't have any money."

"Yep," she says, running her hands through her hair, and twisting it into a knot. "I kept expecting them to ask me to elope all through dinner."

"Maybe it's not a bad idea. Save yourself a lot of hassle that way."

She scoffs at me. "Like you would have done it! I remember how you turned into Bridezilla. Please shoot me if I get like that!"

That hurts. "I'll shoot you; don't worry....Have you looked at dresses?"

She sinks back down on the sofa with me and takes over stroking Rowdy's head. "Just online. There are a few I really like, but now...I guess I'll be readjusting my expectations. Maybe something really simple, like that ivory beaded gown we saw when we were looking at prom dresses my senior year—remember?"

My heart sinks for her. I don't think I could be as complacent as she is right now, were the bridal slipper on my foot. I have a perfectly good Vera Wang hanging in my closet, but we both know it is a couple of sizes too small for Wesley, my little sister who is a good four inches taller than I am, and slightly heavier. Still, I can't part with it, even though it might fetch a price close to what Mama paid for it if I'd knock it down on the wedding gown website. Subliminally, I suppose I think I shall actually wear it someday.

"You know, Ren doesn't care. We can have a sweet little outdoor wedding in a park somewhere with just the families, or have it at the church with the reception in the courtyard with mints and nuts and punch. I really don't care either, as long as we get good pictures so we can remember it all."

"Have you talked about a date yet?"

"We like October," she says, but there is not the excitement in her voice I was expecting.

"I guess you'll be moving to Austin after graduation then?"

"If I can find a job. I'm planning on going down during spring break in a couple of weeks to look around at the hospitals, but I guess I'll be back here until I know for sure. I need to get busy sending out resumes and filling out applications. Maybe you should come, too. Austin's a great place. And there's lots of hot guys!"

"Hmm." Two ridiculous offers in as many days—Italy and Austin. Why don't I jump at either chance? What is wrong with me? I feel the need to shift the attention from myself. "You won't have a problem getting a nursing job. It's not like you're an *art teacher*! You were so smart! You picked the right career path. Jeez, you live in a dorm still, without the hassle of furniture and utilities! You should go and be with Ren after graduation. Elope. Don't waste your time here."

"I like being home. It's the last time I'll get to live here. Maybe Mama and I will have things to plan...."

"Believe me, living at home is not all it's cracked up to be, but I guess there could be worse alternatives."

"Yeah, like being homeless. At least you can keep Daddy company while you're here. He's so worried that he won't find something at his age."

"I know. I can't believe he lost his job. He's competing with people *our* age. He must be so depressed. How's Mama handling it?"

"She just found out about an hour before I got here. I'm sure she's disappointed. You know, she was supposed to retire at the end of the school year."

"Oh, yeah; I forgot about that."

"We were supposed to have a double celebration, you know—her retirement and my graduation."

"That does suck."

"Maybe Daddy will find something and we won't have to worry about any of this."

We stare at the fire for a moment and then she turns to me. "Are you pregnant?"

Chapter 11

CHERIE

Bacon sizzles in the pan, the way Dave insists it should be cooked—another rebellious act against Toots. She hasn't cooked bacon...*ever*. I cook it in the microwave to keep the grease down, but it makes him happy to fry it in the pan. He needs to be happy, I think, as I watch him tend the strips in his plaid pajama pants and T-shirt, hair sticking up in points, whiskers on his face in places they usually aren't. Normally, he'd be singing, but I haven't heard a tune out of his mouth since Valentine's Day, poor baby. I set his coffee beside him as Wesley slips silently into the kitchen in much the same garb.

"Good morning, sunshine!" Dave greets her, and she gives him the first hug. This is new. She's my mama's girl, but Dave has new needs, so she takes care of him first. She will be a good wife, I think, smiling to myself and sipping my coffee.

"Good morning. It snowed last night!" she says, her voice still thick with sleep. There are indeed a good two inches of snow on the ground and I look out the window again, as if I need to check. It is pretty, sparkling like sugar, the way the morning sun hits it—an unexpected pleasure. We don't see snow much; maybe once or twice in the winter. I catch a glimpse of Hope out the kitchen window, in her pajamas, boots, and

Dave's coat, taking photographs of the trees in the snow as the morning sun peeps softly through their branches.

"Yes, it did. Sleep well?" I ask, as she gives me my hug and nods, a yawn having taken over her ability to speak. I pour a mug of steaming coffee for her as she slips onto her barstool and rests her chin on her hand. "What time did you and Hope go to bed?"

"After one or so. We stayed up talking, and I looked at all her new clothes." I cringe. "She has the most amazing new boots. Of course, I can't wear them. Did you see the purse Liam gave her? It's a *Tory Burch*!"

"Mm-hmm. Big whoop; I will *not* have this *shit of a man* become a folk hero! How'd she seem to you?"

"Better than I'd have thought. She's listening to country music, which is a good thing," she says, twirling a strand of her curly hair around her index finger.

"How is listening to country music a good thing?" I ask, feeling out of the loop again. Damn it! I'm not going to be old!

"Mama! The country songs are the best ones. They have the most heartfelt lyrics, especially the ballads."

"Yeah, babe, country music's where it's at," Dave says, winking at Wesley. He knows I hate it when he ends his sentences with redundant prepositions, and he does it just to spite me. I pretend not to notice. He is an otherwise articulate man, another of his attributes that make him such a good salesman. He can talk to the business execs and the good ol' boys and be perfectly comfortable in either's company. "I'm thinkin' I might work me up some Zac Brown and Rascal Flatts songs, in case I get lucky enough to score a gig over at Bimini's."

"For real, Dad? I know Jeff would love to have you play there, now that you'll have time."

"Yep, we been talkin'," he says, trying out his country side, no doubt. I don't know whether I can stand this. My mind brings back all my old favorites growing up: Carol King, Simon and Garfunkel, Jackson Brown, Dan Fogelberg, Bonnie Raitt; those are some heartfelt lyrics for you, to say nothing of the great poets like Elizabeth Barrett Browning and Shakespeare....Dave reads my mind.

"Zac Brown is the new James Taylor," he says with a twinkle in his eye.

"Really?" I ask, knowing he's trying to get my goat as he lifts bacon onto paper towels and gives the pancake batter a stir while I pour orange juice and set out knives and forks for the bar. I'm supposed to stay out of his way when he commands the kitchen. Hope thumps into the mudroom, knocking snow off her boots, setting down her camera and discarding her outerwear, her face still a puffy blotched mess. I wonder whether she stayed up crying after Wesley went to sleep. The sight of her makes my heart ache. At least she finds solace in her camera.

We all murmur good mornings to each other. The girls are looking conspiratorially at each other, which unnerves me. Hope goes to Dave and hugs him around the neck. She will make a good wife, too, I think, feeling a pang of sadness for all of them, with all these question marks floating around the room. I'm the only one in the room with a secure future, I suddenly realize, pushing the tempting thoughts of retirement away once again, trying to remember what I learned the other day at our staff training about how to create and collect assignments online. I will have to pay more attention to things that are going on at work again. I thought I could slip off the horizon quietly before I would be required to immerse myself in technology, but it's not going to happen. I'd better wake up and jump back into the game before I sink. My girls cannot fathom that Dave and I got through college before the personal computer was invented. Even a book is going to become obsolete at some point. I cannot stand it! I live for the smell of old paper and the feel of pages in my hands.

I slide Hope's coffee across the island to her, watching her take a grateful sip. She looks to Wesley, then to Dave, and finally her gaze lands on me. "I guess now is as good a time as any to tell you all this," she begins, looking to Wesley again for the supportive nod she gets.

Oh my God! Here it comes, I communicate to Dave with my wide eyes.

"I'm getting a dog," she says.

At least ten seconds go by as we all stare at one another, before I speak.

"No. You're not."

"But, I am, Mama."

"You can't live here and have a dog. Rowdy is quite enough," I reply, and on cue, our black lab pads into the kitchen from his usual spot by the back door. Absently, Wesley cups his ear in her hand as he sniffs at her bedroom slippers. I remember the ones I had that he ate one evening when we were otherwise occupied; my fifteen-year-old L.L. Bean wicked good slippers, gone in a thirty-minute dog orgasm. Shit.

"Why not? I'll be taking care of it. You won't have to do a thing," Hope continues, and she is nine years old again, giving it her best shot, but I'm getting pissed, feeling her tornado beginning to form. Dave is watching us as if we are two cats about to square off. Maybe we are.

"Right. You'll be working odd hours and Daddy will be the one doing all of the potty training and the poopy scooping, and that wasn't in the deal." Maybe if I put Dave in the middle of this, it will work out better. I have never done this to him before, but it could work! What I really mean is: It will be *me* taking care of this puppy and not her. I am getting no help from Wesley, whose face has gone to mush in an instant.

"Aw! What kind of dog is it?"

Hope is glad to have the support, and I begin to think this scene has been rehearsed last night.

Hope gathers strength from her sister's interest as she continues, "It's a Papillon. Liam got it for me for a Valentine's Day present, in addition to my awesome purse."

"Ohhh! Those are those *cute* little brown and white dogs with the butterfly ears!"

"Yes, and they're very smart, too. Our landlady's daughter-in-law breeds them."

Dave is absolutely useless at this point, and I'm throwing him S.O.S.es with my eyeballs.

"Don't they shed?" he offers pathetically, waving the spatula, as he guards the pancakes he's got going in the pan. Surely, he knows we're being duped.

"Maybe a little, but with brushing, it won't be as bad as Rowdy," Hope says, looking disdainfully at our dog, who is watching her with soulful and loyal brown eyes, wondering about the blow he's just been dealt.

This is pushing the disrespect to the limit and I feel my neck and chest flash with heat. Dave is shaking his head, and Wesley is clasping her hands in delight. "Ohh! When are you getting it? Is it a male or a female?" The girl is jumping up and down! Of course she is; she doesn't live here. She won't have to run the puppy in and out of the house every hour on the hour…in the rain, and the mud, and the snow, *and the cold.* I remember having puppies.

Hope looks victorious. "Liam texted me this morning. They're bringing her up tomorrow. We're meeting at Katharine's at 11:00."

Wesley suddenly looks somber. "Oh. Are you ready to see him… Liam, this soon, I mean?"

"Oh! Come on! Hope. You are *not* getting a dog."

"Mom, Liam's already paid for it."

"How convenient. Now you really can't go to Italy with him, can you?"

The kitchen is silent. The obvious truth has hit the fan, and I am somehow the bad guy in all of this. Hope looks at me as if I have swiped her jugular with my rusty saber. The color leaves her face, and she turns to glance at Dave. Wesley wants to be invisible.

"I'm not hungry," Hope says and walks quietly out of the room.

Wesley and Dave look at me as if I've tossed a bucket of water on the Wicked Witch of the West. *You've killed her!*

"Well…at least we know she's not pregnant," Dave says, setting a plate of pancakes on the island.

Chapter 12

HOPE

As I pull my Civic down the drive of Katharine England's historic Irving Park mansion, at almost 11:00 a.m., I still find it surreal that I actually lived here for the better part of a year. Well, living in the pool house is *almost* living here. I used to pretend that the whole estate was mine, zipping back here to park, and whipping off my sunglasses to sit down under the umbrella with Liam, who'd have a glass of sangria or something equally tempting waiting for me on those lovely afternoons when I'd meet him at home after work. Like I was somebody. As if we were a wealthy, young, and happy couple who couldn't get enough of each other. It could have been the heady feel of this place, or the heady feel of my lover, or maybe it was the combination of the two, but I realize now that I was living in a fantasy world then. Four days ago.

Someone has shoveled the drive. Mr. Sims, Katharine's gardener, has been busy, or maybe it was Liam. The first day he invited me here to see his studio in hopes that I'd model for his painting, I had wondered how he'd scored living here. Anyone who ever read a newspaper in this town knew that Katharine England was a notable arts supporter, as one wing of the university's art museum was named after her. And she had a penchant for encouraging young, up-and-coming talent, so Liam had been next in line to rent her pool house studio when she'd discovered him at a university art exhibit. Of course, I knew about her from my own forays into the art world, and I'd met her once at a local gala. She'd remembered me as well, not because of my impressive photography collection, but because she and my grandmother traveled in the same social circles. That tidbit had scored points for Liam and had earned me a place in the pool house as well when the time came for him to entertain his muse full-time. Katharine had not batted an eyelash. I suppose she understood it was the artist's prerogative to be promiscuous.

No one is about at this hour on a Sunday. I see the SUV that must belong to her son, Peter, and his wife, who have brought my puppy. Katharine is a devout churchgoer, but even she does not venture out in the snow at her age, and with her son here, they have apparently chosen to stay home. I park in my usual spot and emerge, trotting quickly in the cold to the door. Should I knock? Four days ago, I would have breezed right in, knowing it was my place, too. This is all so strange. Does Katharine think I will continue to rent the place? Did anyone ask me? Through the glass, I can see that Liam has carefully packed my framed photographs that used to share wall space with his paintings in a couple of boxes. Our gallery home is no more. Another box holds personal items that are obviously no longer wanted in this house. I knock, looking quickly away, so I won't be emotional when he lets me in.

He is there in an instant. "Hey! Why didn't you come in? It's freezing!" he says, closing the door behind me, extending a hand to me, but I choose to shove mine deep into my pockets and avoid eye contact with him as I step inside. He persists with his glance, but at least he doesn't try to hug me. "I…uh, I have coffee going. You want some?" he asks.

"Sure," I nod. It is always cold in the pool house in the winter because of all the glass, which makes for great lighting. Just the same, we always felt like starving artists, shuffling about in our frumpy sweaters and drinking tea to stay warm in the winter. This part I won't miss. But the summers....

He'd opened the door for me the same way that day, after our first date, when he'd invited me over to see his studio. I'd teased him about living at Katharine's and being her pool boy, but I wasn't far off. She'd promised him half off his rent if he'd clean her pool, something Mr. Sims, her gardener, had never enjoyed. So Liam had learned about chlorine testing, how to use the vacuum, and skimming the leaves off the water.

He'd asked me to stand by the windows and glanced back at me a time or two while he poured our wine that day, a red blend he'd helped bottle at his father's winery in Virginia. I hoped he would kiss me this time, wondering what I'd done wrong the first time, but I was definitely feeling that sizzle again between us. What happened next surprised me. Handing me a glass, he began to lay down the ground rules.

"I hope you'll agree to model for me," he began tentatively. "I've wanted to paint you since the day you walked into the shop. I won't ask you to do anything you're uncomfortable with. We'll work together well, I think." He looked directly at me, eyes softening a bit. "I want more than a working relationship with you, Hope. But, this is going to sound weird...you need to know, I...I don't believe in marriage," he said, a bit sheepishly. He stood close enough so that in the hot breeze I could smell the perspiration beginning on his skin, mixed with his clean hair that was just drying from his shower. It was dark like his eyes, and fell to his collarbone.

After a moment, I asked, "Really?" trying to mask my surprise and genuine disappointment, while doing my best to challenge him. He was taking in my gauzy dress and the way the air stirred my hair.

He looked me squarely in the eyes. "No. I hope you don't think I'm being egotistical or presumptuous, but I think it's best to be honest and up-front about it, from the beginning. I like you, Hope. I don't want to mislead you, if it ever gets to that. But marriage, and settling down; I can't do it. I want to travel and paint all over the world. I can't get tied down. I have to be able to leave whenever the time is right. You need to know that now."

The words should have sounded arrogant, but the sincerity in his voice and in his face made them humble, almost as if he were apologizing. I sipped my wine, trying to think of a reply that would make it sound as if I didn't care. It didn't matter. He wasn't looking for a discussion; he was just telling me the way it was. I thought he'd said these words to others before, making me wonder what else had gone on in this place, besides painting, before I'd stepped inside that day. Still, however intrigued I was, I had to bite my tongue not to argue with him.

"I'm sorry. It's just the way I have to live. Since I finished my master's here, I've been saving my money so that when I'm ready, I can go wherever the muse leads me, preferably Italy for starters."

"Art comes first?"

"Yes. It's the only thing I'm going to do, so it has to be this way for me."

"But what if you fall in love?" I asked. Impulsively, I reached up and trailed my index finger down the line of his jaw.

His eyes were locked onto mine as I watched his brow raise just the slightest bit at my touch.

"That could be a problem. I would never hurt anyone on purpose, especially not you," he said, moving close enough for me to feel his breath on my face. He set his glass on the table by the door and raised his arm, resting it on the wall beside my head.

"Well, love can be tricky. I hope you won't end up getting hurt either," I said, daring him and holding his smoking gaze, tilting my head up to him.

"I'll try my best, if you will."

"Okay," I said, feeling his hand slip along the side of my face. He kissed me then, his lips as soft as velvet, his tongue warm and inviting against mine, making my head spin delightfully. His hand was in my hair and he pressed his mouth harder against mine, making me feel the rasp of his whiskers, even though he'd just shaved. Feeling the door against my back, I gave in to his kiss, as he took my glass and set it on the table, and he wrapped his arms around me, kissing me again, and again....

"Hope?"

"Oh, thanks," I say, taking the coffee he is handing me in my favorite mug.

"Are you okay?"

I nod, taking a sip of the coffee, hoping my face isn't giving me away.

"Come here," he says. Then he takes my cup away and pulls me toward him, enveloping me in his arms, just as I was remembering. I close my eyes and he strokes my hair. "Listen, I know you're angry...I don't blame you."

I sigh. I don't need this now. I want to be in his arms, but I know it will take us nowhere.

He sighs, and I feel his lips press the top of my head before he speaks. "Hope...."

A knock at the door signals Katharine's arrival. "Hellooo!" she says, jovially, stepping inside with her long cashmere coat wrapped around her against the cold as we break apart, in time to see Peter and Carol stepping in behind her. She is a swirl of color and energy, so odd in a person in her eighties—early eighties, she reminds us often.

"Hi, Hope! How are you? Do you remember Carol and Peter?"

"Yes, it's nice to see you again," I say as Peter and I shake hands and Carol grins, and then Peter moves on to greet Liam. Carol has a tiny figure wrapped in a pink bath towel, and all I can see are two arched brown ears and two extraordinarily round dark eyes peering out over the top of the towel. The face emerges next, aquiver with fear, and cold, I imagine, judging by the size of this tiny creature.

"Ohh!" Liam and I say, laughing in unison as Carol holds up her bundle for our inspection. I realize I have clasped my hands beneath my chin, to keep from grabbing her from Carol, who is obviously trying to maintain control over the situation for the puppy's sake, I think. I knew she would be cute, but this puppy has the prettiest face I have ever seen on a dog, Rowdy included.

"Here she is," Carol says, proudly.

"Look at her. She's *beautiful!*" I murmur, stretching out the word for emphasis.

"Yes, she really is," Peter agrees. "She is by far the prettiest of all in this litter. Not the biggest, not the smallest, but definitely the prettiest."

"And I think she's the sweetest," Carol adds, making a move to hand the bundle over to me.

"Oh!" is all I can say as the puppy looks inquisitively into my eyes, crying a little as she leaves the comfort of Carol's arms. I feel Liam's hand under my arm, as if we are cradling our child, but I can't look at him. *Do not be kind to me.*

"I understand you picked her out via this new Skype thing," Katharine says, making us laugh. My head is spinning. *What in the hell are we all playing at here?*

"Yes," says Liam. "They let me look at her countless times. I thought she was the right one. I think I got it right, don't you?" he says, grinning at me, forcing a smile from me, forcing me to look at him.

"Yes, I think you did. Thank you. You did very well." Why do I feel the need to assure him? This is sabotage at best. *Sabotage of my life.*

"Surely, you're not taking this little one to *Italy* with you? When is it you're going?" Carol asks us, as if we are a couple—as if, of course, we are going together. What else would she think?

"Well, no; she's staying here with me. Not *here*," I say, eyes casting about the pool house. Question answered; I notice that there is no confusion on Katharine's part. Obviously, she and Liam have discussed the plans, but this is the first Carol and Peter have heard about it.

"Oh! You're not *going?*" Peter says, shocked that I would pass up a trip to Italy.

I've been conspicuously not invited, I want to scream, but instead I say, "No…well, Liam's plans are indefinite and I…uh, I'll be staying at my parents' house."

"How are they with getting another mouth to feed, or *two*?" Katharine laughs, completely unaffected by the awkwardness of the moment. The other two are looking back and forth at us.

"Actually, they weren't thrilled, but my dad has just lost his job, so hopefully, she will be good company for him," I say as the puppy is beginning to snuggle against me, the shivers having subsided.

Liam looks shocked this time. "Oh! Hope, you didn't tell me…I'm so sorry!" The look of concern is genuine; he has always liked my father. Who doesn't like my dad? *My dad would like to beat the shit out of you right now.*

"Yes. He found out on Valentine's Day," I say, watching my words cut an intimate wound into him. My artist lover tends to wear his heart on his sleeve, regardless of how he pretends otherwise. He is work, thought, and heart all rolled into one being; compassion personified—to a point.

"Oh, that's a shame!" says Katharine. "I'm sure Toots can get him hooked up with someone else very soon. Still, it's a hard thing, especially for a *man!*"

I hadn't thought about my grandmother's helping my dad. My grandmother can be a harsh woman. She has always made us feel as if we were on our own, to make our own destinies, and to pull ourselves up by our bootstraps, and suck it up. You made your own breaks in this world, according to Toots. She certainly did.

"Please give her my regards when you see her again," Katharine says, giving me the distinct impression that I will never see *her* again.

"I will." They've certainly talked and covered all the bases.

Carol begins to drone on and on about the puppy's care, handing me a folder with her records. I've had dogs before. I think I know what to do. Peter sets a canvas bag of her food, her heartworm preventative, and some training treats on the kitchen counter, but I feel so distracted by the creature in my arms, combined by Katharine's dismissal of me, and Liam's hovering, searing presence, now radiating a new surge of emotion my way that I cannot handle. *Do not be concerned about me.* I will not cry, I think to myself, and struggle to attend to the conversation.

"How big will she get?" I ask as soon as there is a lull.

"Maybe ten pounds. Her mother was small, like she is," says Peter, making moves that indicate he is ready to go. They ask me whether I have a suitable vet, and tell me the optimal time to consider getting her spayed, but my head is swimming with Liam and the dog.

"Do you have a carrier and a bed for her?" asks Carol.

"Oh, yes. I went out and bought all that stuff yesterday, and some toys. It's all color coordinated," I manage to say lightly, making them laugh.

We exchange a few more pleasantries, and then Katharine wraps up the visit. "I know she'll be in the best of hands. We're going to head over to the club for lunch before Peter and Carol have to head back to Raleigh. It was good seeing you again, Hope. Good luck to you, dear. And Liam, I'll see you a bit later. Thank you again for shoveling the drive back here."

He continues to serve his benefactress, playing her game until the end. "Yes, ma'am. Good to see you, Peter, Carol. Thanks for everything," he says, shaking hands again, as I manage to stick my hand out from under my new pet.

After they depart, he says to me, "Hope…I'm really sorry about your dad's job. How's he doing?"

"I guess he's holding it together. Oh, and Wesley came in last night. She and Ren are engaged," I say, rocking the puppy nonchalantly, as she's closed her eyes. She smells so sweet. That sweet puppy smell takes me back instantly to my childhood, and the remembrances of puppies we'd had at home. Already I know she is good company. Already, I have someone else to look at and hold while my heart aches, standing in this place for the last time with this man I have loved since the day I laid eyes on him.

"Wow! So he did it," he says of Ren, remembering the phone conversation from our bed, right after Thanksgiving, when Ren told me about his plans. He knows without asking me that this happened on Valentine's Day, the day he hurled my world out of orbit.

"Yep. A lot's been happening." Ha! I have mastered understatement and he gets it.

He nods, watching me. Finally he reaches over and strokes the puppy's head, asking, "Do you like her?"

"How could I not? She's wonderful, Liam. Thank you, again."

"Hope, I didn't get her for you just so you'd have to stay here. You know that, right?"

"I don't know what I know, Liam. I know you have your heart set on going and that's all I need to know." I'm wondering how long he's actually planned this.

"I didn't think I was going to leave when I heard about her, Hope. Then, when it all fell into place, you wanted her, and it all just kind of made sense."

"It's fine, Liam. It's fine." None of it is fine, but I feel as if I'm going to explode.

"What are you going to name her?"

"I don't know."

He watches me carefully, knowing I'm fighting back tears. "Do you want to stay? I can make us something to eat."

Yes. I want to stay as long as you'll let me; I want to eat your food, and take you to bed, and make you miss your plane eventually, but I do have things to do. "No, thanks. I should go. I'm doing a photoshoot with Wesley and Ren—engagement pictures this afternoon before he has to fly back to Austin. So, when are you leaving?" I ask, panicking when I suddenly notice some large rectangular packages and read the labels. *Amelia Fiori* is written in his firm hand, at some address I can't read, then, *Chianti, ITALY.* "Are you shipping Amelia some of your paintings?"

"Yes. But there are some pieces I'd like you to have," he says. Of course—the smaller paintings he did of me that aren't hanging in the England wing of the museum. I was rather famous the semester he exhibited those. "But to answer your question, I'll be driving up to my parents' house in two weeks, after I finish out my notice at the shop. I'll fly out of Dulles on March 10th."

The date lands like a fist in my stomach, makes it final; the plans are made. He is really going. Katharine has probably already leased the pool house to her next protégé.

"Do you know how long you'll stay?" My head is swimming. I have asked this question before, but in my fury at the time, I can't remember the answer.

"No. I'll stay as long as I can make it work, as long as I can afford it. If the job with Amelia's father works out, I'll try to stay at least a year." He speaks as if I am hanging by a thread. I am.

I nod. There is nothing to say.

Carefully, he asks, "Do you have room in the trunk of your car for the paintings…and those boxes?"

He is not asking me to stay again. He is ready to rid himself of all ties to me. "I think so," I say, my voice surreal, as if we are talking about merely transporting a few household items to a storage unit.

"Here, give me your keys and I'll load this stuff for you," he says in the soothing voice I love. He goes to the hall, taking his jacket off the coat tree, the same place where I used to hang mine. I have not even taken my coat off, or sat down, or kissed him as I would have normally done. Four days ago.

As he makes his way out the door with first one box and then the other, the puppy stirs in my arms and whimpers slightly. I kiss the top of her incredibly soft little head and wander about our place, seeing the Valentine card I'd left out for him in the kitchen, on top of a stack of mail. By the lamp on the entry table, I see a picture of us in a frame that he has not yet taken down. A pottery urn made by my college friend, Jillian, that I'd given him for Christmas, stands at the ready by the door, holding our umbrellas. I swipe at a tear when I realize this is the end of my life with Liam—today, in the next ten minutes. I will walk out this door and perhaps never see him again. How has this happened? *Why isn't love enough?* Why am *I* not enough? The puppy sniffs, licking my face, looking into my eyes, showing the first concern for me that she will undoubtedly show me again and again for the next decade of my life. I take her comfort, her compassion, knowing that I will take it again and again.

Glancing at me to see whether I've keeled over, Liam is back for the paintings that are wrapped in brown paper and secured with packaging tape. We say nothing to each other as I watch him go back out to my car and slip the package into the backseat, then ease the seat back, testing it so it won't hurt the paintings. In an instant he is back in, blowing warmth into his hands. I don't wait for him to invite me to go; it is much better that I take my own leave, so he follows me and my new puppy to the car, where I see he has positioned the carrier into the front seat.

"She can ride shotgun on the way home," he says, as if my parents' house has been my *home* all this time. I marvel inwardly as this new decisiveness flows so easily off his tongue. He takes the puppy from my arms and nuzzles her soft head before he settles her in the towel inside the carrier, latching the door, and turns to me. "Hope…" he starts, as my heart begins to pound in my chest. I am shaking, but not because of the cold. Liam sees this and gathers me to his chest, as he always does. "Hope, I'm going to miss you. I wish you all the best."

Burying my face into his jacket, my throat aches with words I can't speak, but I let myself melt into the familiar comfort of those arms. *I want to be happy for you, Liam. I know this is what you've wanted, you asshole.*

"Will you keep in touch?" he asks, lips brushing the top of my head, making this all sound like *my* choice.

"Just…let me know you made it there safely," I say, as if I am his mother. Then he holds me away from him and pushes my hair back from my face, just as my damn tears are brimming over. Thumbing tears off my cheeks, he holds my face and looks at me, his deep brown eyes holding mine as if he'll never let me go, but I know it's impossible to believe it. Then he kisses me, gently, for the last time.

"I love you, Hope. I didn't mean to, but I do. This is so hard. You should be happy. Move on, okay? Don't let all of this get you down.

You've got your whole life ahead of you. Find someone who'll give you what you need. You deserve to get what you want."

I want to hit him, scream at him, and make love to him all at the same time, so I heave the tears back and try to smile, but it's useless. I'm drowning again, in a mix of intimacy, anger, and helplessness, and I need to separate from him as soon as possible. But his arms feel so good, and I want to see his face one last time. I wipe my eyes and pull away. He helps me into my car, and I buckle in, looking at my new little friend who is trembling, watching me with her dewy questioning brown eyes. As I turn the key, the car hums to life, and I crank up the heater. Liam leans in one more time and kisses me quickly. "Goodbye, Hope. Take care of yourself."

Chapter 13

CHERIE

It is the eighth of March in the high school gym, and Audrey and I are sitting in the bleachers, near some of our students. I'm still amazed that any of them acknowledge us, but the buzz is that the English teachers are cool. It is our night to chaperone the basketball game. I'm late, due to Dave's insistence that I eat a real meal before I go, but Walt is even later, and I watch him scoot in and hang by the door, where his presence is noted by the assistant principal who lifts her walkie-talkie in greeting from the opposite door. It's already a sauna, complete with eau de body odor, but we do our due. Walt hates basketball, so I give him an encouraging wave and a grin, watching him greet a couple of students as they squeeze by him. A horn blares, signaling the end of a time out.

"So, how's the puppy?" Audrey asks, tipping her water bottle to her lips.

"Oh, God, she is so cute! She's a little sprinkler, but she's adorable." I show her a picture on my smart phone, a real feat for me, and I even rate a swoon from the students with whom we've been chatting on the bleacher behind us. "See, she's mostly white, but her ears are the color of milk chocolate and her eyes are enormous! Remember those posters of the little dogs with the big eyes we used to have? Oh, of course you don't; I keep forgetting I'm so much older than you!"

"Oh, stop, Cherie! You look about sixteen tonight in those boots."

I snort. "They're Hope's." I'm wearing her tall brown riding boots, and regretting it since I'm smoking in the heat of the gym. And why I ever thought a turtleneck was a good idea….

"See, there are perks to having her home, then!" she chides me in a flattering way; she, who is always the fashion plate, adding to the English teacher mystique with our students, whereas I am the fun mama figure they can all come to for solace and humor.

"Have I complained that much?" I ask, making Audrey laugh. "Well, aside from her wondering about what's for dinner every night, there's an unbelievable pile of cups and bowls accumulating on the dresser outside her room, but Dave and I aren't about to become her room service."

"Are you charging her rent?"

"No. Maybe we should, but Dave thinks the more money she can save, the sooner she can get out on her own. On the other hand, there's that fine line between helping her and enabling her. I just don't know how much generosity to extend to her without ruining her drive."

"Well, you could charge her rent, and keep it in savings for her, or make her pay her bills with it while you have this—hopefully *last* opportunity to guide her."

"God! That's brilliant!"

"What did she name the puppy?"

"Her name is Little Miss. It suits her."

"And Dave, how's he?" she asks as the crowd erupts into cheers when a three pointer from our team swishes through the hoop. We clap and whoop. The shot was made by the boy I tutored last year. *Good for him.*

"Dave is manic," I admit. "He talks on the phone all day, hawks the job websites, and sends out resumes…forgets to bathe, and somehow gets dinner on the table every night when I get home. He's a much better wife than I am. Oh, and he takes Little Miss out to pee every hour on the hour. He pretends not to like it, but I think he's smitten with her. Still, Hope is going to owe him big. He hasn't been to the gym at all, and when I mention it, he just growls at me. It's just so weird to have him home every night, now. He's traveled with his job for twelve years."

"Has he made any contacts yet?"

"Yeah, actually he's got a phone interview coming up. It's a sales job. He had to sign up for a class as part of his unemployment claim require-ment, so he's going to take a cooking class at the community college."

"You are getting so spoiled! Does he do laundry? I'll pay him to come to my house and do all that. He can bring Little Miss, too!"

"Don't swoon, Audrey. He's doing what I'd be doing every day if I were home, and what I *was* doing every day when I wasn't home. But still, I give him that pat on the back because, you know, he needs the encouragement. And it *is* nice."

"Oh, yes. How is Hope doing? Has she seen Liam?"

"I'm worried about her. She's very quiet about it all. She saw him, she says, for the last time, the day she went over to pick up the puppy. She seems really depressed—just stays in her room with the dog when she's home. It wasn't like this when she broke off her engagement."

"That was because she was relieved not to be making a mistake, but this time, she really loves the guy, doesn't she?"

"Yes, she does. I have to say—as much as I'm angry with him for breaking her heart, and I *knew* it would happen—I miss him, too. I loved him, too. He was a good fit with our family. It's a shame he couldn't com-mit. And he was *so* good-looking," I sigh. "Christmas was so much fun with both of the boys around. Ah! I guess it's best not to get too attached to their boyfriends."

Audrey props her elbow on her knee and rests her chin on her hand, sighing. "And then you have this other wedding to plan! Oh, my gosh, Cherie! You really should write a book. How's Wesley handling all this?"

"Oh! Her bubble's been burst. We're just sort of in a holding pattern right now. I can't even give her a wedding budget, you know? They've set a date for October, and we've reserved the church. My longevity payment is coming up next month, so we'll shop for her dress. She's planning on saving her money wherever she can get a job, either in Austin with Ren, or here with us. Or…they could run off and elope and be done with it. Oh, it's just a mess!" I find myself pulling the turtleneck away from my skin and fanning the back of my neck instinctively, knowing the heat is coming, even before it arrives.

"Huh! And here you thought you were the empty-nester!"

"I know! Now, two of them are home, one's thinking about coming back, and I'm the only one who's not there. I was just getting used to being by myself and finally not feeling guilty about it, you know? I just want to run off and take yoga classes like I was, but right now I'm needed at home every night. I'm still their mama."

"Are you disappointed? I mean, I know you were looking forward to retiring."

"Yeah…but I can't let myself be very disappointed. It's a drag, but I have to plan on being here another year. With the wedding coming up, I need to work. If Dave finds something, fine, but I can't keep hoping it will happen when it might not. It's naive to assume he'll find work quickly. Then, it's just the same disappointment day after day. I'd prefer just continuing the way I am and be pleasantly surprised if he gets a job. And then, we'll see about me."

"It could be a while. And the people I know who have lost their jobs end up settling for a job that pays a lot less than what they had."

"Wow, that's depressing."

"I'm sorry. That was insensitive." We are quiet, but I know she is right, which explains my husband's mania. He knows very well what he is up against. He's old, and his competition is not. Age discrimination is alive and well, no matter how it's dressed.

Walt has made his way to our bleacher. "Welcome, friend! Where's our cohort?" I ask, meaning Taylor.

"He uh, has a date tonight," Walt says discreetly, his mouth hardly moving.

"Oh!" Audrey and I murmur. "With whom?"

"I believe it's *Paul*," Walt says.

"Well, I guess coming to the game is out," says Audrey.

"At least you showed up," I say to Walt, "even though you loathe organized sports."

"As tall as you are, I'm surprised you've never played basketball," says Audrey.

He grins ruefully. "Mrs. Brown, I get that all the time. Actually, I did judo in high school, and my mother forced my sister and me to do ballroom dancing so we could overcome our shyness. It was kind of fun, really, and we were surprisingly good at it."

"Oh, really, Grasshopper?" I say. "My mother-in-law is a ballroom enthusiast, too!"

"Cruella, really? Where does she dance?" asks Walt.

"Some studio around here, and in Florida, when she's down there in the winter. The woman has never met a challenge she can't ace, except for Dave, maybe...."

"Dave avoided dancing?"

"Yes, most forcefully. He's never done anything that's met with her approval. He's the quintessential black sheep of the family, and quite proud of it."

"How is Dave anyway?" he asks, and I go over it all again for him. Our lunches have been fragmented these days with each of us going to meetings, or handling phone calls from this parent and that. Every time Walt has required his advanced placement English class to read Ayn Rand's *The Fountainhead*, he has had parent phone calls out the wazoo, complaining about the content, if not the length of the book. The man loves to court danger. I'm still riding high on the heart-wrenching conversation my class had today about the way the father treated his handicapped daughter in *The Good Earth,* but I'm sure it's small potatoes compared to what goes on in Walt's classroom, with his lamps that are so different from most classrooms, setting up a new kind of comfort zone for his students, and highly entertaining discussions. Mr. Hurley is the favorite teacher on our campus.

Walt shakes his head in sympathy. "Tell him to keep his chin up. My brother was out of work for two years."

"See? How weird is that?" says Audrey. "Out of the three of us, we each have at least one family member who is dealing with unemployment, and it's not just the breadwinners. Even the young guns, right out of college, are struggling."

"The best thing he can do is keep talking to people. Networking is the best way to find something. People say it's easier to find a job when you have a job than when you don't. That's because when you're working, you're talking to people, and you hear about what's out there," says Walt, watching the cheerleaders pitch a young lady surprisingly high up into the air. We all suck in a breath as she is caught—barely.

"Whew! Well, that's one thing at which my husband excels; he knows everybody in creation, and he's got the imprint of his cell phone tattooed on the side of his head."

"To his credit, then. Keep him laughing, Cherie. He'll need all the support you can give him," Walt says, spotting his friend, a history teacher, across the gym and excusing himself to go and say hello.

Chapter 14

HOPE

I reach for the Buckshot tap and freeze momentarily, catching a glimpse of Charlie and Kira approaching the end of the bar. They are the last of the artist friends whom Liam and I had in common, and they are here at the upstairs bar, without me or Liam. Did they come here specifically to see me? Maybe they did, or maybe they are here to spy or deliver a message—or maybe they just messed up and this is going to be awkward. Charlie waves at me, and Kira gives a strong smile, as if she is gearing herself up for the inevitable conversation we will have that will be most likely our last. My man is leaving the country, along with my friends on some similar level. I want to be flattered that they've come to see me, but it feels off. Fuck.

"Hey, Hope! We've missed you!" Kira gushes, reaching across the bar to give my hand a squeeze. I know they have both in the past been in Italy with my boyfriend and the woman he is running to, so obviously, this is an awkward situation, and frankly, I don't have the time to hash all this over with Kira. Because she has avoided me, I haven't talked to her in three weeks, so the battle lines have been long drawn, and even though it hurts my feelings more than I am willing to admit, these two are not really my friends but Liam's. Life is like that.

"Hey, Kira! Hi, Charlie! How are you guys? What are you drinking tonight?" I ask. Right now, they are just customers, like anyone else, sitting at my bar. I will make them feel welcome, in case they've signed up to be "shoppers," checking out our service. It is March 8th, and I gather that this is the last night that Liam is in town. These two are probably meeting him and our other friends soon, surely not here, and it's funny how quickly this information passes over my brain as the two of them sidle up to the bar, ordering pale ales, and trying to decide how to play out this scene so it doesn't offend me. I have to laugh, making Kira and Charlie look at me with questions between them. They are assessing my wellbeing.

They order beers and look around. I'm pouring from the tap, wondering what they know of Amelia. I talk amiably with Jessica on purpose, so they'll report to Liam that I'm doing great and looking good—well, at least not moping. I set their beers in front of them on the bar.

"Thanks! You look great, Hope!" says Charlie, paying me in cash. They won't be staying long. "I'm sorry about all that's happened. We've missed seeing you." I think Charlie is the more sincere of the two of them. I'd miss him more than Kira anyway. That's me, a guy's girl. Always have been.

"Thanks, Charlie! I know. It's been a while. How are you guys doing?"

"We're well," says Kira, as if she has to think about it first. Give me a freaking break.

"Where's Liam? Isn't this his last night in town?" I ask, causing them to acknowledge each other, as if they weren't prepared for me to know this. Jeez, they're transparent.

"We're, uh…meeting him and some other folks a little later, over at McCoul's."

Of course, his favorite place. I should have known. "Oh, for a late dinner?"

"Yeah," says Kira, fingering the three rings that pierce her left earlobe. Then she pushes around her short, brown hair with the purple streak, making her look like a fairy from *A Midsummer Night's Dream*. "He's driving up to his parents' house in Virginia tomorrow."

"Oh, right, right," I say. Knowing that Liam and I haven't spoken in a while, they give me sympathetic looks. I have to know their take on all of this. I'm desperate but I don't want them to know just *how* desperate. I direct my question at Charlie. "You've met Amelia. What's she like?" I ask, and it is not too loud in the bar right now, so both of them hear the question. They look back and forth at each other and sip their brews to give them time to come up with an answer. They know me well enough to know how much this all means to me.

"Amelia's great. She'll be able to help Liam get connected with some buyers in Italy, the lucky dog," says Charlie, but he knows that's not what I mean. I can see it in his eyes.

"So, did they have a thing before he met me?" I ask Kira, pointedly, and she does not look away.

She sighs, as if reluctant to spill what she knows. "Liam liked her well enough, but she *really* had it going on for him; at least she did in school, and in Chianti with her family. We stayed at her dad's house, at his vineyard for a few days when we were all there a few years ago. I know she's been waiting for him to come back, you know?"

Charlie looks at her, as if she has said too much, but it's nothing I didn't already know. So I laugh, as if it doesn't bother me.

"Well, who wouldn't want to be with Liam, right? I guess it's her turn now; she can be his next muse."

Charlie scrapes his hand across his chin and glares at Kira. "I think you're still his muse, Hope. Don't kid yourself. It's hard on him, too, leaving you right now."

"Thanks, Charlie."

So, there is division in the camp. It pleases me to know that at least someone thinks I deserve a vote. And that someone thinks Liam loves me. But Kira is uncomfortable because Amelia has designs on my lover, and we all know she will have him by the time the Tuscan sun sets in three days. I have already given up, and I can't let myself care. Did Liam really love me? Apparently not enough to stay with me, or to really put forth the effort to take me along. Without love, what was the point? What kind of farce was I living the past year? How am I supposed to feel about myself? I turn my head away from them and busy myself with the bar towel. I can't let them see how this has destroyed me. They can't know how my head is spinning right now. They can't tell him what he has done to me. I will not let him leave, thinking he has annihilated me. I glance at the two engineers I have been serving from Honda Jet—Chris and James. They smile at me and lift their empty glasses. It takes all I have to wink smugly at Charlie and head down to the other end of the bar. I will make conversation with Chris and James, and get to know the two gay men to their left before Charlie and Kira will get Liam's text that he has arrived at McCoul's across the street. It makes my heart ache to think about him. Maybe it will be easier when I know he is gone. Despite my efforts at nonchalance, I have to turn away from all of them, and take a break to go to the restroom, maybe to throw up.

Chapter 15

CHERIE

It's after 6:00, sunset, when I walk into my kitchen through the mud-room, where laundry is piled on top of the washer, and a wrinkled pile of dry clothes sits on the dryer as well. *Great.* I hear Dave talking on the phone from the den as a basketball preview drones on from the TV; Carolina will be playing tonight. Passing the kitchen sink, I see dishes from breakfast and lunch that have not been rinsed. No dinner has been started, and had anyone called me, I would have been delighted to stop for Chinese on the way home from my meeting with the school newspaper staff. So it's official; *the honeymoon is over!*

Dave's guitar is propped against the couch, and he is currently on the screened porch, the phone in one hand and a beer in the other, not his first, I observe from the other two dead soldiers beside the sink. It is an unusually warm evening and he's standing in Sweatshirt A—the Carolina one—and jeans with Rowdy at his feet, laughing uproariously with someone on the phone; it is Jeff, I think, knowing how his laugh tends to mimic the person's with whom he's talking, a sales thing, I guess. He nods in acknowledgment of me but doesn't make a move otherwise. More laughter.

Great. I place my purse in its normal spot on the desk beside the computer, noticing Hope's purse, keys, and her lunchbox from her day at the boutique, on the kitchen island, and a cute pair of her flats askew on the floor beside the barstools. An almost empty glass of milk stands in a sticky spot on the island near the mail, which has yet to be opened. My neck and chest are dangerously heating up, and I wonder whether this flash of hormones will reach my mouth, making me blurt out something I'll regret later; something like: *What in the hell are you all thinking, leaving this place like a pigsty!*

Climbing the stairs, I'm hoping to find Hope to see whether she has to work tonight. I'll change later, but right now, I wonder whether she might be ill, leaving her belongings in a breadcrumb trail up the stairs. I pick up a small towel she's used to wipe Little Miss's feet with this morning when the dew was heavy in the grass, and a bottle of nail polish, polish remover, and cotton balls. As I open the door, I see that Hope has curled up under her covers, asleep, with Little Miss tucked under her chin. Little Miss looks up at me, barely interested that I've opened her door. Surely it is time to be taken out again.

"Hope?"

"Hmm?" she murmurs without opening her eyes.

"Do you have to work tonight?"

"No…What's for dinner?"

"You tell me," I say, making her stir and stretch, opening her eyes.

"Isn't Daddy cooking?"

"No. And the dishes are piled high in the sink and there's laundry all over the place."

"Oh, sorry, Little Miss peed on my comforter again, so I washed it."

"I need you to write down your schedule, so we can tell when you're going to be here for dinner."

"Here, I'll send it to you," she says, pulling her phone from the covers and sweeping her finger around the touch screen a time or two. "Check your email," she says, hands curling back under her chin.

It's then that I notice a glass of ice water pooled in a circle of water on her bedside table, beside the coaster.

"Hope! There's a watermark!" I cry. But I am wrong; there are *three* watermarks on the antique bedside table that I used when I was a child, from my grandmother's house in South Carolina.

She jumps up irritably and plucks a tissue out of the box, lifting the glass and wiping away the evidence. "Sorry. I forgot." There is almost an eye roll and I want to smack her.

I'm gaping at my ruined furniture as she stares at me. "What? You can get those out with mayonnaise," she says as if I'm mentally challenged.

"That's an antique!" Sighing, I look at Little Miss, who is circling the blanket. "Does she need to go out again?"

"Of course, she does," says Hope, her irritation increasing by the minute, swiveling herself to a sitting position and sticking her feet into flip flops for the journey outdoors. I make my way downstairs to change clothes, where I hear Dave wrapping up his conversation and belching loudly as he enters the kitchen.

"Hey, babe!" he greets me, giving my cheek a smooch.

"Hey. What's for dinner?" I say, giving my best impression of our daughter who has just gone out the front door.

"Uh…" he says, giving his goatee a scratch. "There's spaghetti sauce in the fridge in the garage. I can whip us up a salad."

"Okay," I say, relieved that I don't have to resort to emergency grilled cheese sandwiches and tomato soup.

He waves his fingers at me to shoo me away. "Go change. I'll start on it. How was your day?"

"Long, but good. How was yours?" I call from the bedroom, but I know he can't hear me. "*What have you been doing all day?*" I mutter, passing our unmade bed, slipping off my blouse, the same make and model as all the others I've bought since menopause set in last year, and strip off my trousers, opting for a loose knit top and yoga pants, complete with my bunny slippers. I redo my ponytail and flip on the bedside lamp before I reenter the kitchen, where Dave is setting the pot of spaghetti sauce on the stove. I start on the dishes in the sink while he goes through the mail. "How was *your* day?" I ask, now that he can hear me. His ears have gone bad from years of rock 'n' roll, hunting, and working in the furniture factory, the trident effect on his acoustic nerve.

"Good. I have a job interview in Chicago next week. I'll fly out Monday and probably spend the night up there."

That explains his good mood. Relief floods through me.

"Great, baby! I knew you'd come onto something the way you've been at it," I say, drying my hands on the towel and going to hug him.

"I got the call an hour ago." He slips his arms around my back to give me his best hug when Hope comes in with Little Miss in her arms.

"She peed and pooped!" she says proudly, watching us embrace.

"Daddy has a job interview next week," I tell her.

"I heard! Aren't you proud of him, Mama? See, he'll get a job and you can retire, and Wesley can get married, and life will be good!"

"Life *is* good," Dave says.

"Thanks be to God!" we say in unison, making Hope laugh. I can stand a dirty, messy house and even a little chaos if there is reason for hope.

"You know, Mama, Wesley's flying in from Austin next Friday night. She called and wants to know if we can go wedding dress shopping on Saturday."

I haven't seen the work schedule she's just sent me. "Aren't you working Saturday?"

"Not until 5:00 at Natty's. We could go early," she says, and I catch a little of her old spark, which is a relief—one, because of the ambivalent feelings I worried she might have about Wesley's wedding after her own broken engagement, and two, because of the way she's slunk around in a zombie-like state for the past few weeks since Liam ended things. He's no doubt lounging under the Tuscan sun right now, or probably sleeping under the Tuscan moon; I forget the time difference, but I can only envision him lying beside that half-Italian vixen who's stolen him away, and it makes my neck sweat just thinking about it. My daughter is carrying a ton of baggage at the moment.

"Mama, you're having a hot flash, aren't you?" she laughs, seeing me fan the burn on my face.

"'Cause she's such a hottie!" Dave says, grabbing my butt and making Hope roll her eyes.

"You two need to get a room."

"I'd love to go shopping," I say, ignoring them both, glad that my longevity check is now safely in the bank and I can actually afford a bridal gown this month. I bite my tongue before I reminisce, but Hope is right there with me and we share a wistful smile. Let her destroy my antique table. I don't care. It's all just stuff. I just want my firstborn to be happy. Will she ever trust herself or any man other than Dave or Ren again? I reach around Dave to retrieve the salad bowl from the cabinet on his left.

"So you talked to Wesley? How did her job search go?" I ask, a safe change in the subject, I would say, turning to the refrigerator for salad ingredients.

"She told me she'd met with the HR people at two hospitals there and dropped off her resume. She *really* likes Austin."

"Who wouldn't? I hear it's a great place to live, especially for young people. Maybe you ought to send your own resume out there to some of their school districts." I gesture to her mess on the kitchen island and she moves it with her free hand so I have room to slice cucumbers.

"Maybe," Hope says, her eyes glazing over. It's time for me to back off. Dave is watching her too.

"So, Hope, will you be my fashion consultant for my upcoming interview?" he asks, giving her the charming eyes that can seduce everyone on the planet. She flashes him the old Hope grin of six weeks ago. God, I love this man! He gives the sauce a little stir and tosses the dish towel over his shoulder as he pops the garlic bread he's prepared into the oven.

"Hmm, I'll see what I can do! You really need a haircut, Daddy," she says and pats his belly. "And tomorrow morning you and I are going on a *run*."

Dave groans, and I know he really means it, having avoided any exercise for months. At least I was doing yoga and walking, but he has been virtually sedentary since Christmas. And the drinking has always been a part of his life, but with our current situation, it concerns me. If we have anything, we have our health. For now. "Here, make yourself useful and stir this," he says to her.

"Oh! Mama! I meant to tell you. I met your colleague at Natty's last night!" Hope says suddenly, taking her free hand to push back her hair, while Little Miss observes us all from the elevation of Hope's arms.

I give up trying to pretend I don't know and ask, "Taylor? Yes, he said he met you last night." He's told me about it already, at lunch earlier today, gushing about how beautiful she was, and how she appeared to put up a strong front, but when no one was looking, had the crest-fallen face of the lovelorn. He was so impressed with his observations, even though he knows the whole story. I chop mushrooms for my salad and reach for a few grape tomatoes.

"Yeah, he and his friend were at my bar for a couple of hours last night. He's sooo nice, Mama!"

"Yeah, he skipped out of the basketball game for a better offer."

"That guy he was with is sweet."

"Cute?"

"Yeah, kind of, but not my type. But maybe more of *my* type than Taylor would be."

"Yes, honey, I know Taylor's gay."

"It's pretty apparent. He says he's always looking around to see if his students or their parents are around, and then he either has to watch himself or make a beeline for the door."

"I can imagine. So did you all talk about me?" I ask, opening a bottle of cabernet, knowing I'll be up half the night with burning hot flashes. Red wine is the *worst*, but I'm hoping for a family bonding evening. Maybe I'll just have half a glass.

"Only for a little while. He adores you and Mr. Hurley, and Audrey. So have y'all talked about *me*?"

"In the most *shocking* detail," I say with a smirk and she smirks back.

It isn't lost on me that my colleague is younger than my daughter. I have a startling realization that they could even become friends. Gay men are the best friends. Seriously. They have all the best insights with none of the competition.

"We actually know some of the same people. He did his internship with one of my friends from school. You remember Jillian, right? She was teaching at the high school where he interned."

"Oh, right. I thought she'd switched counties?"

"She did. She's in Winston-Salem now, but they still keep in touch." My daughter has that faraway look that I can't interpret. Is she sad because she doesn't have a teaching job, or does she miss Jillian? When

Liam came into her life, it was evident that she'd walled herself off from some of her friends. Jillian had a pretty steady boyfriend the last I heard.

"Have you kept up with Jillian?" I ask, setting plates on the island and counting out three napkins from the basket on the counter.

Hope sets Little Miss on the floor and I resist the urge to pick her up. She is so adorable, but the puppy really must practice walking. Dave steps behind me to pour pasta into the colander in the sink.

"No, I guess I haven't. I should call her," she says, pouring the wine, and that cloud of sadness darkens her face again; not what I was after, but it's inevitable that most of our conversations will return to Liam at some point. For now, he continues to occupy the sore space in all of our hearts; even Dave is noticing and gives me the eye.

"So, did you have a good night?" Dave asks because neither of us has seen her since she came in late and left this morning without telling Dave about her evening job.

"It was okay. I made $225."

"Wow! Got room for another barkeep?"

"Ha! We get rolling down there about your bedtime."

"Hey now!" Dave says, throwing me a wounded look.

We fill our plates and sit down to dinner, giving Dave the opportunity to launch into his proposal about charging Hope a little rent, with the idea of helping her pay off her debts, or saving her money with our guidance. It goes well, much better coming from him, than if I were presenting it. Hope agrees to the concept and they come up with a plan. He'd told me last night that they had talked and he'd learned that her debt is in the five-figure range. It could take her years to pay that off. God, she will live with us for the rest of her life! I was up most of the night, bending the Lord's ear about all this…and the half-Italian ho! Hope needs to find a rich doctor to sweep her off her feet. I sip my cabernet quietly and promise Him another talk tonight. I doubt I'll be sleeping much tonight either, wondering how we are going to pay for this wedding. Maybe an elopement can be arranged for the right price. Who am I kidding? Wesley should be entitled to have a lovely day. Even though it hurts, I can't help living vicariously through my daughters. Is it a mother's blessing or a mother's curse to do this? Either way, I'm in it deep.

Chapter 16

HOPE

Waking up never used to hurt the way it does now. There is always that split second when I slip pleasantly back into consciousness, still believing that I'm in Liam's bed, and then it hits me that I'm not, and I turn into stone again. Unmovable, hollowed out stone. I believe it's called a tomb. That's me; I am a tomb. It's Friday morning and I can't drag myself out of bed, although Little Miss continues to circle and whine. If I don't get up soon, she will pee on my comforter again so I heave myself to one elbow and rake my hair out of my face as she licks and nudges me to hurry myself along.

"Okay, okay, I'm coming," I say, now aware that it's raining. Typical, the weather is reflective of my mood, sucking me even further under the surface of *just depressed*. At the door, I stick my feet into my mother's gardening clogs and throw someone's rain jacket on as I take Little Miss out into the driving rain. She hates getting wet, and even though I am holding the golf umbrella over us both, she looks at me with that expression of, *Are you freaking kidding me?* Finally, she wades through our yard and pees, and I wait around to see whether she'll take her morning B.M., but she packs it in and hops to the porch like a little rabbit. I'm sure Mama will find her little tootsie roll package deposited on the carpet sometime today before Daddy or I can intercept it. It is bound to happen, just like all the other shit I have to deal with around here. *Have you cleaned your bathroom yet? It's been a month, you know. It will only take you twenty minutes.*

I'm not mad at Mama. I'm lucky to get to stay here, but I wish she'd lighten up about the bathroom. I know I only have to be responsible for *two rooms*, and put my dishes in the dishwasher, but for some reason, it gives me some morsel of control *not* to do it. I don't know why I'm like this, but I just don't care. I guess I inherited some of Daddy's rebellious spirit that makes me not want to do as I'm told. Maybe that's why I'm not teaching; I like control too much. It's the artist in me.

Mama really shouldn't obsess over my nasty bathroom anyway, not when there are worse things going on in the house, like Daddy not getting the job he went after at the beginning of the week. They called him back in three days and told him he didn't get the job. Then he did some digging with his contact and found out that a twenty-six-year-old girl got it. That could be me. A girl who'll be thrilled to go to work, cold calling all over the state for $30,000, a laptop, and gas money, and maybe some benefits she'll have to pay premiums on. She'll be fucking thrilled. Shit, I would.

That, and the pictures of Liam and Amelia on Facebook that I was up half the night looking at. And did I get a text or a message of any kind, saying, *Hey, I made it?* Hell, no! Four fucking words were all I wanted. Or just one, for cryin' out loud. *Here.* He owes me that much out of respect. But no, I have to see his grinning mug stuck to hers all over her Facebook page; Liam and Amelia, toasting with glasses of red wine; Liam and Amelia, laughing, holding hands at a welcome party for him; Liam and Amelia sitting in front of a massive stone fireplace with her dad on one side, an arm slung around Liam like he's the fucking prodigal son. It's too much. *So I guess you arrived safely.* Fuck you.

Aaahh! I can't stand my life. I'm wiping off Little Miss's paws and she looks at me like she's let me down somehow, so I guiltily cuddle her under my chin and slink back upstairs. Maybe my shower will wash my demons down the drain and I can go to work looking refreshed and lovely, selling beautiful expensive clothes to women who don't need them, but can afford them, the way I can't. I can't have anything I want—not a man, a career, nice clothes, happiness, satisfaction, *whatever.* It could be worse. Much worse. *It could be cancer.* As much time as I've spent in the tanning bed, I'll probably have skin cancer one day, too. I could be homeless. I could be married to a sociopath. I could have parents who wouldn't let me live at home. I could be in jail for being caught with drugs. The list goes on. I think of prison camps and those Mexican cults where they kidnap and dismember unsuspecting college students on spring break. I should count my blessings, I know, but I'm unreasonably selfish this morning.

I have promised to pick Wesley up from the airport after work tonight, after her spring break trip to Austin, glowing from her visit with Ren. She will probably have a nursing job prospect as well, and tomorrow Mama and I are taking her wedding gown shopping. It will take me twenty-four hours to gear up strength for such an agonizing trip, given my current state of mind. I will have to muster everything I have to masquerade as the happy, supportive sister of the bride to be/maid of honor, and not think about the hole inside me that nothing seems to fill these days. I can hide behind my camera, and follow her around, and rearrange her train. Nobody will be looking at me anyway. The last thing I ever wanted to become was one of those awful, bitter bitches who have nothing nice to say to anyone, and look at me now. *Ugh!*

As I remove the charger cable from my phone, a message pings. *Surely not!* The bottom falls out of my stomach as I check to see who has shown interest in me. It is not Liam, *quel surprise,* but there are three messages. One is from John, our cook. *Working tonight?* I text back, *no* (with a sad face). The second one is from Taylor, Mama's English teacher friend. *U ok?* How sweet. I don't know how to respond, so I send him a sad face too and text, *it's raining.*

The third one is from Chris Jones, whom I can't quite place. *What are you doing tonight?* Alarm bells go off in my head. Holy *cow!* It's the twenty-something guy from the bar the other night, one of the guys from Honda Jet, the cute one with the stylish haircut and that well-scrubbed look of the men-of-good-hygiene club. And, as I recall, he didn't reek of cologne or sport tacky jewelry or multiple tattoos. He was actually nice in that I'm-really-not-hitting-on-you kind of way. And I also recall giving him my number. Bingo! What should I say? I know tonight is family night, and my presence will be required at home for yet another mediocre home-cooked meal. No, it's pizza night! It sure would be nice to be wined and dined by some competent young hottie genius, but come on, not much notice here, Chris! You should be ashamed, even as cute as you are. Wonder if you're married and your wife is out for the evening? Girls' night, or tennis. Sure, that's got to be it, knowing my luck. So I text back, *sorry, family plans.* I will put him out of my mind as I take my shower and prepare to leave for work. Little Miss sits on my bed and her ears perk up, watching me, as if we are onto something.

There is nothing like a warm shower to wash away the fucked remains of whatever is ailing you, and this morning is no different. *Nice touch, Mama.* She has left the cleaning bucket on my toilet seat. *So subtle.* Anyway, after I have tucked it away in the bathroom corner, I feel better. My pomegranate body wash and extra volumizing shampoo have cleansed the filth from my mind, body, and hair under the pulsating rain of my shower head. It is mystifying to me how this happens every morning, but I know that if I skip my bath, I will be but a mass of quivering humanity, with nothing to contribute to the inane motions of putting one foot in front of the other, simply walking through the funk that has become my life. Toweling off the steam from my bathroom mirror for a glimpse of my pink face, with half-mooned blue eyes peering back at myself, I believe I may be able to pull off a believable shuffle through my day, complete with all the canned, mindless repertoire I need to make it from 10:00 to 4:00 p.m. *Would you like to try those on? Would you like to start a dressing room? How are those sizes working for you? Will this be credit or debit? Are you on our email list? Smile, sigh....* Then it hits me; circling the drain in this mindless way is a whole lot easier than say, teaching sixth graders about perspective in a moldy old art classroom; sixth graders who don't give a shit about art and are circling their own drains. And then there are the Mexican cult kidnappers.... Who am I kidding? My life could be a whole lot worse. *Thanks be to God,* as we say in the Episcopal church.

After filing through the single rack in my closet packed full of clothes and choosing from all of five outfits that would be appropriate for today's weather, I settle on a cream tank, topped with a plum colored loosely woven poncho and some straight leg skinny jeans I'll wear with my new taupe wedge heeled boots and a scarf; casual, rain wear; *who the hell cares on a day like this?* And besides, it will look smashing with my new purse. I know just which bracelet and earrings to wear.

I have dressed, and applied just the right amount of makeup to make it seem as if I'm not wearing any, when my phone pings again.

Chris Jones: *Totally understand. I'm free all week. Just say when and I'll meet you wherever you want.*

Daaang! I'm actually *smiling*. Chris. Chris. *Chris!*

Chapter 17

CHERIE

I have never seen Dave like this. It has only been a month since his termination, and he has plunged from cool and confident to desolate and despairing. In Sweatshirt B and his jeans that I swear could stand on their own at this point, he pours a vodka tonic for each of us, and I do my part, squeezing the limes, wondering how we're going to hold it together in front of the girls tonight. As if the job rejections this week weren't enough, Toots's phone call has completely undone him. We've been invited to an impromptu Sunday brunch in celebration of Eric's sixtieth birthday. He is in from China, and Toots was hoping we were free. Where was her invitation to celebrate Dave's big day in January? Most mothers remember their children's birthdays, like other important holidays, but Toots is more of a C and E; Christmas and Everything Else Is About Toots. Anyway, she was wintering in Florida in January, so Dave was out of luck. As usual.

He sighs raggedly, stirs the drinks with his finger, and hands me my glass. "I'm not wearing a fucking tie over there," he warns me, forever the rebel.

I shrug. "There won't be pictures. She only does that at Christmas."

"I know, so she can send Happy New Year's cards of our *happy family* for all of her people to see. Because she doesn't really give a shit about Christmas. Or us really. Or any of those people either. We're just ornaments. She lives for the show."

"Dave!" He's right but I admonish him anyway. It seems to me that most of Toots's life activities are a game to her, and we are mere pawns in her scheme, with the possible exception of her granddaughters. Toots has an interest in our girls when they are present; although, neither of them has ever been invited on anything more than a shopping trip. Her travels, her business, and her dancing seem to keep her busy enough to preclude any family commitments, having severed her apron strings long ago, if there ever were any. Dave's father was the nurturer of the household. When Philip Johnson died twelve years ago, the family died too, at least from Dave's point of view.

"Going over there is like *torture*," he says, taking a gulp and raking a hand across the back of his neck. He's worried about the conversation they'll have about all of our new circumstances. *Things that Toots has not been told*—Dave's unemployment, Hope and Liam's breakup, the newly engaged Wesley. And then we'll have to hear about Eric's wild successes in the global marketplace, and Toots's latest venture into healthful living. I watch Dave's hand drop from the back of his neck, observing the crisscrossed lines that are drawn across it. I feel as connected to him as if his neck were a part of my own body, his despair my own. If I could take away his distress, I would. I raise my own hand to his shoulder.

"So, did you tell her about your job?"

"Yes." His speech is clipped, dismissive, and I can imagine how that all went. She probably didn't miss a beat and said something inane like, "*Oh, well, I'm sure you'll find something soon,*" as if he were complaining about the rain.

"If you don't want to wear a tie, then don't wear a tie."

He shoots me a look that says, *I'm not her monkey.*

"What is it, honey? I mean, I *know* what it is, but what else is eating you?" I rub my hand across his shoulders and he places his palms on the kitchen counter, stretching out and letting me continue to rub his back.

Dave sighs. "You know how hard I've been looking. These jobs...nobody wants me, I get that. But I don't want them either. I mean, do you really want me to sell insurance and have to move to Texas, or Ohio, or *Baltimore*? I'm not taking an entry-level job, and they all know that. And Cherie—there's nothing out there for me. Nothing. I've been naïve to think I could find something in a month or two, or three for that matter."

I'm shaking my head, not in disbelief, but in agreement, in sympathy for Dave. He removes his hands from the counter and turns to me.

"And to think I have to go over to my mother's house and let her rub my nose in it all. I can usually put up with her bullshit, but not today, and surely not tomorrow."

"Don't let her get to you. Honey—you and Hope are just victims of the economy right now. You will both rise above this. There is a job out there for you, and you *will* find it when the time is right. We have so much going for us. We can start renting Mama's beach house if we need the income," I say, making his eyes widen. My mother's modest beach house on Sullivan's Island is all I have left of my parents, and as I am an only child, my last tie to my native South Carolina low country. We'd refrained from renting it over the years, just saving it for ourselves, and sometimes my Aunt Sophie's friends, as a last vestige of my mother and my grandparents, but if it even came to having to sell it, I'd do it to spare us this anguish. If it got to that. If it got to the point where I'd have to succumb to some nasty people rolling around in our beds doing God knows what, or throwing up in the bathrooms, or the kitchen sink, or on the *carpets* no less, from too much house partying.

We look at each other and blink. "No," says Dave. "That's not happening on my watch. Estelle would be rolling over in her grave. Hell, the whole Porcher family would haunt us for the rest of our lives if we let that house out of the family."

He's right. I sigh. He sighs. A vivid image comes to my mind of a July day six years ago—Mama and me sitting in the rocking chairs on the back porch, the sea breeze blowing the tied ends of her scarf. She'd looked so fragile with her head wrapped up that way, with no eyelashes or eyebrows, but telling me stories just the same, all the stories she knew that I couldn't have remembered but needed to hear, of bringing me there, to the beach when I was a baby, and the oyster roast my grandmother had hosted when my daddy was introduced to the family. I knew then and there the sale of our house was not an option.

"Well, why don't you take a break? Just—I don't know, go to the gym, play some golf. Maybe you just need time to clear your head before you throw yourself back into the fray."

He looks at me, his eyes softening. "Thank you. Not all wives would be this understanding. I'm not asking you for time off."

He didn't get my dig about the gym, but that's okay, as long as he knows I'm trying to be supportive. My heart is pounding inside, but I make my face relax and smile at him. "Get Jeff away from the restaurant and go play golf."

"As if I could concentrate on hitting a ball. I can hardly bang out a tune on the guitar anymore." He strokes his goatee, thinking. "I've been talking to Jeff a lot lately. We've been cooking up a deal, and I think it's time to run it by you."

"What have y'all been discussing?"

He sighs and takes a slurp of his drink, turning around to lean on the counter and crossing his arms over his stomach. "Do you remember the night we were at the restaurant and Jeff said he needed to start a seafood sales business?"

"Yeah, Valentine's Day."

"Right. He wants to start up a kind of fresh caught seafood stand that could operate on the weekends in a busy location. The farmers' market might be the perfect spot, where people can just pull off the road, get it and go; kind of a shrimp at the blue jeep kind of thing, but better," he says, referring to the guy who used to sell shrimp out of his old blue jeep down at the beach years ago. He'd set up on a street corner and sell out in a matter of hours, and his shrimp was always the freshest you could get without standing around the docks. Dave watches me and nods, "Yeah, you'd have to be at the beach to get it any fresher."

"Okay, and how do you play into this?"

"He wants me to set up his website and construct his promotional materials, which I can do easily. I thought about getting Hope to design the logo."

"That would be great!"

"Yeah. And the other part is that I'd be the one going down to the coast, bringing back the shrimp and fish, oysters, and what have you, and selling it at a roadside location."

"How? From coolers in the back of your car?"

"Yeah, well, we'd have a large tent with our signage, and some tables, with lots of coolers to transport it all, and I'd need to buy a trailer to haul it back."

"A tent? You'd be a *fishmonger*?"

He looks at me; not the reaction he was hoping for, I'm sure. "Yeah, sort of. This would be temporary until I can find something else. And it would give me time during the week to explore other possibilities, *and* an income while I'm looking. With Jeff's seafood brokers and his contacts at the coast, it's workable. And with his customers here, and the right kind of marketing, we could make it work. There are lots of people who'll pay top dollar for the freshest seafood. I'd also be responsible for maintaining the website, establishing the customer base, and sending out emails every week for our repeat clientele. We'd post recipes and that sort of thing. It'll be like a running blog once a week."

I can see that he's been busy planning all of this, and it's probably one reason he hasn't been sleeping lately; neither have I really, with all of his tossing and turning.

"And what is Jeff's role in all of this?"

"He'll help me set it up and match whatever I can invest."

"Invest? With what?" I am beginning to feel my chest close in as the talk turns to money. Every time we discuss our financial situation, I get a serious case of the flutters. Uncertainty is not my friend, I have discovered.

"Babe, I've got the severance we can work with."

"But—that's money to live on until something comes up. And the *wedding?*"

"I'm trying to make this work, Cherie, and it will pay off after the initial investment. We can put the wedding on credit cards if we have to."

What? My conservative husband, who's lived his life out of budget envelopes for the last five years, is willing to plunge himself into credit card debt for the happiness of our daughter. "How much money are you talking about?"

He shrugs, "Probably five thousand from me and the same from Jeff."

"A tent and some coolers will cost ten thousand dollars?"

"We have to have a business license. There are some promotional expenses, and the property rental to consider. It's all itemized. I've been working on the business plan. I might need to switch out the SUV for a truck if we do as well as I'm hoping."

"A truck?" I can see him now, barreling down the coastal highway in some big old pickup truck, his windows down, hair blowing, and the country music blaring about suds in the bucket or some such thing, and

I want to laugh. But I can't. *He is damn serious!* Wait till his mama gets wind of this shit! Holy *cow!*

He reads my face immediately. We have been married too long. "Babe, support me on this, okay? I've had two no-call-backs and one rejection. I promise you I'll keep looking, but I've got to *do* something. I'm going crazy, and it's only been a month."

We hear the door open and our giggling girls spill inside, returning from the airport where Hope has been to fetch Wesley. The pizza man should be right behind them.

"Hey!" the greetings go all around as well as the hugs from the girls. Wesley looks exhilarated, but she can sense the discord in our midst. I try to refrain from fanning my face, a dead giveaway that there is trouble.

"What's wrong? What'd we miss?" she asks, depositing her rolling suitcase at the foot of the stairs.

"Nothing, sweetie. How was your trip? Do you need to do any laundry?" I ask to throw her off our trail. She will leave Sunday evening to return to school, for the last leg of her college journey. I notice Hope beside her, looking exhausted as she often does these days, from the sag of her shoulders. It is not from fatigue, but the downtrodden look of the brokenhearted. I cannot *stand* this! My family is falling apart in front of me, well, some of them, but we continue to tiptoe around it and put on a brave front for the one who is trying to enjoy her happiness.

"The trip was great! Daddy, aren't you watching? The game is coming on in ten minutes!" Wesley says, checking her watch. March Madness is in full swing, as the ACC tournament is about to get under way, with Carolina taking on Maryland in the Dean Smith Center—what we Tar Heels affectionately refer to as the Dean Dome. Even I am into it, although at my ECU, it was tradition to pull for anybody but Carolina. (Those people are called ABCs.)

"Yep. I was just getting ready to turn it on," Dave says brightly, all pulled together as the doorbell rings. I still cringe at uncomfortable memories of Hope as a toddler, upon hearing the doorbell ring, intoning in her silvery little voice, "*Pizza!*" regardless of who was at the door.

"Pizza!" she says, giving me her little wink, and I give her an extra hug as Dave goes to the door, whipping out his wallet for cash, not the plastic card that Hope assumed was magic, back then as well. Did we not do a good job of teaching her about money? And now look at us—a credit card wedding? What is happening to us?

"So, darling, how is Ren?" I ask, circling my arm around Wesley, while Hope gets plates out of the cabinet and sets them on the island.

"He's wonderful! I met all of his new friends. It's going to be great living in Austin. There is *so* much to do. I've learned my way around the city. That was comical, let me tell you!"

We all laugh. Wesley is not known for her sense of direction, as proven by the little notebook of directions still stashed in her glove box from high school; directions from school to the mall, from the mall home, etc. She rolls her eyes at us and continues. "We have smart phones now that can get you anywhere you need to go, so I'm all set. Anyway, Ren made me drive him to work every day and then gave me his car, so I visited all the hospitals while I was learning my way around. I dropped off three resumes and even got an audience with the HR person at the women's hospital. She was encouraging. Labor and delivery is my first choice, and I let her know that, but that I'd be interested in other areas as well. She said they'd look over my application and call me."

"Good for you!" I say, setting out napkins and parmesan cheese as the others listen attentively to her hopeful news. Dave sets up the TV trays in the den so we can all watch the game, and my chest begins to loosen up, now that we are all together, and the talk of his new endeavor is sinking in. It is workable. It is possible. It is an option. It is *something*.

Chapter 18

HOPE

Maybe I am turning the corner. My dad is at the door with Little Miss at his heels and clinking two cups of coffee together—his signal that it's time to wake up. I did not hear him come in at first, but he must have taken her out for her morning pee and poop.

"Hey, sunshine," he says, sitting beside me on my bed and taking a sip of his coffee. I stretch and attempt to wake up. It's not so bad today. Running my fingertips over my face, I realize there are no remnants of tears in the dark this morning. I manage to pull myself to a seated position so Daddy can hand me my coffee, and then he lifts Little Miss back onto my bed.

"Morning, Daddy. Thank you!" My voice is hoarse from staying up late last night with Mama and Wesley, talking about Ren and their wedding plans. I can't help but get sucked into her happiness. I think it is good for all of us, judging by my dad's rested face. The usual dark circles under his eyes are reduced to pale half-moons this morning.

"What do you need, Hope?" he asks, those earnest, steel blue eyes that are just like mine probing me for total honesty. His question makes me smile; he has asked me this countless times during my life. It is his test for keeping me grounded in reality—and humility. It still works. What do I need?

"Nothing," I say, and it's true. I really need nothing. I am rested, fed, warm, safe, and loved. I have a small amount of money in the bank and I have made payments on my debts. I will use my camera today, practice carrying my sister's train, and hug my mother as we find the perfect dress when Wesley has her bridal moment. I promise myself I will clean up my mouth. I might even scour the bathroom. "I need absolutely nothing, but this coffee is really hitting the spot. How about you, Daddy? What do you need?"

"Absolutely nothing. A job would be nice, but I'm working on that." He winks at me, just like old times.

We laugh. "Me too, Daddy. I'm going to update my resume this week-end and start looking at the school districts again. Now is the time," I say, and we toast with our coffee cups.

"There you go," he says, grinning at me for the first time in what seems like months. Maybe both of us are turning the corner.

Wesley's curly head appears in my doorway and she joins us on my bed, scooping up Little Miss in her arms.

"Morning. Ooh, coffee!" she squeaks, through a yawn.

"Morning, angel. Why don't you hop in the shower and I'll bring you a cup. Mama's already in, and she was hoping you all would get go-ing early so you'll have plenty of time to shop before Hope has to go to work." My father sends her a wan smile, evidently envisioning her mod-eling a wedding gown or two in his absence.

"'kay," she says, oblivious to his look, giving Little Miss a kiss on her fuzzy head, and depositing her back on my bed. Wesley kisses the top of Daddy's head as well. She closes the bathroom door, and I chuckle when I hear the thud of the cleaning bucket as she sets it on the floor before the whir of the water comes on. Mama has upgraded her hint from subtle to obvious!

Wesley's diet has worked, resulting in her fitting into the sample sizes of most of the gowns she's tried on. I have to admit, my sister is a freaking knockout, with her peaches and cream complexion, and curly blond hair wrapped in an elegant chignon. I've brought her pearl earrings and a matching bracelet to dress her up a bit for the pictures. So far she has selected vintage style ivory dresses that accentuate her classic looks, thinking that the old fashioned refined styles will go well with the pared-down setting of our church and the simplistic reception that will follow in the courtyard. But my sister is worthy of so much more than this, so we take a break and I go to work combing the racks for just what I have in mind. Finally, the correct dress lands in my hands—a layered silk organza dream of a ball gown with a ruched sweetheart bodice. There is a pale lavender sash with a delicate rosette at the waist. I pull it off the rack to the oohs and aahs of my sister and mother, the bridal consultant, and another lady in the shop who is shopping with her young daughter.

"Oh, yes!" says Margaret, our bridal consultant. "This gown could go either way, formal or less formal, depending on whether or not you want to wear a veil. It would be perfect for a garden wedding or a small church ceremony." So Wesley is off to the dressing room, while the little girl is attempting to take a photo of her mother with the lady's phone. Margaret returns to the lady, whose name I've learned is Cayenne, to arrange her train on the modeling pedestal.

"May I help?" I ask the daughter. After a tentative moment of regarding me, a stranger, the child sends a questioning glance to her mother, who nods, so I squat beside her, giving her a safe distance. I think she must be about six, judging from her missing front teeth, and help her focus the phone camera, looking through the viewfinder at what she is seeing.

"Make sure you don't see your finger in the viewfinder," I say gently, urging her forward for the best shot. "When you're ready to snap the picture, hold your breath so it won't blur. You don't want a fuzzy picture of your pretty mama in that beautiful dress!" The girl smiles shyly at me and takes a shot, then holds the phone up to me for my review, as Cayenne mouths a thank you my way. "That's very good! Let's have her turn around so you can get the back of her dress, too."

Margaret has gone into the dressing room to assist Wesley and Mama, so I help Cayenne position herself and arrange the ruffled train of the gown she's chosen. The daughter takes another photo and we review it as well. "Let's do that one again. It was a little fuzzy. What's your name?"

"Lena," replies the girl.

"Wow! That one was great, Lena!" I say, viewing her next attempt. Both of us are giggling.

"You're good at this," says Cayenne.

"Oh, I photograph brides professionally," I say casually, maybe hoping for a job. *You never know!*

"No, I meant the way you're helping Lena. Are you a teacher?"

"Actually, I am. An *unemployed* teacher right now, but I teach art when I can. Photography is my first love, though. Would you like me to take a few photos? I can send them to you." *Along with my business card.*

"Sure, if you don't mind. I don't have a photographer yet. We're getting married in Wilmington in September, so I need to get moving. Things are a little tight right now..." Cayenne says, her voice drifting off.

"I certainly understand that," I say, and snap a few photos. "Is it a beach wedding?" I ask, thinking her dress will be just right. She nods, but the pressures of the wedding planning must be getting to her. Capturing her vulnerable expression makes the images much more poignant. I think she will like these. With her dark skin and almost black hair, the white dress is the best choice for her. I wonder what Lena will wear, and whether she likes her mother's fiancé.

My sister emerges from her pink dressing room curtain, making us all suck in our breath. She has transformed into a fairy tale confection in the gown I've found. Judging by all of our faces, the impression is unanimous. "Ohhh..." we all murmur in unison, with our hands at our mouths; thus all three of us Johnson women are sharing our collective bridal moment, accompanied by tears and smiles. Even Margaret is beaming; Cayenne too, and Lena is jumping up and down with her hands clasped around the camera phone. I raise my camera and begin to snap shots as Cayenne steps off the pedestal to trade places with Wesley while Margaret tends to the skirt. Wesley looks hopeful when Mama asks the price again, and we all breathe a sigh of relief that it is in line with our budget.

The gown is purchased and we are ready to roll, after looking at a few hideous bridesmaids dresses that I would never be caught dead in, and I think Wesley is about to burst out of her skin with exuberance. A text comes across her screen as she's changing in the dressing room, and I watch her hands shake as she wipes a tear from her cheek.

"What is it, hon?" I ask, my hand going to her arm.

She looks up at me with large hazel eyes full of tears beginning to brim at her lower lids.

She whispers so Mama won't hear through the curtain, "It's a text from Ren. He says his mother just found out there is a cancellation at the Duke Gardens for the third Saturday in June. She says they can make this happen for us if I want it to."

My jaw drops. The Duke University Gardens in Durham is about the most beautiful place in North Carolina for an outdoor wedding, and the most coveted. I would imagine it would take nothing short of royal birth to secure a date there in June. Mrs. Henry's most extravagant offer could be viewed as a godsend, or as the highest insult to a man who has just lost his job. I love the Henrys, but this is not what our family needs at this moment. How to bow out gracefully?

"Oh *wow!* Don't tell Mama!" I hiss in my most restrained whisper.

"Oh, believe me, I wasn't planning on it. What do I *do?*" Wesley whispers back.

"I have no idea. Let's think about it before you respond. Damn!"

"I *know!* Damn! What is Ren thinking? He doesn't even care about all of this..."

"Then tell him to grow a pair and tell his mom to forget it."

"Really? But, it's *Duke Gardens.*"

"No, don't say that," I say, running a hand through my hair and beginning to sweat. News like this will cause spontaneous combustion when my mother hears it!

Wesley is crying silently now, and I reach out to hug her. This new drama is so unnecessary!

"Things were so great until two minutes ago!" she blubbers into my shoulder. I hope she's not getting mascara stains on my yellow blouse. They will never come out. As gently as I can, I hold her away from me.

"It will be fine. We'll come up with a tactful way to get out of this."

"But Duke Gardens..."

"*Really?* You really want to emasculate Daddy like this?"

"No...of course not. Our church is fine. I love the courtyard."

"Oh, I love the courtyard too! It will be so beautiful, and the second weekend in October will be so lovely with the leaves changing. We do need to talk about flowers."

"I think I want lavender snapdragons."

"And those pretty coral cabbage roses for the bouquets, maybe to tie in the autumn color scheme."

"Yeah," she says as we emerge again from the curtains, where we find Mama reapplying her lipstick. I wonder what we'll find for her to wear. She looks particularly fetching in lavender with her blond hair, but it's usually not my color. Maybe I'll choose a darker shade of plum or an *aubergine*. There is plenty of time for this, especially since we have until October.

"Honey, have you been crying? What's wrong?" Mama asks, her face going pale.

"It's just overwhelming, that's all. I love the dress! Thank you, Mama!" Wesley covers.

While Mama and Wesley settle the details for the subsequent fittings with Margaret, I seize the opportunity to show Cayenne the engagement photos of Wesley and Ren on my camera. She loves the snow series in front of the red barn, with Ren swinging Wesley around in her cowboy boots. We wrap it up and say goodbye to Cayenne and Lena after exchanging emails and giving her my business card. As we buckle into Mama's Civic, I get a ping on my phone, signaling a message. Great! I hope it's Chris getting back to me about Thursday night. I look at the display on my phone, indicating that there is a Facebook message, and my jaw drops yet again.

Hey. Missing you. You and your camera would love it here. Liam

FUCK!

Chapter 19

CHERIE

It is an oddly quiet ride with my two daughters as we leave the bridal boutique. I thought everything went so well, but they are acting as if someone has died, rather than their snagging the most beautiful gown in the shop. And for the price, I know *I* am ecstatic. What's with these two? I have certainly gotten an education with them today about what the young people wear, or more to be exact, what they *don't*, for example, the *thong*. I've never understood why they think the thong is a comfortable alternative to underwear. I thought thongs were something one wore when pole dancing or modeling for a particular kind of magazine, but my daughters wear these lacy diminutive undergarments on a regular basis. Why? And on top of that, it's apparent that they *do away with all of their body hair*, south of their eyelashes.... *Ugh*! And then, I come to find out that the boys are doing it too! *Ew!!* For what purpose? Of course, I can imagine, but the reasons have brought my understanding of what they must be doing to a whole new and uncomfortable level. It conjures up images I wish I wasn't picturing. If this is what dating is like in the new millennium, then I'm glad I'm happily married to a man who is as clueless as I am...or *was*. Dave would die if I did away with everything south of my eyelashes! It makes me relieved to be an old person. I don't want to be young if that's what is required these days. Still, it makes me sad that I'm old school and my girls are new age. We really are so different, and it's not just because they cut their teeth on the technology that scares the crap out of me. I glance at Wesley in the rearview mirror, and then at Hope, who's chewing the cuticle around her thumbnail and looking out the window from the shotgun seat. *Something isn't right.*

"Okay, I can't stand it. What's going on with you two?"

Hope swings her head around to share a look with Wesley, and then she begins to spill the beans.

"You aren't going to believe this, Mama. Ren's mother offered to host the wedding at the Duke Gardens for the third Saturday in June!"

"*What?*" I am sure my face has blanched, but then just as soon as the color has drained, I feel the heat start to take over my entire being. "When? And what did you say?"

"I haven't responded yet. Ren sent me a text right before we left the boutique."

"Well, tell him thank you very much but tell Missy Henry it's absolutely out of the question. Your dad will shit."

"Of course. I will—respond, I mean, but I'm just trying to think how to word it."

Hope takes up the narrative at this point. "And then, as soon as we left, I get a Facebook message from *Liam!* He says he misses me and that me and my camera would love it there."

"My camera and *I,*" I correct through my shock and disbelief.

"*What?*" Wesley shrieks. "You didn't say anything! When did *this* happen?"

"Right after I buckled my seatbelt," says Hope.

Oh boy. Our perfect day has just been ruined. Two annihilations in one day are unacceptable, and with the technology at hand, they have attacked with lightning speed. How blissful we would all be if we would lay down our smart phones, lending new meaning to the phrase, *ignorance is bliss!*

I have to admit we make a smashing looking group, standing at Toots's door. We were even able to get the girls up to go to church this morning, a real coup, but both of them realize the importance of reacquainting themselves with Father Roger, as the wedding approaches more rapidly than I can process. It is nice to see Dave dressed up again, in something other than Sweatshirt A or B. He looks back to normal with a nice black shirt under his black and tan houndstooth jacket, hair combed and freshly shaved, except for the goatee. All of us vetoed his notion to shave it. My husband is indeed a memorable looking man! He even smells successful. Maybe it will serve him well on the job search trail.

Eric and the housekeeper, Martha Jane, answer the door together and invite us inside. There are birthday wishes for Eric, and hugs all around, as Eric explains that Toots is on the phone. We haven't seen Eric since Christmas, but usually it's only at Christmas when he makes it home at all. I have good feelings toward my brother-in-law, but he is quiet and reserved, so I can't say that I know him very well. Living in China, he must find us hopelessly provincial and boring with our—until now—uninteresting lives, and like Toots, his intelligence intimidates me. He leads us into the kitchen where Toots and Martha Jane have laid out a lovely and healthy brunch. Eric pours the girls Mimosas from the butler's pantry, and I settle on one myself, but then he begins mixing Bloody Marys for himself and Dave. I change my mind and ask Eric to change my order. I'm getting an unsettling aura of the kind of day it will be. Even the girls seem to have the jitters.

Toots appears, with her hand over the mouthpiece of her phone, and waves to us. "I'm so sorry! I'll be just a few more moments," she says in a stage whisper, so the person on the other end might not hear. She motions us off as she retreats to her sunroom to pick up her conversation. Dave and Eric choose the opportunity to slip into their father's study as the rest of us follow.

Unlike the rest of the house since Philip died, nothing in this room has changed, making me wonder whether Toots ever visits this room. The elk head mounted high on the wall is still the focal point of the grand room, while the other hunting and fishing trophies adorn tables and bookshelves. My favorite, a colorful wood duck mount, sits peacefully at the edge of Philip Johnson's burl wood desk as the antique clock chimes majestically from the wall. Displayed next to it on the dark green wall are the remnants of his sons' past achievements in chronological order, beginning with Eric's baseball plaques, and then Dave's: most improved player, team record for RBIs in a season, most valuable player, etc. Their baseball trophies are displayed proudly in a trophy case beneath the plaques, along with framed articles about the boys in high school, and then Eric in college. Autographed baseballs used to punctuate the trophies, but as Philip's collection was divided between his two sons, those are the only missing items from the room, as I remember it from thirteen years ago when Philip still commanded this castle.

Absently, Dave fingers an antique key on a console table, the old iron kind of key that locked a door from the late 1800s most likely. I touch his arm as he's lost in memories of his dad. It makes me sad, but I understand why both of the brothers gravitate to this room whenever they are here. It is where they find their father. At least Toots has had the good sense to leave the room untouched, for whatever reason—lack of interest possibly, inability to move on, which is doubtful, or consideration of her sons, which I'd like to believe but don't.

"What's that key to? Do you remember?" I ask.

Eric answers. "It's a key to the smokehouse on Granddad's farm in Virginia," he says, smiling placidly. "Louisa County, somewhere in the middle of the triangle of Richmond, Fredericksburg, and Charlottesville," he fills in for the girls. "I remember going there so many times as a kid. The older we got, the more we realized how out in the middle of nowhere our grandparents lived. Granddad always spoke as if he'd been to college, even though he hadn't been. But our Uncle Ansel was a different story. We'd have to sit in the living room on those nights when we'd visit. Uncle Ansel would stand there in his overalls by the wood stove that was as tall as a man, telling stories in his heavy Virginia accent."

Dave picks up the story for the girls who have never heard these tales. "Ansel was Dad's brother-in-law, as all of his family was much more articulate. Ansel would usually have a big chaw of tobacco in his cheek, and at the end of his rant, he would open the vent and spit tobacco juice in the stove. I never knew half of what he was saying, but you could tell his mood by how hard he spat into that stove! Dad used to laugh about the accent too, and called it 'Bumpass talk' because that was the name of the township where they lived. When Dad was young, he was so determined to get off the farm, he began to take correspondence courses and later joined the army. He dropped most of his dialect, refined his handwriting, and developed the best table manners you've ever seen. He was a bit of a rebel, I suppose you could say."

"Hmm. It ended up with his moving to High Point and starting the furniture company in 1949. Rebellious nature must run in the family," says Eric, grinning at my Dave. Their rebel spirit brings to mind Toots as well. With all that rebellion in the family, my husband was doomed!

"Possibly," Dave says, raising his glass to Hope, who feigns shock at his assessment of her. It is true, though. She is definitely our rebel. Artists are naturally rebels, seeing the world in a different light from the rest of us. As Liam has shown us, artists can be self-centered. They tend to make their own rules, rather than following the ones we do. Artists don't always make the best teachers, as teachers are expected to follow the rules, and teach the rules as well. A teaching artist seems to me to be the most gifted and respected of educators—an oxymoron at the very least.

I've watched my husband grapple with that same dichotomy many times in his life, leaving his music behind as a minor interest, in favor of taking a job that would support us as a family. Hope is molded from the same clay, I think, searching for what she can live with that will simultaneously earn her a living. It is so much easier to play by the rules. That is why she couldn't make it work out with Matt, a P.E. teacher who always played the game of life by the rules, and she just couldn't do it. He saw the world as black and white, but she sees so much more color and texture in her universe, and she is prone to shooting from different angles and in different light. If she doesn't like what she sees today, she will go back tomorrow and try again, determined to find the shot she wants. That is Hope. So, with Liam hopefully out of the picture, who is going to forever win my daughter's heart? It will take a special man. It will take a guy like Dave, if she is lucky enough to find him. Don't we always look for our fathers?

Toots finally appears, splendid in her raspberry sweater dress that reminds us how slim she is from her good health choices and hot yoga practice. Her bright smile lights the room and she waves enthusiastically with her elegant hands. "Hello, everyone! I'm so sorry to have been so rude and to have kept you all waiting!"

She comes to us, giving me the first hug and a European style kiss on each of my cheeks, then embraces Dave and the girls, telling Hope how exquisite she looks.

"Everything all right?" I ask, somehow delighted that she's picked me first to hug.

She waves a hand dismissively, but her face clouds over. "Oh, it's just a little snafu in my upcoming black tie event that I *really* was not anticipating, but I'll tell you about it later. It's just exasperating!" she says and plants a large smile back on her face. She looks stunning, and I watch my girls' reaction to her larger-than-life presence in the room. They have managed to keep their mouths closed, but I can tell they are transfixed by their grandmother, who looks about sixty, with the help of an excellent dermatologist and a great hair colorist, leaving me to wonder whether she's chosen more radical and artificial means to preserve her looks, besides the obvious dancing and exercise. Maybe she's had one of those miraculous new face-lifts they are always advertising on TV, I think, consciously stretching my upper lip to even out the wrinkles.

"Oh, let's go ahead and serve our plates before all this gets cold, and we can catch up around the table," she says, taking obvious note of Dave's midsection and my hips, and Wesley's entire physique as we all lift our bone china plates and dip into the buffet—a vegetable frittata, fresh fruit salad, an assortment of muffins and scones, and to my delight, stone ground *grits*! Toots probably won't eat more than a spoonful of grits herself, but she does know how to make people feel welcome at her table. She declines a drink, choosing a tall glass of water with lemon from her beverage table, as we arrange ourselves at our seats. I find myself breathing a little easier; maybe this won't be as bad as I'd feared.

"So, what has been going on with all of you?" she asks, grinning broadly, folding her napkin across her lap. We all wait until she lifts her fork to begin.

Oh, here we go. Of course, she already knows about Dave's job loss, so she is pointedly looking at the girls for better news.

Wesley swallows a bite of scone and smiles. "I'm engaged, Toots! Ren proposed on Valentine's Day," she says proudly, holding up her left hand so Toots can inspect the ring.

"Oh, how wonderful! What a lovely ring!" Toots says, slipping an unmistakable glance toward Hope, who appears to be trying her best not to notice. "This is grand news! Have you and Ren set a date?"

"Yes, October 11th, so mark your calendar. The wedding will be at our church, and we're planning to have the reception in the courtyard afterward." Only our family can discern the tentative tone of her voice, despite the certainty of her words.

Toots blinks at her, contemplating the scene. Our church is understatedly elegant and simplistic; low church, as it were, as she has seen on the occasions when she's visited for the girls' baptisms, and as I remember, she was underwhelmed with the whole Episcopal concept we've embraced as our religion. "Oh! Well...wonderful! Will your little church hold all your guests?"

"It's going to be small, but yes, I'm sure it will be fine," says Wesley with a hint of defensiveness that only Dave, Hope, and I would recognize, but maybe I'm wrong. There is a glint in Toots's eye.

"Or...you could have it here. The gardens are lovely in the fall, and you could come down the staircase and have your ceremony right here in the living room. My friends in the symphony guild can perform in their string quintet and it would be so lovely!" She thinks a moment, taking a bite of her frittata, while I feel Dave bristle beside me. "And...if you wanted to have it in, say, September, it would be even better. The weather is so delightful that time of year!" Toots is smiling in that *game on* way I've seen so many times, producing the desired reaction in her younger son that is palpable in the room. Hope sends me a raised pair of eyebrows as she sips her second Mimosa. I take a swallow of my Bloody Mary as well, wondering what to do next, but Toots is on the dialogue before any of us can respond.

"Just think about it. Let me know. You know I love to plan a party, and this would be such fun! And Hope, what about you and that handsome young man of yours? How is Liam?"

"I think he must be doing fine. He's in Italy, painting and promoting his work."

"Oh? And you didn't go with him? What a shame! That would have been such an opportunity for you, dear!" she says, shooting Dave a look as though he's failed once again in providing this kind of opportunity for his children.

"Well...I wasn't invited along this time," Hope says, downplaying the situation nicely. "And Katharine said to tell you hello when I saw her last."

"Oh, I'll have to give her a call. Have the two of you ended things?" Toots asks, sounding sincere, but I don't buy it for an instant.

"You could say that. And it's fine. I'm looking for a teaching job right now, actually."

"Wonderful! You can begin teaching at the same time your mother retires!"

Oh, she is fishing now, but I won't play her game.

"Possibly. Here's to all of us," I say, raising my glass and winking at Dave.

"So tell us about China, Eric," I say to cast the attention onto him.

He begins to drone on about the success of the company, and how many Americans are living in Beijing now. The girls are hanging on every word. I'm sure it would be interesting if I really cared, but like Dave, I'm still angry that the company is there. As I tune back in, I hear Eric lament that there is nothing workable from the States for which Dave would be suited, which we knew all along, but if he didn't mind traveling to China, it would be a different story. The conversation goes back and forth with Eric, Toots, and Dave about the business. Toots fills us in on her latest string of speaking engagements, leaving us duly impressed.

"So what happened with the dance gala?" Eric asks.

"Oh!" Toots says, rolling her eyes and shaking her head. "My partner, Fred Newlin, has fallen and broken his hip! Can you believe that? Honestly, men just don't take good care of themselves!" she says, casting a distracted glance at Dave, who is enjoying the last of his grits. "Anyway, we have our annual red carpet event in a month, and I'm fresh out of a partner at this point. This has never happened to me, and I certainly don't want to have to back out now!" she says, and I notice the appalled expression on Wesley's face. Here is a man Toots has danced with for over five years, a friend, supposedly, who has been seriously injured, requiring surgery, and her main concern is how he has inconvenienced her.

It is out of my mouth before I can catch myself. "I know a man who dances."

She looks completely skeptical. "Really, Cherie? Who?"

"My colleague in the English department, Walt Hurley."

"Have you seen him dance?" she asks, taking a bite of kiwi.

"No, but I believe he must be quite good. He and his sister used to win trophies for ballroom dancing." I think this is what he said. *I am too far in it now!*

"What does he look like? Is he handsome? How are his teeth?"

"I think he's quite handsome. And he has nice teeth, a very nice smile."

"Oh...is he tall enough for me?"

"Yes, definitely. He's upwards of six-something at least."

"Do you have a picture of him? How's his foxtrot? Do you think he owns a tux?" She has a myriad of questions, and I find myself scrolling through the pictures on my phone, like one of the girls. They are giggling at my attempt, as I've had to pull out my reading glasses from my purse to see the darn thing. *Oh, Walt, what am I doing to you?*

"Here he is," I say, finding a picture of Walt at the last honor society ceremony, posing with one of our favorite students, whom we'd both taught.

Toots takes the phone from me and borrows my readers, squinting at Walt's picture as I wait for the verdict. "Attractive! Balding, but in a distinguished way. He's *very* attractive, and even taller than Fred. He just might do. I'll call him, if you can give me his number. But check it out first. Then let me know if he's interested."

What have I done? As if under her spell completely, I nod foolishly, having just sacrificed my friend to this player of a woman. Dave sends me a look that says I should have known better.

Martha Jane enters the dining room to begin wordlessly clearing our dishes, but the girls greet her and thank her when she removes their plates. Toots scarcely acknowledges her as we all adjourn through her expansive living room, which could be the lovely setting for Wesley's wedding, and into the sunroom, where we decide it is warm enough to venture out onto the veranda. For the end of March, the weather has taken a nice turn, making us hope for the little lamb that is supposed to usher in the spring. A wedding reception would be quite nice here, under the pergola, with the views through the trees of the rolling golf course and the water hazard, complete with a fountain and flanked by weeping willows that would lend beautiful green waving fronds, sweeping the ground in September.

Martha Jane has brought out a large tray with coffee and a small birthday cake. Toots leads the singing of the birthday song, and Eric modestly blows out his few candles that are meant to represent sixty years. Suddenly, I feel sorry for him. How lonely it must be to live on the other side of the world, and have a foreign family—us. Hope takes a picture with her camera phone. He looks as though he's enjoying himself, though, as Martha Jane hands him a plate with the first slice of cake and a candle to lick. We've brought a present, a pair of shoes that Dave has discovered, that are incredibly comfortable and airport friendly. Toots has presents as well: books and a pair of expensive cuff links that he will enjoy wearing. Eric dresses well, as she does, and he appreciates all the gifts.

As the girls and I chat with Martha Jane, Eric has excused himself, so I notice Dave and Toots wandering toward the edge of the veranda to have a private conversation. I'm sure he is telling her about his upcoming foray into the fresh caught seafood business. The breeze catches her dark hair, long for a woman her age, making me imagine her with Walt, gliding about the dance floor in a Viennese waltz, wearing a gossamer gown, exuding such grace and charm that none can look away. Then her persona changes as I hear the timbre of her voice, edged with ridicule.

"Selling fish in a tent by the roadside? This is not the vision I had for you, Dave. This is beyond unacceptable even by your standards. Your father would be so disappointed! You have no idea what you're getting into."

The comment about his father stings. She really knows how to hit below the belt.

"It's a *business*," Dave replies impatiently, with his back to me, giving me the impression that he is valiantly holding his shoulders up, trying to speak quietly to her without turning toward us. "You're only upset because it could make you look bad." Still, he continues to explain, trying to convince his mother that this is a temporary solution, and one in which he can job search while bringing home some income. They argue indistinctly, although I am straining to listen. Finally, I can make out the words as he tells her that he wasn't seeking her advice, and he makes it clear that we are perfectly capable of hosting Wesley's wedding ourselves, which has become clear enough for the rest of us to hear as Eric returns to the veranda. Hope looks awkwardly at Wesley, who widens her eyes and rubs her arms as if a chill has come over her. Discreetly, Martha Jane begins clearing the dessert plates while we hug Eric, wishing him happy birthday once again, and ready ourselves to leave. Toots congratulates Wesley again, and reminds me to contact my friend about the dancing, which means I'll have to talk to her again. I was hoping she'd forgotten, or at least abandoned the idea. We walk through the house with tension in the air, so thick it makes my stomach hurt, as Toots bids us goodbye, dismissing us with a frozen smile.

Chapter 20

HOPE

Chris Jones is quite a catch, I think to myself, as he helps me into my car after our first date. We've just finished bar bites and glasses of red wine at Bravo, as well as a pleasant but bland ninety-minute conversation about what he does and what I'd like to be doing. He acted almost disappointed that I'm underemployed. When most people hear my story, they seem at least sympathetic, but not this guy. I am a loser. I can tell by the chaste peck on the cheek he gives me before tucking me inside my Civic that I've left him as flat as he's left me. No chemistry. Nada. Part of it is my fault because I was so distracted, first thinking about my Facebook reply to Liam, *hmm, saw you arrived safely,* (along with the latest pictures of him with that woman), and secondly, recalling those awkward images of Uncle Eric's birthday luncheon at Toots's house last Sunday, and how she dissed each of us in her own way, except my mother, whom she's using to advance her dancing career. So, I just wasn't into this date with Chris. He smelled kind of funny too, musty, like some kind of icky dandruff shampoo, and I know that's shallow, but when you've had the best, it would be hard for him to measure up, even if he is what I need, and even with his six-figure salary, which under normal circumstances would have made little dollar signs bounce up and down in my eyes. To me, my disinterest in him is a good sign—a sign that I'm growing up, but my mother will be heartbroken that I'm letting an engineer slip through my fingers. I am not what he's looking for. He looked so disappointed, as if my foot hadn't filled the glass slipper he'd held in his hand.

Gallantly though, Chris waves me out of the parking lot ahead of him, so I circle around and park for a moment when I see that he's gone the opposite way. The night is still young, and I am too restless to go home, keyed up from the wine, and yearning for a different kind of conversation. My buddies from Natty's are working tonight so I pull out my cell phone and finger the screen, sending a message to John.

I'm coming by. U working?

In less than a minute, I'm rewarded with a response: *off—just sat down at the bar, saving you a seat*

I smile. A moment later, my phone pings again and there is a picture of an empty bar stool. I grin this time, pulling my car into the evening traffic.

John has indeed saved my stool, as the crowd has picked up, the way it usually does on Thursday nights.

"You look nice," he says, unaccustomed to seeing me dressed for my day job, in a dress from the boutique and my favorite wedge heels. He helps me off with my coat, as he looks away from the TV screen where I notice Kentucky and Butler are going head to head in tonight's NCAA tournament game.

"Thanks. How was work?"

"We were slammed earlier, but the food traffic has slowed down. I'm first off tonight." John smells like French fries since he is a line cook in the kitchen, and his shirt sleeves are rolled up, as though he's been hot all evening. I'm getting a whiff of laundry detergent as well, and it's not offensive. Jessica is tending the bar and greets me as soon as she can get away.

"Hey! How was your date?"

"Hey, Jess. It was unremarkable. I'll have a Wildflower, please."

She gives me a sympathetic pout. "Sure, coming right up."

"What date?" asks John, and I see an unmistakable glint of interest in his blue-green eyes.

"Oh, I went out with an engineer from Honda Jet. He was nice, but..."

"Not your type?" he asks, taking a sip of his Guilford Golden.

I run fingers through my hair, feeling myself relax, listening to John's easy voice. There's never any judgment from him.

"He should be, but I couldn't get into him. I don't know why. I don't know what I'm looking for," I say, and it sounds more desperate than I wanted.

"That's why it's dating. You checked it out, and it wasn't for you. Maybe you're not ready. Now you'll just have to figure out how to brush him off without hurting his feelings," he says, angling his eyes my way.

"Oh, I don't think I'll have to worry about that. He was none too impressed with underemployed little me, either."

"Then he's not as smart as he should be."

"So, why aren't you hooked up with some nice young lady?" I ask over the din, squeezing the orange wedge into my beer and taking my first sip, realizing I'm in the right place.

He scoffs, running a hand over his wavy brown hair. "Too busy, I guess. Life has a way of putting things like that on hold when you can't handle it."

"What are *you* so busy with?" I laugh.

"I *was*...rather busy with some family issues, but that's behind me now. And I know what you mean about being underemployed."

"What'd you used to do?"

"I was a civil engineer in Charlotte. My dad got sick a couple of years ago and I came home to help out. My sister couldn't deal with it...you know, taking care of a sick man, condom catheters, and all. Sorry—way too much info. She was living at home, going to college here, and with her in school, he didn't have the money to get the kind of help he needed, so I bagged the job and came home."

"Wow. What about your mom?"

"She took off when we were kids, so you can imagine how freaked out my sister was. She has serious abandonment issues."

"What's your sister doing now?"

"She works in a bank."

"And your dad?"

"He died not long ago. Molly and I are keeping the house."

This news makes my heart sink into my stomach. When did this happen? I'm trying to remember how many months he's worked here. I had no idea what he'd been dealing with and I've painfully underestimated this guy. I need to remember that people aren't always what they seem.

"Oh, John...I'm so sorry." Any words I might say would be so inadequate. "You must miss him so much." He nods slowly. I was right; being this obtuse is embarrassing. "But...now you can move on?"

"Yeah...I could if I could find a similar job. It's not easy these days."

"I know. My dad's out of work, too. We send out resumes together over morning coffee."

"That's cool. Can I join your club?" he chuckles. "What are you... looking for a teaching job?"

"Yep. It's too bad I don't teach English. My mama wants to retire. I could take her job. I'd be cheap labor. If I taught English, or math, I'd have a much better shot."

"Well, I'd say that guy underestimated you, Hope. Anybody who works two jobs and does freelance photography on the side is pretty impressive."

"Thanks, John. And I'm really sorry about what you've been through."

"I didn't tell you to make you feel sorry for me. I told you because you asked."

Apparently there are a lot of questions I should have asked this man, I think, looking at John with a new level of understanding, and compassion. Shame burns my face; shame for my past assumptions that he was a loser. Like me. I have felt that same sentiment directed at me just this evening, so I'm sure he has gleaned it from me at some point since we have worked here together. Being perceived as the loser doesn't feel good, despite my own delusions of self-worth. My Eliza Doolittle voice takes over inside my head; *I'm a good girl, I am!* But maybe I'm not so good.

Jessica is back to chat. "What's wrong? Your face is bright red."

"Must be my wine flush from earlier," I offer, combing my hair back from my face with both hands to allow the air to cool it. Is this what my mother goes through twenty times a day? *Ugh!* John is grinning.

A gust of wind swooshes by me as a man takes the seat around the corner from my barstool and faces me directly. The intense eye contact he throws my way is vaguely familiar, and then I recognize Mama's colleague, Taylor Kimbrough, alone on the barstool.

"Hope! God, I was hoping you'd be here!" he gushes, looking as flustered as I feel.

"Oh! Hey, Taylor. Taylor, this is John. John and I work together here."

John extends his hand first, and they shake, a firm, manly grip, I notice, wondering about John's opinion on homosexuality. Watching his discerning gaze, I sense instant recognition, followed by nothing, as if he has realized that Taylor speaks English or something. "Good to meet you, Taylor."

"You too, John." Taylor, on the other hand, is conflicted, as his elbows go to the bar, and he drags a hand across his mouth, letting it support his chin in a sign of conundrum. He drums his fingers on the bar and glances back and forth at John and me. As usual, I cannot escape the intensity of his eyes, along with the energy that is radiating off him like heat lightning.

"What's the matter?"

"I need a beer," he says as Jessica looks back our way, and he orders a pale ale. Taylor glances at John, who is watching Butler getting its ass kicked by Kentucky, and decides to go for it. "I just left Paul," Taylor says under his breath as his glass is set before him. He takes a gracious gulp and continues, meeting my eyes full on. "He's *married!*" he hisses.

"*What?* To…?"

"A *woman.* Yeah. They have two little kids!"

"Shit!" I knew the guy was straight…or bisexual, or whatever.

"No shit!" says Taylor. By now John's attention has shifted back to us and he has caught up in a nanosecond.

"*Shit!*" John says as we all take a drink. "That really sucks," he mutters, signaling that Taylor's sexual preference is a nonissue for him. "I'm sorry. I couldn't help but overhear."

Taylor looks relieved. "Not a problem. You don't work for the public schools by day, do you?"

John snorts. "Nope, and I'm pretty good at keeping secrets, too."

"Good, because tonight there is no way I can keep this in. And I'm going to need a *lot* of alcohol to drown all this crap," Taylor says, rubbing his forehead with his fingers.

"You came to the right place," I say, placing a hand over his.

"Thank God! Friends!" Taylor says, as the three of us raise our glasses together.

"Friends," echoes John, and already I am glad he is here with us. What a crew we are. John orders Fireball shots for all of us, leading me to believe there is no way I will be driving all the way to Pleasant Ridge tonight, so I will need to crash with Jessica tonight after she gets off. And from the looks of it, Taylor may end up there as well. My mama will have a freaking cow!

"Jeez-o-pete! I never saw that one coming," Taylor says, shaking his head.

"Really? To be honest, I did. I thought Paul was straight from the get-go. But I'm sorry it didn't turn out like you wanted."

"I don't know if it ever will. It's like being a salmon, swimming upstream in a creek full of brown trout!"

I have to laugh, and so does John.

"I'm used to it, don't get me wrong, but I just want all the same things that you want. I wanna be like your mama and daddy. I'll bet they still hold hands," he says, wistfully, his chin sinking into his hand.

"Yes, they still do."

"That's sweet," says John. We all exhale, a sad little trio of sexually underserved lonely hearts, who all want the same thing. The shots arrive and we drink—to holding hands.

An hour, another shot, and two more beers later, Taylor leads the three of us deep into conversation about our favorite movies and books, and John, who has switched to drinking Coke, is holding his own about *Jane Eyre*, which surprises me again. I need to go back and reread it, as I've forgotten some of the lines he's trying to quote. Taylor knows the one he's thinking of and recites it, *"If all the world hated you and believed you wicked, while your own conscience approved of you and absolved you from guilt, you would not be without friends."*

"That's the one," says John, nodding and running the tip of his thumb across his lower lip.

"It's my mantra. It has been since I read that book in the seventh grade. Is it any *wonder* that I always identify with strong female protagonists?" asks Taylor who notices me check my watch. He checks his phone for the time too, exhaling in a soft whoosh. "This has been fun guys, but it's past my bedtime. Thankfully, tomorrow is Friday so I might be able to cruise through the day." He collects his car keys and signals to Jessica that he's ready to close his tab.

"Are you okay to drive?" I ask him.

"Actually, I could just walk. I don't live far," he mutters, signing his tab.

"Lucky," I say, about to ask Jessica whether she'll let me stay with her when John interjects. I've just noticed he's laid down cash and paid my bar bill.

"You can bunk with me and Molly. I just live two miles from here. Taylor, I can drop you off at your place on the way."

"Thanks. I guess I can walk to my car in the morning."

And with that, I am apparently on my way to spending the night with John—without Taylor. Seeing the sudden deer-in-headlights look on my face, John begins to backpedal.

"Or, if you want, Hope, I can drive you home," he says gracefully.

"It's a thirty-minute drive from here, John. Why don't I just stay with Jessica?"

"Her brother and sister-in-law are staying there."

"Oh, that's right." I had forgotten that they were in town for a wedding, and taking extra time off to look at houses in town. In her one bedroom apartment, they would make a crowd, so they wouldn't need me crashing their party.

John's face softens into a smile. "Don't worry. Molly's home, so I can promise I won't be putting the moves on you. And I'm sure we have a spare toothbrush. She's thorough that way."

"No John sandwiches?" I blurt, wishing I hadn't, but I'm trying to remember the guy I thought I was with. He just grins and shakes his head. I am used to being taken care of, but I wasn't expecting this from our line cook. Again, I have miscalculated.

"We can come over for your car in the morning so it won't get towed."

"Okay. Thank you." After sending my mother a text that I'll be staying in town for the night, we pile into John's truck, an old model Ford with a bench seat, not at all what I expected, and he murmurs while starting the engine, "A *Hope* sandwich. Even better, right, Taylor?"

"It could work, especially after the night I've had," says Taylor. A set of army dog tags swings conspicuously from the review mirror, and I try inconspicuously to make out if that is John's last name on one of them. I wonder if the tags belonged to his father.

"My dad's truck...he served in the Gulf War when I was little," he explains. In three minutes, I notice we are magically in front of Taylor's apartment complex on the other side of the train tracks, and he bids us goodnight, thanking John for the ride. They bump fists and we are off again. The ride is a dream cloud in which I've closed my eyes, but I pretend to be wide awake at intervals.

In what seems to be five more minutes, we are pulling into an alley and crunching over gravel, parking inside an old wooden garage, like nothing I have ever seen. It is early April and warm, making me wonder whether there could be snakes afoot yet as I step out of the truck. John waits and escorts me through a gate along stepping stones across the backyard of an old brick two-story home, using the flashlight on his phone. Maybe I'm not the only one worried about snakes. We enter the screened porch, whose door creaks open and bangs shut like in *Sounder,* another one of my favorite books. At the kitchen door, John sets the security system to *stay* mode. The kitchen is small and cozy, containing almond-colored appliances, consistent with a 1980s remodel, complete with butcher block countertops and lace curtains, but the plaster walls still retain the older charm, along with millwork, and ten-foot ceilings, and compartmentalized rooms. Lamps are lit in the living room, and over a stair landing that divides the downstairs is a bedroom to the right of the bathroom, where John has gestured for me. In it is a charming mix of beaded board paneling and blue and white ceramic tile that sets the stage for the porcelain sink and bathtub with a handheld shower attachment. I emerge after relieving myself and washing my hands, finding John talking at the staircase landing with Molly about my toothbrush and the possibility of pajamas.

Molly is cute, younger looking than her early twenties, with her pale blond hair pulled back into a ponytail, her face pink from having just been scrubbed, and she smiles at me, extending a hand for me to shake. We are introduced and she tells me she has clean pajamas I can wear and there is a new toothbrush in the upstairs bathroom. Before John can say goodnight, Molly grins.

"Wait, I have to share something. Ready for this?"

"Absolutely," he says.

"I was promoted to loan officer today!" she says, beaming. When he hugs her automatically, I realize how close they are, and that he is not only her brother, but her father figure as well.

"That's awesome! Congratulations! I'm so proud of you," he says, kissing the top of her head. In a flash, his eyes dart upward and then close before he releases her, making me look away. Too much family intimacy.

I offer my congratulations, and as we are all exhausted, John explains that I'll be upstairs in the guest bedroom. After working out our morning departure time and setting the alarms on our phones, we say goodnight. I follow Molly upstairs where she shows me my toothbrush and a towel in the bathroom at the top of the stairs, next to large windows that look out over the backyard, the kind my grandmother used to keep open all summer—the kind you had to hurry and close in a rainstorm so it wouldn't rain in. The smell of the old house and creaky wood floors not only take me back to another time and place, but connect me to John and Molly. She leads me around to the left, down the hall where another lamp glows at the end of the hall, and into the guest room, turning on a lamp, promising to return with nightclothes for me.

I touch the coverlet, a patchwork quilt done in earth tones, and gratefully toe off my shoes. There is a picture of a man wearing a huge grin and desert camouflage, holding a little boy, wearing his camo cap on the bedside table. Books are stacked on the table: *Robinson Crusoe, Hatchet, Snow Treasure*, and a worn paperback copy of *Ender's Game*. One of my own favorite books, I pick it up to inspect it, and a dog-eared ticket falls out—an Atlanta Braves game from 2003. There is a poster of Rascal Flatts on the wall and an old Braves cap on the dresser—John's old room. As I remove my coat and lay it on the bench at the end of the bed, Molly is back with a clean pair of cotton pajamas and curiosity illuminating her young face.

"Here you go," she says, handing them to me. They smell of the same pleasant detergent I smelled on John earlier. She watches me in her brother's room. He has taken over the master bedroom, apparently.

We must shift the focus off of me. "Thanks. That's great news about your promotion."

"Thanks. It will take a load off of John. He's waited a long time for me to get on my feet, especially after our dad died."

"I'm sure it's been hard on both of you."

"For John, it was worse. He had to take care of me. I was kinda stuck in a bad place," she says, a faraway look on her face. How fragile she seems, not just young, but almost lost. I feel as though I should tread carefully.

"I can imagine. I didn't know until tonight what had happened."

"He doesn't dwell on it. It's his way of dealing with it. We're real different. But he sold his car so I could finish school, and I guess you know, he gave up his job so he could help me take care of Dad."

"Well...it will be good for both of you to move on."

She looks at me and smoothes a strand of blond hair behind her ear. "Shit or get off the pot."

"Excuse me?" Maybe she is not so fragile.

"That's what my dad used to say. It's time for both of us to shit or get off the pot."

Me too.

Chapter 21

CHERIE

Lunch in the English department office today is oddly fragmented by our random explosive conversational topic changes. First, Taylor has regaled us with his break-up with Paul and the horrifying revelation that Paul is married with children, and then he broadcasts the startling news that he has spent the last evening imbibing with my daughter, who has apparently spent the night with a man I have never met. I can hardly digest my cottage cheese! Of course, this drama trumps the dreaded proposal I've waited all week to present to Walt.

Now, Audrey is complaining about the latest staff meeting we've realized is on the calendar for this afternoon, so I stir my peaches into the cottage cheese, waiting patiently for a segue into my topic. I try to set my face like Hope when she's getting ready to tell me something I don't want to hear, and then the lull presents itself.

"Walt, I wanted to ask you a favor. Actually it's for Toots."

"What is Cruella up to now?" he asks, effectively knocking me off kilter. He has heard a plethora of stories about my narcissistic mother-in-law, and as usual, he is spot on in his assumption.

"Well...how long has it been since you've done any ballroom dancing?"

He shakes his head with a chuckle. "A while."

"Surely you've missed it!" I suggest, gathering momentum.

"It's been a while. Why?" he asks, narrowing his eyes, aware he's about to be set up.

"Toots's dance partner fell and broke his hip, and she needs a partner for their upcoming black tie gala in about a month. Would you be interested in helping her out? It's here in town at the convention center."

All three of my colleagues regard me with wide eyes.

Walt takes a minute and clears his throat. "I assume this is an evening affair? An *early* evening affair for the blue hairs before they all turn into pumpkins?"

He makes me laugh, and formidable as Toots is, again he is spot on in his assessment. "Exactly!" Realistically, it almost sounds harmless. I have to throw in the charity aspect of this to sell the thing. "It's their annual fundraiser. The proceeds go to...somewhere, I don't know, but I'm sure it's a worthy cause. Scholarships to their dance chapter—that's it."

Walt nods, contemplating his turkey sandwich on pumpernickel. "I could consider it. What dances is she talking about doing? I'm not getting out there and tangoing with her."

"Oh, of course not! Ew! I heard her mention the foxtrot. Maybe a waltz. And she's in great shape for a woman her age. I'm sure she'll be very nice to you for helping her out. She'll want to talk to you and get together for a little practice session if you'll agree to it."

"Are you going to be at this event?"

I hadn't given it a single thought. "Of course! Dave and I will both be there." Oh boy, Dave will kill me. That means I've got to get an evening gown. Consignment shopping could be in order. "I've got her number and you can call her, or she can call you and set it all up."

"I'll do it if I'm free," he says, making me exhale a grateful breath.

"She wants to know whether you own a tux," I throw in, now confident, making Taylor sputter with laughter.

"Not one that I could possibly fit into anymore, but I have a nice black suit that ought to suffice."

"You're a prince, and I will owe you big, Mr. Hurley."

"It will be my pleasure," he replies, that enigmatic look of easy challenge on his face. Of all the people I know, Walt will be able to handle Toots, and he knows it.

It is Saturday morning before I see my daughter. And still she has not cleaned her bathroom, so last night I resorted to setting the cleaning bucket inside the tub shower again where she can't possibly miss it. The nerve! Live here, don't make your bed, eat our food, bring home a dog; the least she could do is clean the dang bathroom! What if we had company and some unsuspecting lovely person had to use the facilities? I'd die of embarrassment!

Dave is outside with Little Miss, who has mastered potty training at last, and I can hear him speaking to her in that hilarious animated baby talk he uses with our four-legged family members. I'm sure the neighbors must think he is crazy, but he has become very attached to Little Miss. She is good company for him while Hope and I are working. Rowdy has been relegated outdoors when Little Miss comes downstairs because he is much too rowdy to interact with her safely, so not everyone is happy with the arrangement.

"Who is John?" I ask Hope as she trails through the kitchen in search of coffee, her head wrapped in a towel after her shower. I know she has not had time to clean the bathroom.

"Oh...a guy from work. At Natty's. He's a cook. He let me stay with him and his sister the other night after I'd had too much to drink at the bar."

"Oh." A cook. "His sister and *him*. What about Chris? I thought you had a date with the guy from Honda Jet?"

"I did, but he was just okay. We didn't really hit it off."

My face falls, and she sees it. "It was just a date, just one guy."

"I know, sweetie. Don't feel like you have to rush it."

"I don't," says Hope, turning to go back upstairs with her coffee.

"I heard about some job openings in the county," I offer, while I'm unloading the dishwasher, hoping to give her a bit of good news.

"Any art positions?"

"I don't know, but now is the time to check it out. They just announced the request for transfers."

"I know. I checked the website last week and sent in an updated resume. Daddy and I are all over it. Oh, and he's asked me to design the logo for his new business venture. It's called *Catch of the Day*. I'm doing a cartoon-like fish monger-looking guy with a huge tuna in his hands."

"That's great." *How about the bathroom?*

"Oh, and also, Cayenne, the woman from the bridal boutique, the one with the cute little girl, has approached me about doing her engagement pictures."

"How about the wedding too?"

"Maybe, if she likes the engagement pictures. She knows I'm not booked out, so...maybe."

"Good. Can you clean your bathroom today? I don't live upstairs, so I don't think I should do it."

"I agree. But I beat cha to it. I did it this morning."

My mouth is hanging open.

"Come upstairs and look in my room. I'm trying to put together a new portfolio in case I get to show it at any upcoming interviews."

"Okay." This is new...or *old*. The old Hope is back. Praise the Lord!

Dave is back in with Little Miss and hands her off to Hope as she goes back upstairs, coffee in one hand and puppy in the other. It is a relief to have felt no reference, mentioned or not, about Liam this morning. And with this new focus, maybe she is moving on.

Dave meets me at the sink and pours more coffee for us. He starts helping me put away the pots and pans. "What have you got planned for today, sugarplum?" he asks, letting a kiss linger behind my ear, reminding me of last night before Hope came home. We're back to planning when we can fool around outside of our children's comings and goings. It's so weird, having to sneak around in our own house!

"Yoga at 10:00 and then I'm planning on vacuuming the house and cleaning our bathroom. I need to order Wesley's graduation announcements too. Don't let me forget." No shopping. I haven't been shopping since the beginning of February. It's kind of a relief. Saying no to things we can't afford is somehow freeing. It's less to worry about. If all I have to do is buy food and keep the place clean, being mother bird isn't a bad gig. Anyway, mother birds shove their chicks from the nest once and they are done, so I don't know what I am, except a clean-your-bathroom nag. Then the wedding comes to mind, creating an uncomfortable wave of nausea. I need to call the caterer whom Wesley and I are considering, to schedule a tasting. There is a wedding cake to order as well. The guest list continues to grow, and Ren's family is matching our guests two to one. Dave's band has agreed to play, pro bono, which is a relief. But I'm wondering how in the world Hope is going to manage her maid of honor duties and shoot pictures, even with a friend to assist her.

"And you?" I ask my husband brightly to mask my panic.

"I'm going to work on the website this morning, and go over to Bimini's later on to meet with Jeff. I'll bring home some shrimp. Feel like shrimp scampi tonight?"

"Sure, maybe with just a Caesar salad. Let's keep it light, okay?" I say, thinking about my weight on the scales this morning, and he gives me a kiss. I swear I'm going to burn that sweatshirt when Dave gets a job. I reach for a bottle of pinot gris in our wine rack and place it inside the refrigerator to chill for tonight's meal.

After a moment, he takes his coffee and retreats to the living room that we call his office, and I hear him on the phone with Jeff. Curiosity propels me upstairs to Hope's room, where I get a rare chance to hold Little Miss. Even I have succumbed to her cuddly charms, and I let her snuggle into my bathrobe as I breathe in her puppy smell and nuzzle the soft fuzziness of her head. If she were a cat, she would be purring. Strewn across Hope's bed are the framed pictures from the box she brought back from the pool house, along with her laptop, open to a slideshow of her photos.

"Oh, my! You've been very productive this morning. How long have you been up?"

"I know. I couldn't sleep, so I got up about six and cleaned the bathroom, and then I started looking at all of this before I took my shower. I almost forgot I have to work today, and tonight." She looks at me while running a large-toothed comb through her wet black hair. "It's time for me to get on with my life, you know? You know, shit or get off the pot?"

"Oh. Got it." I've noticed that Hope has been cleaning up her mouth, but it will doubtlessly be a work in progress. Then again, Dave and I are not the best models of decorum, especially in these times of duress. But she will definitely need to control her outbursts before she starts teaching children!

A framed photo catches my eye, a black and white shot of Liam, slouching by a window on a cloudy day, an unmistakable glow in his eyes as he gazes at his photographer. It is heart-stopping in beauty as well as composition and lighting, and gives one the impression of an intrusion into an intimate moment between lovers. The other framed pieces are paintings of Hope, giving off the same sensation. She notices me watching and begins collecting the frames and stacking them against an empty spot on her wall.

"Have you decided what to do with these?"

"No, but there's no rush. I *have* decided against burning it all."

"Good choice." I sit down on her bed, repositioning Little Miss in my lap, to look over Hope's digital portfolio. My cell phone rings from my robe pocket, and as I check the caller ID, my happy mood sags. This can't be good.

"Hi, Toots."

Chapter 22

HOPE

I feel happy. For the first time in a couple of months I can say I feel upbeat. Although I don't understand all the reasons completely, I have a sense of control again. A week has gone by, and after cleaning my bathroom, I feel as though I have jump-started my life again. I am officially off the pot. Spring is here, and I have come to that annual understanding of why green is my favorite color. That is a large part of my change of heart. And at last I have begun to create solutions to my problems. My debt is down to four figures and I'm making steady monthly progress on beating it down, thanks to my living situation. I have Cayenne's photo-shoot to do in Wilmington next week. Currently, my resume is on file in over seven different school districts in North Carolina and at three private schools. I've even begun drafting a grant proposal for integrating a digital photography component into whatever art program I connect with and the social studies or science curriculums. It can't hurt to think ahead, go outside the box, and create a win-win situation for all involved. With students being able to access tablets with digital cameras now, my plan should be a no-brainer, and any school district would be foolish not to look my way. My father has coached me on leaving a memorable impression, apart from wearing red shoes, so this has to be it. Pick me!

I'm a keeper! I am a self-starter and goal-driven. I can hardly freaking wait to interview. A performing arts middle or high school would be my first choice, but I won't be too picky. My goal is to get a foot in a door somewhere.

Tonight I'm working the downstairs bar at Natty Greene's and we are *slammed!* It's not even five and the tip jar is filling rapidly. I love nights like this, and Jessica and I are on a roll, making drinks, pouring draughts, and racking up tips from the furniture market people who are in town this week. I glance through the window into the kitchen and watch John, sautéing his heart out, forearms pumping under the heat lamps. He catches my eye, cocking an eyebrow as he flips steak and onions up and over in the pan in one fluid motion with his right hand. He knows we lust after his forearms. Jessica massages them with extra-virgin olive oil every so often after a busy night. He loves it. I think she has a secret crush on him, but she would never acknowledge it. But after our unexpected pub pal bonding last week, he's been treating me differently, backing off as if I'm off limits somehow. At my age, it seems silly to wonder: does he like me; do I like him? like a twelve-year-old would. Maybe I know too much about him now for his comfort level, but with what he's been through, he is emotionally defensive. I get it. So am I. Still, I think he worries about his sister, and I wonder how long he'll be tied to cooking on the line, in this place, a job he is overqualified to do. Like my dad, and me, we do what we need to do to get by.

My parents and my sister are coming in this evening, as they mentioned, and I have put in a reservation for four, in hopes that I can join them for a brief moment, but that looks unlikely the way it's going so far. I sneak away for a moment to the restroom and see that Wesley has called so I return her call. She answers after the second ring.

"Hey! I'm getting gas and running an errand before I hit the road," she says.

"Hey! Glad you're coming in for dinner. What's the occasion?" I ask, sticking my finger in my ear so I can hear.

"Duh...Hope. You know I wouldn't miss Mama's birthday. I'm going to get her present now."

A moment goes by and I realize I am screwed. I have forgotten my mother's birthday for the first time in my life. "Fuck."

"Oh, my God, Hope! Say you didn't forget Mama's *birthday!*" It is a pronouncement no one ever wants to hear, but with it my sister has demoralized me in one sentence. Seconds go by before I can respond. No wonder my dad seemed miffed at me for not being able to get off work tonight. I can't believe I forgot. We just talked about it last week, and it completely slipped my mind to ask off.

"Shit."

"Hope! Did you make the reservations? Daddy said you did."

"Uh, yeah, for 7:00, but he didn't even say that's what it was for."

"*Well*...did he really have to?"

"Oh, God, stop making me feel bad. I'll pull something together. A cake or something. What are you getting her? Get something good and I'll go in on it with you."

"That's thoughtful. Okay. I'll see you in a couple of hours."

"Okay. Bye." Fuck! I am seriously screwed! It's one thing to be preoccupied, but another to be self-absorbed. The only one in our family who ever gets away with that is Toots, so I am extremely and seriously fucked. I feel another one of those hot flushes coming on; Mama's wrath on me to be sure.

I'm standing at the kitchen window, looking over my last ticket before I clip it to the rack, when I feel John's eyes on me.

"What's wrong, chick?" he asks, seeing the flush and the dilemma on my face.

Should I lie? What good would it do at this point? Besides, he already knows how I am.

A sigh pops between my lips and I give him that look that says, *I'm screwed.*

"I just forgot my mama's birthday, and she and my daddy and sister are coming in here for dinner in a couple of hours. What am I gonna do?"

He winces and gives me a sympathetic look. He steps back from the stove, taking the moment to remove his baseball cap that he typically wears backward, and wipes the sweat off his brow with the back of his arm. "Well, we have cheesecakes by Alex; that's always a hit. Pick out her favorite and we'll stick a candle in it," he says with a shrug, and checks his watch. "Hold on a minute. Cover me a sec, will you, Justin Bieber?" he asks the other line cook, who resembles the young pop star.

He goes to the back of the kitchen where it is quieter, and I watch as he makes a call on his phone. I return to my job, pouring four Wildflowers for the server at the end of the bar, and preparing to mix Margaritas, when I see him gesture to me at the window.

"Look, everything's taken care of. Flowers are coming from the Farmer's Wife around the corner. Get Caitlyn to put those on their table and you should be good to go."

"What?"

"There will be an arrangement of yellow roses and irises in a glass vase here in about thirty minutes. I know the guy who works there. He'll drop them off on his way home. Believe me, I've used him in the past, and he does an awesome job." How could he know my mother loves yellow roses? What have I possibly said in our past conversations that would have tipped him off? *Ohh*...now I vaguely remember something in a conversation with Jessica...but it was months ago.

"No. I'm sure it's great, but how? I mean, how do you know about this stuff?"

"Molly needs flowers from time to time, okay? Look, all I did was make a call. Hopefully, it will save your ass."

"Thank you. I meant, thank you. That's so sweet...that you're going to save my ass. I—I'll pay you back, too," I say, sounding ridiculously pathetic.

"Hope, I've done plenty of boner moves like this before. I'm sure you'll be forgiven."

"At least by Jesus, right?"

He snickers, "Yep. Jesus knows me, this I love! *My* mantra." He is back to tossing chicken and onions in his skillet and prepping two Elm Street Phillies in baskets in front of him, and checking the next ticket, as if I'm not here.

Luckily, tonight we are featuring the Creme Brûlée cheesecake from Cheesecakes by Alex, which will make Mama feel special. I *am* thoughtful, when I remember to be. I've found a sparkler in the kitchen that will make her celebration even more exciting, so I am feeling better about what will transpire later. The boys in the kitchen are singing along to Brad Paisley's "The World," making me laugh. It's a funny song and has everybody shaking their hips. John is singing country music to the peppy bass line and seems to know all the words; who would have thought! He is full of surprises.

Chapter 23

CHERIE

On the way to my birthday dinner at Natty Greene's with Dave, I have to laugh; Toots and I are texting. My new best friend. She'd called last week to thank me for setting her up with Walt, exclaiming how charming he is, and that he'd been at her ballroom club meeting the next day, making an impression on the other women as well. She even gave him rave reviews on his dancing skills. I owe the man big. But now, the problem is that Dave is being such a pain in the butt about it all. He won't be my date for the evening because he's picked that Saturday—in two weeks—for the grand opening of Catch of the Day. Of course. It's such a passive-aggressive move on his part. I'm glad he doesn't treat me the way he treats Toots. Still, it's disconcerting that I'm going to have to represent the family all by myself. I've explained it all as diplomatically as I can to Toots, and I can tell by her text that she's perplexed by his behavior, once again, no doubt. I really don't want to be in the middle of yet another family squabble, but at least I'm finding myself on her A list. What a new turn for me!

This is our first evening out to dinner since Valentine's Day, so I feel special, although a little guilty. We don't need to be spending the money, but at least we are sort of all together, since Hope is working. We arrive at the restaurant right on time, and we are escorted to our table by a woman who introduces herself to me as Caitlyn as she shakes my hand and then wishes me a happy birthday. Hope has flowers waiting on our table, which I really wasn't expecting, but her thoughtfulness is touching. Wesley has a funny look on her face as Hope gets away from the bar momentarily to say hello and happy birthday, and she tells us it's unlikely that she'll be able to join us for long, as they are extremely busy. She will come back by when I am ready to open my present.

At dinner, Wesley fills us in with the news on her job prospects in Austin. She'll fly down after graduation to stay with Ren and start interviewing. The wedding plans are falling into place, so tomorrow, she and I will visit the caterer for a tasting. Hope and I need to start looking at dresses. Dave has connected with his band members and has set up some rehearsals in High Point. I remember those rehearsals all too well, and the hangovers that usually followed!

Hope is making her way to our table with a small entourage of staff to help sing "Happy Birthday" to me. She is carrying a large piece of cheesecake with a sparkler that lights her face as if she were Lady Liberty herself. Caitlyn, Jessica, and a man in a white apron with his ball cap on backwards are singing along with her. Dave and Wesley join in, all hamming it up for the other customers. I get quite an ovation from the crowd, complete with whistles, as I blow out what remains of the sparkler. Hope introduces John, the cook, as the others have wished me a happy birthday and left. He's cute, and seems genuinely interested that I'm enjoying myself. I notice Hope smiling at him as he leaves and she sits down. Then Wesley brings out an envelope. The card they've chosen is sweet, and where it says *I*, they've marked it out and written in *we*. There is a gift card to one of my favorite shops, and I am thrilled to get a chance to go shopping again.

"Oh! I get to go shopping! Yay! I need something to wear to Toots's black tie thing. And a date!" I add, shooting Dave a look, but he is unaffected.

"Ask Taylor, Mama. He's dying to go. I'll go too. I was planning to be off all day for Daddy's grand opening. By the time we need to get ready, I'm sure I'll be ready to wash off the fish and come out for a good time."

"You could come, too," I say to Dave, who rolls his eyes. I moan with delight after taking a bite of the creme brûlée cheesecake, and pass it to Hope for a bite before she has to return to the bar.

"I have a band rehearsal that night. You could all come over there afterward. You'll be all dressed up. I'll still smell like fish, but it will be fun."

"Man, I wish I were going to be here!" says Wesley, who would prefer a party over studying for her final exams. I smile at her. Even after graduation, she will have her nursing boards to pass before she can get a job. I'm hoping she'll stay with us while she studies and sits for the exam. It will give her an opportunity to help with the wedding planning. And as Audrey said, it will be the last time I'll have her to myself.

We finish the cheesecake and Hope gets ready to make her exit, giving me a kiss on the cheek, and a hug with one more happy birthday wish. Her phone pings and she checks it before she turns to leave.

Her face goes ashen.

Chapter 24

HOPE

I cannot believe what I'm seeing. On my phone's screen is another Facebook message from Liam. *Sold a painting. Would like to buy you a plane ticket to Chianti.* He has apparently not been affected by the tone of my last response to his other message. My hand goes directly to my mouth, as if to contain my insides. I sink back down into my chair, hearing the restaurant buzz about me, knowing I've overstayed my allotted time, and that Jessica is probably freaking out at the bar, but I can't move.

"What's wrong?" Mama asks, as Daddy is finishing off the cheesecake. Wesley has allowed herself only a taste, in anticipation of fitting into her wedding gown in six months.

I can only show her my phone, and she regards it gravely, then passes it to Wesley, who passes it to Daddy.

"Holy cow!" Mama says, all three of them going as white as I feel. The table is silent for a moment; then, so like her, Wesley draws out something positive with a wave of her hand.

"He sold a painting. That's great!"

"Yep. That's what he went there to do..." I murmur.

"Well, he must have gotten a good price if he can make this kind of offer. You aren't considering going, are you?" Daddy asks.

"I—I don't know. I have to deal with the shock of this first."

My mother is looking grim. Doubtlessly, she's thinking I'm about to get my heart broken again. We're all thinking it. One thing is obvious to me, but I can't say it to them out loud. Liam and I need closure. Something inside me wakes up and yawns seductively, surprising me even further. I have got to get away from my family before they see that I'm somehow pleased about Liam's offer. I can't even believe it myself. I shudder with the butterflies that are scattering throughout my body.

"I've got to get back to work," I mutter, running fingers through my hair, giving them hugs again while I try to hold myself together.

Jessica is barely holding down the fort and is glad to see me return.

"Can you catch these new people at the bar? I've got the servers lined up down there, screamin' for drinks."

"Sure," I say, going to greet the patrons who are drumming their fingers while they wait. The work is a good way to take my mind off my newest dilemma. A glance through the window tells me that John is too busy to look up, as I watch him arranging sautéed sweet potatoes on a plate while he scrutinizes the next ticket on the line. The next lull comes an hour later, which gives me the opportunity to get Jessica's take on the situation. As always, she listens with great empathy, and she extends her hand to my arm as she replies.

"You're not done with him, are you?"

"I thought I'd moved on, but maybe I really haven't," I admit. It's only been a couple of months, after all.

"Well...here's your chance to go for a few days and see where you stand with him. It must mean something if he's sending you a plane ticket, right?"

That's what I think, but it's scary to entertain such notions. I give a weak shrug. I've never seen Italy. I could do some major damage with my camera there.

"Girl, if you don't wanna go, I'll take that ticket. Do you think he'd mind if I showed up instead of you? I'd really make it worth his while if you're not into this!" I almost think she's serious, until she breaks into that big grin of hers.

"I should be pissed, right? My parents will croak if I go."

"So? It's not their life. But I think they'll understand. What have you got to lose?"

John's head appears in the window.

"So, how'd it go? Was your mom duly impressed?"

"Yes," I grin. "She was. Thank you for saving my ass. What do I owe you?" I ask, reaching for the tip jar.

"Nothin'. It was worth it, seeing her face when you brought out that cake with the sparkler on it." He is gone before I can protest. Jessica twists her lips.

"Girl, you *do* have a problem."

Chapter 25

CHERIE

I am going to burn this red satin robe, I mutter to myself, wandering conspicuously back from the neighbors' house in broad daylight. If I had just waited until I was fully dressed to feed Rowdy his dinner and let him use the bathroom, I wouldn't be standing here like a two-bit ho on a street corner, trying to break into my own house. But then, I didn't want Rowdy jumping on my new evening gown. Of course, when I went out the mudroom door, it slammed shut in the spring breeze and locked me out. And, of course, some fool I live with forgot to put back the spare key under the old coffee can I keep on top of the shelf in the garage, in case someone gets locked out. Okay, maybe it was me who forgot to return the key, but oh well, here I am. To top it all off, when I went out the doorway from the garage, it locked behind me as well. I don't know why I didn't check it before I closed it, but the garage door is down, and I am shit out of luck right now. Also as my bad luck would have it, my neighbors are the only ones with a key to my house, and they are out at their boys' baseball game, so I am standing around, contemplating how to break into my own house without attracting too much attention. I have no phone with me, as I'm in my robe, and nothing else, so I can't call for help. I was almost dressed except for my new dress and shoes before I got caught out here like some college freshman who's forgotten her key. *Damn!* I have forty minutes to get dressed and drive the thirty minutes into town to the black tie gala, where Taylor and Hope will be waiting for me, not to mention the expectations of Toots and my dear friend, Mr. Hurley. Hope got dressed at Jessica's since it was closer. I should have gone with her.

The garage window is partially open. If I can knock out the screen and raise the window the rest of the way, I can attempt to climb in, but that still leaves the lock on the door that I'd have to jimmy to get into the house. I've never jimmied a lock, so I have no idea how that will all go down, and I'm fresh out of bobby pins. Jeez, all I need is a cigarette hanging out of my mouth and I would look just like Carol Burnett in *Annie!* I could go to the other neighbors and ask them to call a locksmith, but they have teenage boys who don't play baseball, and they really don't need to see me like this. I glance left and then right and manage to pry off the screen with a gardening trowel I've found stuck in the flowerbed I'm now standing in. Maybe I can use it to pry open the door as well!

Next, I have to go back to the yard to find something suitably tall enough to stand on, so I can heave myself through the window. If I rip my robe in the process, I won't have to burn it. I come across the largest terra-cotta flowerpot I can find and turn it over to empty it out. I haul it over to the window and set it upside down so I can stand on it. As I'm wondering how to climb in gracefully, I hear a car slow to a stop, and then it turns into my driveway. *Oh, good, it's the police!* Now I feel even better. Crap! This is all my mother-in-law's fault. I've met Karma, and she doesn't play nicely with others.

"Good afternoon, ma'am. I'm Officer Griffin with the Guilford County Sheriff's Department. Is there something I can help you with?"

"Hi," I say, brushing an errant curl off my face and extending my hand, while trying my best to look poised. My hand has dirt on it from the flowerpot, and now, so does my face, I'm sure. "I'm Cherie Johnson and I live here. I'm trying to break into my house," I say and laugh, but he's regarding me carefully as if I'm an escapee from Dorothea Dix, the mental hospital a couple of hours down the road. Then I notice he's sizing up my bare feet and what I'm not wearing underneath my red satin robe, and I am almost overcome with embarrassment, but at this point, I have to press through it. Thank God I'm not wearing my bunny slippers! He is wiping his hands together to rid them of my dirt. "I could show you my driver's license if I could get back into my house. I'm going to be late for an important engagement as it is," I explain, trying not to sound like the White Rabbit from *Alice in Wonderland*. I am definitely in someone's drug-induced fantasy! The way Officer Griffin is regarding me, he must think so too.

He nods, waiting for more, so I continue. "I was getting ready to climb up on this flowerpot and go through the window, here." At that point, Rowdy rounds the corner, and upon seeing my new acquaintance, begins barking. "Hush, Rowdy!" I admonish my dog, and then explain to Officer Griffin that he is harmless. "He'll lick you to death before he'd bite you," I tell him, although he doesn't look convinced.

But he seems to believe me about living here, so he offers to go through the window. For good measure, he checks the door beside the window, and shakes his head, confirming my escape from the nut house. I can*not* tell him that I am a teacher. I would never live it down if he ever saw me again. Carefully guarding his holstered pistol, he lifts one long leg over the sill and pulls himself through with the skill of a gymnast, making me laugh with relief. Walking over to the door, he pushes the garage door button. The door raises so I can enter the garage gracefully, clutching my robe around me. Next he asks my permission to pick the lock, and after I nod, he goes to work with a pick he's produced, and in less than a minute, my door is standing open. I thank him profusely, and offer again to show him my photo ID, and he lets me show him, probably just for kicks, but he seems satisfied that I am who I say I am. Officer Griffin looks at me with the ghost of a smile, sending my face scarlet.

"Thank you so much for rescuing me!" I thank him again, seeing him out.

"Not a problem, Ma'am. Glad to help. Have a good evening."

As I close the door behind him, I shudder with relief and whip myself into overdrive, running back to the bedroom to wipe off the dirt from my face and the sweat I've produced from my frenzy, and I repair the makeup damage before slipping into my new midnight blue gown. My birthday gift card from the girls paid for half of it. I am too keyed up to care how I look at this point, so I forgo the up-do I had planned for my hair and stick my feet into Cinderella sandals, grab my clutch, check for a tube of lipstick, and I'm off.

As I'm careening around the kitchen corner and through the mud-room, I remember to grab my cell phone while commanding Rowdy to sit and stay as I back my car out of the garage, all the while carefully thinking over each maneuver so I don't pull another brainless move. I can't afford to be stupid at this hour. I gun my car up the street, and then I realize I'm speeding, and I don't want another encounter with Officer Griffin, who I now notice is parked at the crest of the hill, checking for speeders like me. I give him an enigmatic smile and wave casually as I glide by in my Civic. Maybe he won't recognize me fully clothed and in my Ray-Bans.

Halfway into town, I know I'm already late, and right on cue, my phone begins to ring.

"Mama? Where are you?" It is Hope, of course, wondering where her usually punctual mother is.

"Hey, darling. I'll be there in fifteen minutes. I had a little incident. I'll tell you about it later. How is it so far?"

"Really nice! It's like a prom for old people. Toots looks awesome, and so does Mr. Hurley. And the place is filling up quickly. Our names are on the list, so just check in at the door. Taylor and I have saved a place for you at our table. It's number sixteen. We'll be looking for you."

"Okay, thanks! See you shortly."

I open it up on Bryan Boulevard, and in the estimated fifteen minutes, I am pulling in the parking lot at the Koury Convention Center and entering the building. I follow the signs to the appropriate ballroom and check in at the table. There are many more people than I've expected, and the tables are set with white tablecloths and elegant floral arrangements. I pass a table with raffle items, noticing the numbers on the tables, when Hope and Taylor are at my elbow, grinning at my deer-in-headlights face. I have hardly recognized them!

"OMG! Cher, you look amazing!" Taylor croons, giving my shoulders a squeeze.

"Oh, really? Well, I wanted to put up my hair...."

"Mama, you look *hot!*" says Hope, and I can tell by her face that she's impressed. But so am I with the two of them; Hope is in her elegant black dress with gold trim, large gold bracelets, and hair in a high ponytail, hanging straight down her back. Taylor is in a dark suit, which I've never seen, and he looks sensational.

"You two are definitely Oscar-worthy yourselves!"

"Come and sit. We fixed you a plate," she says, leading me to our table. On the way, a handsome man in a black suit catches my arm.

"Mrs. Johnson! You made it!" It is Walt Hurley, looking like a dreamboat, and my face breaks into a grin.

"Wow, Mister! You look great!"

He indeed looks quite comfortable in his new persona, as opposed to the rest of us in the room, who are acting like we are dressed up for a masquerade ball, preening and strutting around to beat the band.

"Thank you! And you look smashing! Have you seen Toots?" he says, loudly, above the talking and laughter, as well as the music in the background, "String of Pearls," I think it is.

"No!"

"Look for a vision in red at table twelve. That's where I'm headed. See you later!"

"Okay. And break a leg!" I add and he chuckles on his way back to his table. Walt is perfect for this. I only wish it were Dave. Dave, whom I left earlier in the day, up to his ears in shrimp, with a line five deep as long as I was there. They'd bought plenty of shrimp, knowing that they could sell whatever might be left over tomorrow, but I think they surely must have sold out if business was like that all day.

I sit beside Hope, and Taylor returns to the table moments later, handing me a glass of white wine. We sit and enjoy Swedish meatballs, chicken satay, and mini spanakopitas while the program gets underway. The lights dim as a spotlight makes a moon-like circle on the podium, where I assume a Master of Ceremonies will emerge momentarily. Then, a dark-haired woman in red chiffon with a rhinestone brooch on the single shoulder appears, grinning broadly as the applause begins. Hope digs her elbow into my ribcage. It is Toots. In all her glory, looking my age, but of course, taller, and skinnier. *Damn* her!

She welcomes everyone to the annual red carpet event. I am at a loss to attend to how many years, and who the beneficiaries are, as well as any of the words she is saying, so stunning is she in her bright red gown. Her voice slides gracefully over every word, as if she waltzes in her speech as well. She invites us to continue to eat, drink, and be merry, and to view the items for silent auction, and she lets us know that the dance program will commence in thirty minutes.

I glance at Walt, who applauds appropriately, looking proud of her, as we all should. Then I meet Hope's eyes, and she is grinning along with Taylor.

"She's something, isn't she?"

"Yes. Think of all we've missed over the years," is all I can say. Think of all Dave has missed. Think of all Toots has missed. It suddenly makes me sad, and I take a sip of my wine, thinking I should go and find her. I eat one more spanakopita, and take one more sip of wine, and excuse myself to search her out. Her red dress is easy to spot and I find her in a tête-à-tête about the program with one of the other ladies who is dressed in royal blue, and she catches my eye.

"Oh! Cherie! I want you to meet Katharine England! Cherie is my daughter-in-law. You know, Hope's mother. She is also the angel who sent me the divine Mr. Hurley, with whom I'll be partnered tonight."

"Yes, Cherie! How nice to meet you!"

"My pleasure as well, Katharine. Hope is here tonight, in fact."

"Oh, yes! I saw her. It's so good to have met you, Cherie," she says, holding out a finger and making her exit.

Toots turns to me. "I'm glad you came! I wish Dave were here. How did it go today?"

She seems genuinely interested, but looks as if she's surely expecting me to say, *dismally.*

"I think it went well. Much better than he expected. I got a little way-laid coming over here, so I didn't get the final report, but they were covered up the whole time I was there earlier."

"Huh! Well, that's great news. I hope he doesn't have to do this for long. Can you imagine smelling like fish all the time?"

"Oh, I'm sure it will suit him just fine, until the right fit comes along."

She dismisses me with a stern press of her lips. "Mmm. Well...have a good time, dear. I've got to run along and check on a few things. Enjoy the show. And do a little dancing!"

I meet Taylor and Hope back at our table. None of us has the available cash to bid on the silent auction items, so why bother to tempt ourselves? Taylor is back with another plate of food to share—a man after my own heart.

"I met your former landlady," I say to Hope.

"I know. I saw her earlier. She was just cordial."

"*Just* cordial? No more?"

"*Just.*"

What a bitch. Whatever. Hope has decided to visit Liam in Tuscany, and Dave and I have ambivalent feelings about it. She needs closure, but whatever it is he needs is unclear. I can only imagine. Still, it scares me for her, but it is a free trip and she could use a break if she is about to take on a new school year. I have to remind myself that she is a grownup and can make her own decisions.

"So, how do you think Daddy came out on the grand opening today?"

"They *killed it*," Hope says. "It didn't hurt that everybody and their brothers were out in force to buy plants at the farmers' market after the dreary winter we've had. I took down over 120 email contacts in just the four hours I was there. People are literally eating up this business. I knew it would go over as soon as I got out there and saw the lines forming. People were squealing tires to pull off the road and take a look. He's going to need an assistant. Jeff won't be there every weekend."

"Well, Taylor, are you looking for a summer job?" I ask, half-seriously.

"Too much heat stress for me," he laughs, dodging any form of commitment. I will dodge it too, if it comes to that, maybe. I don't work in the summers either. I would be free labor—with fringe benefits, as Dave would remind me.

"Maybe he can get Wesley involved after she graduates."

"Maybe. And I have to say, my logo looked awesome, on the tent and our T-shirts, didn't you think, Mama?"

"Yes. And on the recipe cards too. That was a good idea. I'm impressed with the whole thing. I hope he remembers to wear his sunscreen next week," I say as the lights are flashing, reminding the last minute bidders to return to their seats.

The show begins, and I am immediately aware that Toots is a major attraction, along with other more widely known ballroom dancers she's invited to perform. The actual MC takes the podium and the show begins. There are many exciting tangos, lovely foxtrots, and sultry sambas, but my favorite of the evening is the dreamy waltz to "Moon River" by Toots and Walt. If she had just not worn *red*, it would have been perfect, but my hat is definitely off to my colleague. The consummate gentleman, he floats as easily across the floor as if he has done this with Toots a million times, and she looks truly tranquil in his arms, not just the plastered-on smile I have seen enough times to know when she's faking it. They are magical; their performance transcends who they are, making me feel as though I do not know them. Everyone else seems to be in awe of them as well. When they are finished and take their bows, there is a standing ovation. I even see some of the women wiping tears from their eyes. They catch our eyes and all three of us shout out, "Bravo!"

After the initial performances, there is more dancing for everyone, appropriate for even beginners like the three of us, so Taylor takes each of us out for a twirl around the dance floor. I've had just enough wine, and the lights are low enough for me to be brave enough to try. This is not the kind of dancing I usually do, nor is it for Hope, but with Taylor to guide us around, we are believable impostors on the floor. It's a nice change, but by 9:30, I've had enough.

"Mama, let's go over to Daddy's rehearsal and crash their party!" Hope says, with mischief in her eyes as Taylor squires her back to the table.

Toots must be involved with the auction at this point, as people are beginning to move toward the tables, placing their final bids of the evening. I haven't seen her, or Walt, in a while. We look around for a moment and decide to leave. She's in her element; she will never miss us.

"Well, the night is young, so why not?" I laugh, surprised that I'm not tired. It has already been a long day, but we are just minutes away from drummer Gary Porter's house. Gary has offered his man cave in High Point for the rehearsals.

Hope is talking on the phone already. "Wanna get *wild?*" she's asking someone on the other end.

Chapter 26

HOPE

I get through to Jessica immediately and she is all over the invitation. She is crazy about the old rock 'n' roll, so she's got her car keys in hand as I instruct her to bring cold beer and end the call. And she's bringing John.

I look down later at my phone and there is a picture of the road with his message, *I'm coming*. I laugh and show Taylor the picture. It's funny, but John has not talked to me, personally, after he heard I was going to Italy. I guess it wasn't my imagination that there was something between us after our night at the bar. Enough of a something that now he's hurt because maybe he thinks I'm going back to Liam. Or, then again, I could be imagining it all, but if he won't talk to me, then how am I supposed to know? *Boys!* This is so middle school!

As Taylor and I pull into this well-to-do neighborhood in his car, we can hear the thumping beat of the music from the top of the street. I'll bet the neighbors are having a stroke, but then I see that I'm wrong; it's a fricking *concert* at the back of the house. The band has set up in the outdoor kitchen, and people of all ages are standing in the driveway around the patio and in the yard, tapping their feet in the moonlight and having a rowdy good time. We have definitely been at the wrong dance party!

Mama follows us in, holding up her skirt with her shoes in her hand, looking cuter than I've ever seen her. I'm checking out the outdoor kitchen, something I've never experienced outside a showroom, and thinking it was a good thing these guys didn't quit their day jobs, but they sound pretty good for a bunch of old guys!

Taylor agrees. He's shed his jacket and lost the tie, rolled up his sleeves, and looks a lot more comfortable. We look like we've just ditched the prom. Finally through the neighbors, I can see the band, and my dad who is ripping out the guitar riffs to the Beatles's "Back in the USSR"— in his Catch of the Day T-shirt, looking like a twenty-something young gun on that black Fender. It's a classic, as he's reminded me many times. I remember the band being good. But I had no idea he had *this* in him!

I gaze open-mouthed at him, and then turn to Taylor. "That's my dad," I shout in his ear.

"The *guitar player?* Yeah, you look just like him!" he says, drawing a proud grin from me. My dad is pretty freaking cool!

Mama is looking at him, too, with a smile that means more than memories. Then he sees her and plays to her until the song is over and he laughs. She goes over to him and he takes off his guitar, picking her up and swinging her around like he is twenty-something. The crowd is whistling and clapping. Daddy whispers something in Mama's ear and winks at her. She makes the rounds through all the band members and finds someone, Gary's wife maybe, and starts talking. Someone hands her a beer, so she switches her shoes to the other hand and accepts the bottle. Then Daddy straps the guitar back on, and the band confers momentarily. A new song, Bruce Springsteen's "Born to Run," starts up while Taylor and I congregate, wishing we had a beer, like some of the neighbors. It's the next song, "Brand New Man," before Jessica and John arrive.

"This is the band that was supposed to play at my supposed-to-be-wedding," I explain to Jessica, and she nods, impressed. "Now they're going to play at Wesley's."

John is in on the conversation and I point out my dad.

"Damn! He's good," says John, who's pulsing up and down like everyone else in the yard. I recognize no one else. Jessica and John have brought beer so the four of us make it our own party.

"This is so much more fun!" Taylor says.

"I know!" I say, thinking none of us have checked our phones in almost an hour. That's a sure sign it's a good time. Jessica and Taylor are laughing at two little girls dancing with abandon, the way I used to do when I was little, with my twirly skirt. Always a twirly skirt. If it didn't twirl, I wouldn't wear it. This makes me happy. My father is making people happy. People are dancing, some of the older ones, but some of the teenagers are getting in on the act as well. My mother is talking to everyone, and I don't think she's even touched her beer. I can feel John's eyes watching me. I look and he smiles. I might as well start this conversation. He won't ever do it. It's darker where he's standing, out of the porch lights. I take a couple of steps backward and speak directly in his ear.

"How are you?"

"Good! This is so cool. I'm glad you asked us over here tonight. Beats sitting at home."

"Are you okay? We haven't talked much in a while."

"Yeah. Everything's good. You know," he says, and I think I do. "You're going to Italy, finally," he blurts.

"Yeah. I was invited this time. And my tickets are paid for."

"Tickets?" he has to shout in my ear so I hear the plural.

"Well, yeah. I'm coming back. In time for Wesley's graduation. And then I'm hopefully going to have a job."

He searches my face, maybe wondering. "Leaving the nest again?"

"Absolutely."

"It's good that you're ready to spread your wings. Healthy."

"I know, right?"

"You should do it. You should go after what you want," he says, looking back at the band and tilting back his beer.

I stare at a man's knee as I think about this. What *do* I want? Last week I was so sure, and now with Liam's invitation, I'm unsure again. What if I get to Italy and don't want to come home? What if I get to Italy and Liam doesn't want me to leave? Nah, it won't happen. I can't let myself think that. I might really have a shot at a solid future if I stay here and follow my plan. Travel is for vacations. Vacations you've earned by working hard. I'm thinking about this as the cool breeze lifts my hair slightly. I glance back at John.

"It's okay, Hope," he says, watching my hair, and then he leans in and kisses the side of my mouth. His kiss is soft. Gentle. I want more, so I kiss him back and it's nice. John is kind. I don't want to hurt his feelings. Tears leap into my eyes and he sees it. I turn away, realizing the music has stopped and there is more applause. My dad is beside me, his hand on my shoulder. He actually does smell like shrimp, but it's not a bad thing.

"Hey, beautiful," he says, then addresses John. "John, right?" he says, shaking John's hand.

"That's right, sir. The band is righteous!"

"Thanks, man," Daddy says, and it hits me that they could bond, and be friends. My head spins.

"I played bass in my garage band in high school," says John. "I always wanted to be a session man. Wanted to go to Nashville, do the whole thing, you know?" he says, and now he and my dad are lost in conversation.

Jessica is watching me so I go over and stand with her, feeling suddenly awkward.

Her green eyes invade me again. "I know you're going to Italy next week, but please don't hurt John."

"I'm not planning on it. Listen, Jess, if you want him, you should do something about it," I say.

"It's not that. And he's really not my type, but just...go easy on him, okay?"

Mama is beside me now with her phone at her ear, a finger in the other, and a look of alarm on her face. "No! When? Where are you?" she cries into the phone.

Chapter 27

CHERIE

After I've disconnected from Walt's phone call, I reach for Dave, anticipating that the evening will be closing down around us all in the next moment. Seeing that the last moment's mirth has evaporated from my face, he touches my arm, saying, "Babe, what is it?"

"I just got off the phone with Walt. He's with your mother in the emergency room. She's having some stomach pain, and they're trying to figure out what it is."

Hope and John are listening in as well, as it takes Dave a couple of eye blinks to process what I've just told him.

"Didn't you just leave the party?" asks Dave, confused.

"We did, but we didn't see either of them around right before we left. I thought she was involved with getting ready for the silent auction, so we slipped out without saying goodbye." I'm feeling worse than ever about my *faux-pas* now, realizing the purpose of good manners in the grand scheme of life. You should always be able to say, *She was fine when I left.* Crap! It's Karma, back from the dead.

In the darkness, Dave searches through the people in the yard, trying to locate Gary, and making mental plans. "Okay, look, let me tell Gary we're leaving and then we can go over to the hospital."

"I drove. Do you want me to drive us there?"

Dave looks at me and thinks better of it. Good thing he doesn't know about my earlier lapse in sensibility as well. "No, we'll take the truck."

Hope chimes in. "Taylor brought me over here, Mama. Do you want me to drive your car home? I'll need to pick up my car from Jessica's tomorrow."

"Okay..." I say, feeling my head swim. Dave is walking through the crowd of neighbors to Gary, explaining the situation, as I glance at Hope. John is reaching for her hand and asking whether she wants company. What a nice guy.

Dave is back with his guitar case, fishing car keys from his jeans pocket. "Let's go. Which hospital?"

"Cone...."

Dave leads me by the hand as we hug Hope, who's just catching Taylor up to speed.

"Thanks, Taylor. It was all great. Thanks for coming and being our date. I'll see you Monday."

"Maybe. Call me. Take care, Cher." He lifts crossed fingers and winks as Dave and I are heading down the driveway.

We are in the truck, Dave's not so new purchase, a Dodge Ram pickup, and I almost giggle when he turns over the engine that sounds like a cigarette boat growling to life. What a sight we are, me in my evening gown, and Dave in his James Dean best! I fasten my seatbelt and realize that now I can't lean over to get my shoes on, but Dave is backing carefully out of the driveway, trying not to kill Gary's friends, and then guns it up the street. It takes over a half an hour to reach the hospital, and I attempt to calm Dave's nerves by asking him about the grand opening, telling him how great the band sounded tonight, and giving him a color-ful minute-by-minute account of the gala, so he will be filled in, thinking Toots will likely grill him when he arrives.

Walt is sitting in the waiting room, looking every bit the lone sentry when we arrive. I give him the bear hug he deserves. "Hey, Walt."

"Hi. She thinks I left. I was ordered to go home, but I didn't think that was wise," he says, shaking Dave's hand. "Hi, Dave. They don't think it's appendicitis. Her pain is on the wrong side for that. They mentioned diverticulitis, but I have no idea what that is. She's waiting to have some tests done but there's a crowd tonight. It could be a while. Between you and me, she didn't seem very surprised that this was all happening to her, so I'm wondering whether she might have had some of these symptoms and didn't mention it to you."

"Yeah, well...that's so much like my mother. If you know anything about her dietary habits, she's a health nut. It's not like she would ever eat anything that would give her indigestion."

"A case of nerves, maybe?" ventures Walt.

"Nah, the woman has nerves of steel," says Dave, and Walt imme-diately concurs. "But thank you so much for helping her get situated tonight, and waiting for us. You've gone way beyond the call of duty. I'm sorry for all the trouble."

"Not a problem. She knows you were on your way. I had a great time, and I thought Toots was rather delightful. I know it comes as a bit of a surprise, but we got along quite well."

That's her MO—good company manners, I think to myself, but now is not the time for sardonic humor. Instead, I say, "Walt, thank you so much! We really didn't mean to suck you into this much family drama tonight."

"Like I said, it's no problem. I hope I'll see you Monday, Cherie," he says and leaves us to find the attending doctor.

It is 2:30 a.m. when Toots is released from the hospital with pain medication and doctor's orders to follow up with a gastroenterologist, as her preliminary tests have shown a blockage in her colon. She was glad to see us for her ride home, but she would not tell Dave how long she had been experiencing her symptoms.

"Really, you two are over-reacting. I may have a twisted colon or something. It happens to people on rare occasions. I'm as healthy as a horse."

Of course, Toots knows all this medical mumbo-jumbo. Dietary health and nutrition are her fields, and she's spent the greater part of her life treating people and chairing seminars on the very topic. She is even socially and professionally connected with Dr. Wharton, whom she is supposed to call on Monday. The irony of Toots's dilemma is not lost on any of us. Toots Johnson is the last person on earth I would have ever expected to have colon cancer, but that may well be what is going on here. None of us wants to say she could have cancer, even the ER doctor, but Toots is presenting herself as someone in denial, and we know she's just trying to get rid of us for the night. Dave has given up trying to coddle her, so we take her home in her red chiffon evening gown and help her up the steps into the house, uncomfortable as she is. She refuses to let us stay with her, claiming exhaustion, promising not to die tonight, and that all she wants to do is get a good night's sleep. I insist that we stay until she is changed and ready to get into bed before we leave. Dave warns her that he will check on her in the morning, and contact her on Monday morning to follow up on her follow-up. It is good that he is not working full-time so he can attend to her needs.

I send Hope a report by text, in case she has gone to sleep. After the day he's had, Dave is dog tired himself, and his face is pinched with what I assume is worry, refusing my offer to drive us home. Sitting in the shotgun seat as we roar down the isolated road, I can't help but feel irritated at Dave and Toots, both pushing against the other as they dance the *paso doble* that has become their life. It is late in the game, she may be too sick, and they are way too smart to be this pissed off at each other.

"Sooner or later, you all are going to have to come to terms with each other," I murmur, staring out the window at the crescent moon that follows us home. My voice is quiet, but my tone is serious. "It's absurd.... It's like watching two bulls face off every time the two of you are together. I'm tired of it, Dave. Aren't you?" I ask, turning toward him in the dark.

Dave's arm stretches over the steering wheel but he says nothing, staring at the road until we pull into our own driveway.

Chapter 28

HOPE

It is two o'clock in the afternoon when we land in Firenza. I have lost track of how many hours I have been up, but I think it is over twenty. My eyes are dry and my shirt has a little stain on it from where I threw up as we landed in Atlanta. Of course, with my luck there wasn't a barf bag in sight. The man beside me was kind enough to offer me a plastic bag from an airport gift shop purchase. On the way back, I'm getting Dramamine.

Rolling my carry-on onto the concourse, I am submerged in the mass of people departing the customs area, amidst the squeals of those finding their loved ones, and I wonder how my reception will be. Will they be late? Did they forget about me? And then I spot Liam's head above others in the crowd. Amelia is standing beside him, texting, in a feminine short-sleeved blouse and a pencil skirt, taller than I'd have thought in her outrageous stilettos with expensive sunglasses on her head. She is much prettier in person. Fuck.

He sees me and bursts into a grin. When our eyes meet, it is electric. I believe it is as if we left off the day before I saw Amelia's Facebook message. Nothing has changed, from the ripped jeans and rumpled button-down shirt to his hair, today pulled back in a ponytail. Liam looks hot as hell. And he is glad to see me.

"*Ciao, mia bella!*" he moans, engulfing me into his arms and lifting me in the air. "*Mi sei mancato molto!*" I had forgotten his strength.

"I have no idea what you just said!"

"I've missed you...so much!" he says, letting go of me and giving me a kiss on my cheek, not what I was hoping for, but he does seem glad to see me. I am trying to gauge their relationship at once.

Amelia is smirking beside him as she wraps up her text message and presents herself to be introduced. How weird is this going to be? I still don't know where I'm staying. Is this like going away to camp, or is it more like a rendezvous with my lost lover? Liam kisses my head and turns me to meet Amelia.

"This is Hope!" he says, as though I am his masterpiece. I get it, though. He has painted me so many times, my reputation must precede me. Turning to me, he introduces her, with a wave of his hand. "Amelia Fiori," he says as she and I shake hands.

"*Buongiorno*, Hope. *Benvenuta*," says Amelia, in the lilting lovely rhythm of the language, making me realize the few Italian phrases I've studied on the plane have already vanished from my memory. They have said five words to me in Italian and already I am cowed! Worse than that, I think Amelia is devilish; I can tell by the look in her eyes, and that smirk again. God, this is going to be a long week.

"How was your flight?" Liam asks.

"I...got here. Customs was a little intimidating, but I didn't get strip searched."

"Good. We've been working all morning. Come on, let's go and have some fun! Is this all you have?" he asks, still grinning, and commandeers my rolling bag. I nod, and he can't believe it; clothes horse me, here, with only one fifty-pound bag. I am too cheap to pay the extra bag charge. As we head down the concourse, I'm tuning in to the flight announcements given in Italian and then in English. I am all aflutter with excitement and terror at the same time. Maybe I will be okay as long as I don't get separated from them. I latch onto Liam's arm and he does me one better, circling his big arm around my waist. I've missed his protectiveness and the sheer masculinity of his presence.

It is warm and comfortable, almost hot in the bright sun as we exit the doors of the airport. As they lead me across the parking lot, I realize I will be like a baby here, knowing nothing about anything, and totally reliant on these two people for my every need for the next seven days. I try to relax through the fatigue that is making me feel as though I am in a Fellini film. We stop at a slick little red and black Fiat that can't possibly be big enough for the three of us, but Amelia aims the remote and the car beeps twice. She opens the passenger door and looks at Liam.

"You're driving," she orders, flipping the seat back forward, and somehow inserts herself despite her tight skirt into the backseat, so I can ride shotgun while Liam drives. He looks unsure, but he settles his tall frame magically in the driver's seat and off we go.

"Nice car," I comment, noticing the new car smell.

"My papa's incentive to get me to move back over here. It worked," Amelia says.

"You have to direct me—in English too, if you expect me to get us home," Liam says, as he leaves the parking lot. The road signs mean nothing to me.

"Ha ha! *Vada dritto! E poi giri a destra!*" she laughs again as if her control over him is so hilarious.

"*Right*, right?" he gives it back to her and swerves the car back and forth quickly, sending her into a fit of giggles.

"Yes! Go straight and then turn right."

I'm going to vomit again if it's going to be like this all week. Liam looks over at me and takes my hand, saying, "Poor baby. How was your flight?" he asks again and laughs at his redundancy.

"Long...I threw up."

"Ugh! We'll get you some coffee. It's best if you try and stay up with us. Then tonight you'll sleep like a baby." He winks at me. He has always been skilled at knocking me out. My insides ripple at the thought of sleeping with him again.

I smile at him gratefully and he squeezes my hand. If I didn't know better, I'd think he was Italian. So far he fits right in here. Amelia is screaming directions in English this time. The traffic is crazy, but he manages to zip across two lanes of traffic as she swears from the backseat.

"She makes me drive her everywhere. I'm her *slave*." He grins at Amelia in the rearview, giving her his smoldering look—my look.

"Yes, you are. It's the only way to learn," she mutters from the backseat, texting again.

"How is the family?" he asks.

"Daddy's working, selling fish in a tent by the road."

"No kidding?" he laughs as I shake my head.

"Oh, yeah. He doesn't sleep half the time, he's got so many ideas going on in his head. The band is back together and they're awesome. I'm photographing brides, and sending out resumes for next school year. Still working at Natty's and the boutique.... Oh, and Toots has been sick. She's going in for surgery tomorrow. Something's wrong with her colon."

"Oh, no. That can't be good."

"No. It might be cancer, but nobody's saying the word yet. Of all people, Toots with colon cancer...I don't understand, but...."

"Oh...that's ironic, isn't it? Hard to believe Toots could be so sick. I'm sorry to hear that."

"And I saw Katharine England last week. At a dance thing we went to with Toots."

"How's Katharine?"

"Snobby as usual."

He laughs. "How's your puppy? What did you name her?"

"Little Miss."

He chuckles at her name. Of course, he doesn't know. We haven't talked much since that day when I left the pool house, other than arranging this trip, and that was on Facebook. "Little Miss is great. Everybody loves her. And Wesley is going to graduate from Carolina next week when I get home." There is probably more to tell, but I can already feel myself slipping out of my life at home. I yawn and close my eyes momentarily, but the way he is flying along the cobblestone streets, I feel the need to look. And the scenery is amazing in the city. The spectacular colorful architecture, the people, and the mad traffic; I don't want to miss a thing. I crane my neck to see everything. It's a million times better than the pictures.

"Is this your first time in Italy?" asks Amelia.

"Yes. Florence—*Firenze* is beautiful!"

"You'll like our farmhouse in Greve as well. It's much more tranquil than the city here. There are lots of people around with my family and the guests in the agriturismo, but it's nothing like this. I think you'll find it very relaxing and beautiful."

"I thought you lived in Chianti."

At my confused expression, Liam explains, "Greve is a village in Chianti. Agriturismo means guest accommodations. The Fioris have different guest houses on the property and tourists stay there as part of Amelia's family's business, along with the vineyards and the cantina at the winery."

"So what do you do there?"

"Whatever they need me to do. I helped prune the grapevines when I arrived, and then there's general cleaning, fixing, and moving stuff around. We've been bottling a lot, getting ready for the wine festivals.

They host parties there all the time. Soon the weddings will start. They let me help in the cantina sometimes when it gets really busy."

"Liam is our American chick magnet. He's very good for business. And he's sold a painting or two in the winery."

"That's good."

"We like it that he adds another flavor to our concept. And it's not your typical American *vanilla!*"

I am slightly offended. I also believe Amelia is sexist. Or maybe she is just pulling his chain, but Liam seems unfazed by her remarks. I wonder whether she has a boyfriend. I *hope* she has a boyfriend. And I really hope it's not Liam.

"There's a lot to do with the wine festivals coming up this month. You're here at a good time. You'll get to see what the vineyard is all about," says Liam.

Finally I get up the nerve to ask.

"So, where am I staying?"

"With me, of course. If you can stand the close quarters," he says, shooting me his smoldering glance, and my heart does a distinct flip-flop. And I thought I was over him! Holy smoke! It is like we never left each other. Was I so mistaken about his feelings for me? Have I put myself through hell for nothing? "My house is very small, but it's all I need. There's a beautiful view of the vineyards, and birds sing all the time there. You'll love it."

Small house, small car, big man. My man. I'm excited. Or confused. I can't tell. I don't care. I am in freaking *Italy!*

After a brief stop at an outdoor espresso bar where Amelia orders me something wonderful and frothy, and a little window shopping, they take me on a mini-tour of the city, promising to take me back another day when they are out dealing Liam's art. Amelia explains that most of the legwork for promoting Liam as an artist is done online, then by phone, but the real contact is made face to face in the cities and villages where she can work in appointments. In this small car, however, I wonder how anyone will ever be able to appreciate the magnitude of Liam's work, without seeing the real thing.

In the short drive from the city, the scenery in the countryside softens abruptly to beautiful rolling hills bathed in golden sunlight, covered in grapevines that dot the landscape like patches on a quilt. We have headed southwest, past the city of Siena. Tall cypress trees and olive groves add a new texture to the farms and small villages we pass that are always denoted by their characteristic churches and small stone houses and buildings. Verdant fields separated by dirt roads lead to tranquil communities nestled in the gentle hillsides, making me wonder which one will eventually be our destination.

Liam speeds around every corner, obviously enthralled with this fun little driving machine, as Amelia becomes my tour guide, continually rattling off our locations and the history of the region, pointing out the ruins, and how each community has its own animal symbol that depicts the region. We are passing signs with black roosters, the *gallo nero*, which means we are in the Chianti region now. An occasional car or Vespa careens past us on the other side of the lane, making me gasp, but Liam seems ready for anything, motorized or not, that might land in his path. Amelia points out unusual black pigs with wide white strips around their bodies, as if belts have been painted on them. They are rare native swine called cinta Senese that are indigenous to this area, she explains. If Liam would slow down, I feel as though I could be lulled into the most pleasant sleep, but the espresso, Amelia's travelogue, and his driving are keeping me awake. I'm glad; I couldn't possibly miss any of this.

We turn into a dirt lane lined with cypress trees, marked by a sign, also with a black rooster, that reads Fattoria Casa Fiori, and all of us are smiling. Liam takes us past the vineyards and the olive groves as the road winds around, opening into the entrance of the fattoria itself, a sprawling stone home, painted golden by the afternoon sun. A part of the earth itself, with the terra-cotta tile roof, it seems to beckon us home. I can tolerate Amelia if I get to stay near this place. A sign to the right directs guests to the guest houses, but Liam parks in the drive under a large tree with other cars and an old truck where we emerge. I hear chickens nearby and people about, as I stretch my legs.

A flutter of anxiety takes me again, knowing I'll be meeting new people, and hoping they like me. Liam is at the back of the car, retrieving my bag and Amelia's laptop, which he dutifully carries up the drive. We enter a terrace which was private from the drive, with its vine-covered walls. A pergola overhead is thick and fragrant with wisteria. We hear a door open and a woman begins to chatter in Italian as she approaches us. She is small in stature, but her robust nature makes her seem larger, and she immediately throws open her arms to welcome us. I wonder whether she is a newly arrived relative, with her sparkly brown eyes and matching smile.

Amelia goes to embrace the woman who kisses her on each cheek, and then moves to do the same to Liam after he releases my carry-on to participate fully. They are laughing and talking, Liam doing his best to keep up with the language, glancing at me, making me keenly aware that I am the topic. Liam extends his arm and circles it around my shoulders, introducing me to Mara, Amelia's stepmother. My family is never this enthusiastic after only a few hours' absence!

Her hands go to her mouth and she croons to me, "Ah, Hope, *benvenuta, bella*!"

I inhale, bracing myself for the foreign conversation that will likely leave me feeling left out, a feeling I should probably get used to, but then she embraces me with kisses as well, saying, "How was your trip?"

"Oh!" Relief floods through me as I realize she speaks English. Maybe I will be talking to her a lot if Liam and Amelia ditch me. "It was very long, but I'm so glad to finally be here. I'm very pleased to meet you. Thank you for having me here. Your home is so lovely." I realize we are holding hands and she is gazing into my eyes, and I am already aware I have met a friend.

"Liam tells me you are a photographer," she says, noticing my camera bag that I've slung over my shoulder.

"Yes. This will be beautiful countryside to photograph while I'm here."

In the breeze, Mara brushes strands of dark hair, streaked with gray, away from her cheek, as insects start up their slow evening conversation in the trees overhead, dream music for later. She gestures toward a small stone house across the terrace. "Liam, why don't you take Hope to freshen herself and be settled in the house. I'll bring coffee out to the terrace in a few moments. Does that sound nice to you, bella?"

"Yes, coffee would be wonderful," I reply, wishing I could plant my face into a pillow and see them all tomorrow, but I feel obligated, and I truly want to be in the moment with Mara.

"Do you want to go and try to roust your papa?" she says to Amelia, who has sensibly stepped out of her stilettos and walks easily across the flagstones to the house.

"Sure. Is he still in the winery?"

"I believe he is still. They have been cleaning up from the bottling."

A savory aroma of meat and herbs is coming from the house, making my mouth water. Liam smells it too. "What are you cooking, Mara?" he asks.

"Roasted pork with rosemary. We'll have a little salad, a little bread, a little cheese..." she says, laughing, her hands moving, teasing him with each item she mentions. "And your special favorite, my tiramisu!"

"Wow!" he says, taking my arm and guiding me to his cottage as Mara heads back into the house. Vines cover the porch on Liam's place. He opens the door for me and gestures for me to precede him, and then lifts my bag over the threshold. It is cool and peaceful inside, the walls plastered with stucco and the floor tiled with the same terra-cotta they have used for the roof. I take stock of the small but efficient kitchen that opens onto the dining area and living space, where Liam's studio looks out onto the terrace in the front, and vineyards behind the house. The afternoon sun pours in the front windows, lending warmth. He leads me through the studio to a small bedroom and a bathroom, where I go immediately as I hear him deposit my bag in the bedroom. When I emerge, he takes his turn, giving me the chance to observe his residence more privately. The bed is double size, and old, with a cheerful red duvet and comfortable looking pillows. Beside the bed is a plain but antique dresser and lovely ornate oval mirror on the wall above it. There are pegs on the wall to hold his jacket and raincoat, and a small open closet holds the rest of his clothes, a black blazer for dress occasions and gallery hobnobbing, and a winter coat, along with a few shirts and two pairs of slacks. A painting of me hangs on the wall opposite the bed, as well as one of a vineyard I recognize as his home in Virginia.

I resist the urge to nosedive into his bed, and instead, I walk out to the studio, where I see he has displayed several studies of a work in progress, a picture of the Fiori's house. Before I can snoop for paintings of Amelia, he appears behind me and wraps his arms around my waist. His strong arms devour me deliciously, and the fatigue from my body fades into his being as he's breathing in my scent, his face at my neck.

"Do you love it?"

"Yes. It's beautiful. I'm already relaxed, just being here. And meeting Mara. She's so sweet."

"She is. And you'll love Vitale. He's Amelia's father. He's much older than Mara, but he acts like a young man.... It has to be the place," he shrugs, watching for my reaction. We hear them, assembling at the table on the terrace, Mara and Amelia laughing at a man's voice. We go outside to meet Vitale.

He is tall and slender, with gray hair and a white beard. His skin is tanned and smooth and his dark eyes are calm and friendly. He also embraces me and kisses me, and thankfully, speaks English to me, repeating everything he says in Italian. I am starting to feel the language, letting it roll pleasantly through my head. No wonder Italian is the most romantic language; I feel it in my heart, even though I have no idea what's being said. We all sit at the table that is covered in old damask, and Mara hands the coffee around to each of us as they all seem to talk at once. Instead of the cups I expected, she hands me what looks like an earthenware cereal bowl, and then she passes a small decorative pitcher of cream and a small matching bowl of raw sugar. I sip eagerly. It tastes wonderful, and in a bit, I begin to perk up as Mara passes fig cookies around. No one uses a plate, and I watch them set the cookies and her bread on the tablecloth, where crumbs fall untended on the damask. The cookies are heavenly, reminding me of Fig Newtons, but so much more delicious, and Mara tells me they are made from their figs, at St. Joseph's Day, and that they freeze exceptionally well.

I am relaxed. It is wonderful to sit back and listen to the friendly banter of the family, as birds appear on the walls and the tile roofs. The doves coo while the people talk, and even though the coffee helps me stay awake, it is all like a lullaby, and I can pick out Liam's soothing voice as he contributes occasionally to the conversation. He is learning Italian and they indulge his mistakes with good humor, expecting him to learn. They include me, too, but I am content to listen, while taking in the beautiful scenery around me. Amelia has ceased to irritate me. She has appeared in jeans and a loose blouse, her feet bare, and she has become more palatable around her family. A boy called Nicolo appears from the winery, bringing a carafe of red wine and small tumblers to the table. He pours for Amelia and himself. He has the same laughing eyes and wavy dark hair as Mara, and he jumps right into the conversation, which has something to do with a funny thing that happened in today's bottling process. He appears to be in his early twenties, and he is riveted to Amelia, who humors him well.

Liam leans over to me, explaining that Nicolo is Mara's son, and once again, I am introduced. Nicolo reaches across the table to take my hand, and he gives it a gallant kiss, making me grin. I have been smiling since I've arrived.

Mara gives me a sympathetic smile as she begins to gather the cups with Amelia's help.

"Why not rest a bit before dinner, *amore*. You will feel so much better later if you rest."

"Thank you," I say. There is that unmistakable moment I've been expecting, when Amelia glances at Liam, and there is a frisson of betrayal in her eyes, and an instant of rebuttal in his. Liam stands to help me with my chair and takes my hand, but not before Vitale collects the ends of the damask cloth, snapping the crumbs out into the terrace. Gracefully, the birds flutter down from the rafters and off the wall to partake in their afternoon treat as well, their bodies pink in the fading light. I am happy.

Chapter 29

CHERIE

Everything always happens at once. Dave starts a new job, Hope is across the globe, Wesley graduates in five days, and Toots will have surgery tomorrow. Dave and Martha Jane have played tag team with Toots, taking her back and forth to her visits to the oncologist and then the thoracic surgeon. I go to work each day, only because Dave insists, reminding me that there may be many more days ahead when I might be needed elsewhere. At least summer is coming in about a month. Teaching helps to divert my attention, and I'm able to lose myself in my classes and whatever is going on with school, but still it is hard to concentrate when I'm not in class. I walk into the hospital room where Toots and Dave are chatting quietly, amiably, about their visit with her attorney regarding her will and other affairs earlier in the afternoon. Eric is expected this evening, and he will stay at Toots's house to keep Martha Jane company. Toots's illness has taken a toll on her as well.

"Eric wants the house in Florida. You should have the house here, because if you want to sell it, it will be so much easier for you, being close by," she says matter-of-factly, as Dave stares at the bedspread, taking in the possibilities of what might transpire, once the doctor opens her up tomorrow morning.

"It's not fair, I know," she continues.

"No, it's not, Mom," he says, resigned to the guarded prognosis we heard about last week.

"That's not what I mean," she says impatiently. "I'm talking about the houses. The house in Long Boat Key is worth so much more than my house here. And the business that Eric will inherit...makes it unfair to you."

"I don't care," says Dave. "It's not about your money."

"I know. And to make you the executor of the will is not a job I'd relish either, but you're here, and well..." she says, lifting a hand. "Oh, hello, dear," she says, noticing I've walked in.

"Hi, Toots," I say, going to her and squeezing her hand, giving her a kiss on her forehead. "How are you feeling today?"

"Better since I gave up eating and did all that cleansing. This IV drip is doing the job, but it makes me want to go to the bathroom all the time. They'll be taking care of that, too, a little later, I guess," she says, meaning the catheter she is promised before the surgery.

Dave straightens paperwork and places it in a folder while I lean over to give him a kiss on his lips. He smiles. They have somehow moved past their differences at least to act like business partners, rather than a mother and son, but even this is progress. On some level it seems to be easier without the raw emotion I remember with my father and then my mother when they were ill. Dave remembers it too. As difficult as their relationship has been, knowing that Toots is our last living parent makes me want to hang on to her even more, and I'm happy that we've become amicable. The nursing staff must think we are an odd set of folks, but I'm sure they have seen it all.

"So, tell me something good!" she says, giving us a bright smile. I'm glad I can contribute.

"Hope sends her love and prayers for your surgery tomorrow. I saw it on Facebook where she's been posting more pictures from Italy."

"Oh, let's see!" says Toots, looking at Dave's laptop, as he pulls up Facebook and turns the screen toward her.

"Oh! These are spectacular! What a lovely place. And this is what's his name...oh...!" Toots says, looking over Hope's pictures and comments, and Dave and I murmur our agreement. "How's she getting on with her fellow over there?"

"I think it's good," I say, glancing at Dave, but of course, neither of us really knows. "Her travel logs are not very personal. She does tell us that the woman of the house is a wonderful person, and she's teaching Hope to cook. They spend lots of time in the kitchen together when Hope's not helping Liam in the winery."

"What a marvelous experience for her. And Wesley is graduating on Saturday?"

"Yes," Dave says, grinning. "Four years, in and out. That's pretty good these days. She sends her prayers too."

"Who's going to be manning the fish tent this Saturday while you all are celebrating?"

"Jeff is going to be there, with another friend who's thinking about going in with us."

She doesn't take the opportunity to say something degrading about Dave's having to work on the weekends, the way she would have done a month ago. I've held my breath needlessly. Toots and Martha Jane had surprised Dave by showing up at the tent on Saturday, and they took home the largest purchase of the day. He was pleased that she'd come out in support of him, and he didn't even realize she'd been there in the crowd until she was standing right in front of him, looking over the inventory clipboard and recipes before placing her order. All of us were pleasantly surprised at the turnout for their second weekend, and now Dave has all he can handle at the moment.

We visit a little longer, the two of them updating me on the doctor's report from the day, and then she tells us she's tired and would like to rest before Eric arrives later. As if dismissed by the boss, we promise to see her early in the morning and head toward the elevator. When the doors close, giving us privacy, Dave sighs raggedly. I slip my arm behind his shoulder and give his neck a rub. This is the most emotion I've seen from him during the whole ordeal, but I realize it is far from over. We have been here too many times. We get to our cars, both too drained to talk.

"Why don't we get something to eat before we head home? I really don't feel like cooking tonight, and I'm sure you don't either," says Dave. We stop in a place that offers soup and sandwiches, comfort food that we need to make it through this night and tomorrow. Dave won't sleep, if it's been like the last couple of weeks. The man has so much going through his head—with Hope gone, and Wesley preparing to make such a huge transition in her life, and now with his mother, not to mention the business ideas he's always coming up with—that I worry for his health. But I don't nag him when he orders the roast beef sandwich and baked potato soup—with chips. Like I said, it's comfort food he needs.

I'm ordering a salad and vegetable soup, when a girl about Hope's age taps me on the shoulder.

"Excuse me; are you Mrs. Johnson?"

"Yes," I say, gazing into the face of one of Hope's friends, but I can't place the girl initially.

"Hi, I'm not sure if you remember me; I'm Jillian, Hope's friend from college."

"Oh, of course! I remember you very well. It just took me a minute, you know; you're out of context..."

"I know!"

I introduce her again to Dave and we all shake hands, and then she asks after Hope. I'm telling her about Hope's trip to Italy, and she looks confused, saying, "Oh! I thought they broke up."

"Well. I guess they needed some closure and he sent her a plane ticket so off she went with her camera! But how's it going with you? Are you still teaching? You know, I work with your friend, Taylor Kimbrough, and he and Hope have become good friends."

"Oh, I love Taylor! Yeah, I'm teaching in Winston and loving it. I'm glad to have a job!"

"I'm sure. Hope is sending out applications again, so if you know of anything, please let her know."

Jillian's eyebrows raise a notch. "Actually, I just heard about an opening at one of the magnet schools. It's an art position at a middle school, and they do a lot of work with the arts center as well as on their own campus. They are the kind of school that's doing things outside the box, you know. Tell Hope to call me when she gets back and I'll give her the lowdown."

"Thank you, Jillian, I will. Send her a message on Facebook. I'm sure she'd love to hear from you. She could use a girls' night—if you think about it."

"Sure, I will. I'll want to hear about her trip, too! It's good to see you both!"

We get our food and sit down, and before I lift my napkin, I'm on my smart phone to send Hope a message. Dave is rolling his eyes at me, and I start to text. "It can't hurt," I mumble.

He covers my hand with his and says, "Stop, Cherie. Let her enjoy herself."

Chapter 30

HOPE

I feel safe here, not like that first day in the airport in Florence, wondering what I'd do if Liam and Amelia hadn't materialized. Liam's place is cozy, but my favorite spot is in Mara's bright and earthy kitchen, watching her multitask between her bread baking, stirring her gravy, pasta making, and running the guest houses from her laptop computer on the corner desk. Mara is sweet and gregarious, reminding me of Mama, and we spend time talking about our families while she has me chopping and stirring, teaching me about the Tuscan cuisine, and life too, I think. Our conversations remind me that I have grown up enough to enjoy living in my parents' house again. Mara wanted to hear all about Liam, including all the shameless details. She is fascinated with the situation between us and Amelia. I have to admire her for not judging either of us, nor Amelia for that matter; although when the topic is Amelia, she listens intently. Amelia is not her daughter, but they seem to have the kind of mother-daughter bond that most of my friends have with their mothers; a lot of encouragement paired with a little kidding around, and some nagging thrown in for good measure.

Mara understands my confusion about my feelings toward Liam. She tells me she was divorced once, so she can relate to my issues with integrity and my longing for security. After her divorce, she and two girlfriends set out from Rome, coming here to chill out at the fattoria and celebrate their freedom. She met Vitale, whose wife had left him and taken Amelia back to the States five years earlier. "I liked him tremendously, and we had...the *spark*, you know? So I never left!" she says, brown eyes dancing.

"Happiness will come to you as well, *mi amore*," she says. "It will be like a butterfly landing on your shoulder, when you least expect it."

I am keeping two photo journals while I am here; one is a travel log that I'm posting on Facebook, and the other is my private diary, which I've written by hand and hidden under Liam's mattress. It's paired with private photos, like shots of Liam in the early morning light, sleeping sprawled on his stomach, barely covered with the sheets. I'm still on American time, and I find myself waking early. The morning is the best time to stroll the grounds of the farmhouse and vineyards without any-one but the chickens to distract me, and the lighting is perfect in the hour just after sunrise. My camera and I are loving it here, and from time to time, I fantasize that I could chuck my life and live here, but it is more complicated than that. Who has the luxury to do that, besides Liam? Even he has ties he doesn't discuss with me, and I believe he is treading a thin line with Amelia.

She is obviously interested in him, no matter how indulged she is with Nicolo, whom she is not related to. Nicolo adores her, and they must have had a relationship before Liam came, but it is hard to tell what she expects of Liam. She still has her smirky moments, although we are find-ing it easier to talk, possibly because of Mara, and she seems impressed with my photography.

It is Tuesday, and this morning we are returning to Florence and Siena for a day of sightseeing, and gallery visits for Liam. How Liam has gotten any painting done with all the distractions here, and the work, is beyond my understanding. I return to the house, smelling the coffee I made, and peek in on Liam, who has not budged, breathing in the untroubled deep rhythm of the sleep deprived. As so he should with all of our nighttime activities! Sleeping with Liam is an oxymoron.

I pour a cup of coffee, thinking of my parents, and Toots, who will be having surgery today. Wondering about her makes me think of John and how he must have gone through the same range of emotions when his father was ill. John. I feel almost guilty being here, I think, sipping my coffee, and gazing out the window as two barn swallows build their nest in the porch eaves. John works hard. John would like an escape like this. I don't even know whether he's ever been to Europe. There is so much I don't know about him.

I hear Liam stir so I return to the bedroom, where he opens sleepy eyes and rolls to his side, pulling back the sheet and making room for me in the bed. Wordlessly, he watches as I undress and slip in beside him and feel his warmth in the cool dim room, the smell of springtime moving delicately through the windows. "*Sei figa*," he murmurs into my ear, rolling on top of me. He pushes my legs apart with his knee, grasping my hands and sliding them over my head into the pillows. I am looking into his dark honey-colored eyes, and he has me once again under his spell.

"What does that mean?"

He kisses me before he answers. "You are one smokin' hot babe!" We laugh and it starts all over again. He is heavier than I remember, doubtlessly the result of Mara's good cooking, and his muscles are firm, the result of his labor in the vineyards. His skin is sun-kissed from being outdoors, and it feels warm when I kiss his face. Our lovemaking was tentative when I first arrived, but he seems to be as invested in me as he ever was, leaving me more confused than ever, so I find myself holding back somewhat. If he notices, he doesn't question me.

"*Ti amo!*" he sighs when we are finished. I love being ravished in Italian, but I cannot say the words back to him. We lie together, knowing we should be preparing for the day, but aimlessly, I stroke the small of his back, staring at the curtains that dance gracefully in the morning breeze.

"Why did you bring me here?" I finally have the nerve to ask.

He moves his head to look at me, and he strokes his fingers over my hair.

"I love you, Hope. I wanted to share all of this with you."

"But...I know you're not asking me to stay here. And I can't. What good does it do us to go here again?"

"Why not just enjoy it, for what it is...today. I can't ask you to stay. It's not my place, sadly. This is all I can give you. I can barely take care of myself. And it will be this way all of my life, probably, unless I give in and settle down to teach somewhere."

"You'd do that?"

"I think about it from time to time, especially when my money gets low. Not everyone can live like this."

"No," I agree, wondering whether he has health insurance. What would happen if he got sick, or hurt? I know that his parents don't help him, something I cannot fathom.

"It's hard for me sometimes. I have to do what I have to do," he says, and I don't really know what he means, but it's nothing new. His commitment to his work is something I've never questioned, as he made it clear to me in the beginning. After all, this time I know he wasn't exaggerating.

He strokes my face, and turns it up with his hand so I have to look at him...and his eyes. "We have three more days. Lose yourself in them with me, okay?"

Chapter 31

CHERIE

We sit in the waiting room, joined by Eric and Martha Jane. Each of us has our diversion; Eric and Dave are tapping away on their laptops while Martha Jane knits a baby sweater for the grandson she's just learned will arrive at the first of next year. I'm grading papers; poems that should have been returned yesterday, but I can't help being behind. There is always that one over-driven student who calls me to task, so of course, I feel guilty that I have a life. After thirty years of teaching, I still can't say, *It will be ready when it's ready*. I take a break after one class set to check my phone for text messages from Wesley, and a Facebook message from Hope. Today, they are in Florence, touring the art museums and shopping. They are having lunch alfresco, and she swears she is not buying anything, so I am relieved that she has learned to restrain herself. I marvel at the ease with which we can communicate while she is overseas, which makes me increasingly irritated that Liam could not have kept in touch with her any better than he did. Of course, I realize, too, that he wanted to keep her at a distance, but why the sudden change of heart to have her join him? I will never understand it.

I text her a message about running into Jillian and the possible job lead she'd mentioned. Hope is interested and will follow up when she returns. Again, this instantaneous communication from halfway around the world has left me vexed at Liam.

Eric is talking to the doctor when Dave and I get off the elevator after a hurried lunch in the cafeteria. Martha Jane signals to her that we are coming, so the doctor starts over when we are there. Toots's surgery went even better than expected. The mass was contained to one location, and the surgeon was able to resection the colon without the need for a colostomy bag, which was Toots's major concern. Not that she could die, but how it would look to be carrying around a bag of waste! Stage one cancer, as it was, is the best scenario, and we were so lucky that Toots caught it in time. Follow up with the oncologist will determine her next course of treatment, but for now, the only lesion appears to be gone and Toots should be able to return to a normal life after the recommended recovery period.

Normal for anyone else, that is. Dave and Eric are discussing the need for Toots to retire. Martha Jane has been on her for years to cut back her workload, but Toots thrives in the limelight. Now may be the time for limiting her practice to part-time hours in her office instead of spending the remaining time traveling all over the country doing her speaking tours.

Martha Jane, Dave, and Eric spend the next hour talking about tag-teaming their support while Toots is in the hospital. Dave travels to the coast every Thursday now, to collect the fresh caught seafood and whatever else has been flown in from other locations for the weekend sales. Our upcoming weekend will be filled with graduation festivities. We'll collect Hope at the airport on Friday, and then on Saturday, we'll take Eric with us and drive up to Chapel Hill for the ceremony. We'll leave early in the morning to spend as much time with Wesley and Ren as possible. Martha Jane will hold down the fort while we're gone, and then the real fun will begin when Toots comes home.

Toots has insisted on hiring a nurse for the week of recovery at home, to Dave and Eric's relief. Martha Jane will have enough to do handling the visitors and cooking, as she normally does. Toots is expecting a multitude of guests to pay their respects, so she has already set the schedule for visiting hours, which will apply to us as well. Eric will stay at the house for the next week, so he is excluded from any restrictions, which suits us just fine. The relief is palpable in the waiting room as a nurse comes to inform us that Toots is in her room where we can visit.

As we gather around Toots, awaiting a word from her, she opens her eyes to view us all, flanking support on both sides. Expecting her to smile and exclaim that she is glad to see us and to be alive, without the colostomy bag, I'm somewhat surprised at her words.

"Go home," she says.

Praise the Lord! She's back. I have to text Walt.

Chapter 32

HOPE

I hear Liam cracking eggs into a bowl and placing the skillet on the stove as I'm emerging from his tiny shower. Wrapping a towel around my hair, it makes me a little sad thinking that I will be back in my parents' house and a much larger shower in just two days. I will miss this lovely place and my new friends, Mara, Vitale, Nicolo, and even Amelia. I come out into the bedroom in search of my clothes when I hear Amelia's voice greeting Liam at the kitchen door. Pulling the towel off my head to cover myself, I peer around the door that is usually open since it's just us in the house.

"*Ciao, principessa!*" he greets her good-naturedly, making her laugh. I can see her, stepping into the kitchen, handing him a cup of coffee and a note, the morning sun shining around her pretty brown hair. He accepts both and gives her a kiss on the cheek.

Princess? I murmur to myself, watching.

"Buongiorno. What's this?" he asks, looking at her smiling face, opening the small piece of paper.

"It's a note from Papa's friend, Vincenzo. He wants to commission you to paint his winery. He saw your work in progress and wants you to do the same for him."

"Cool! Thank you! Did you do this for me?" Liam asks, and they take their conversation to the porch. I lean farther out the door to listen and watch. They drink their coffee, watching the barn swallows' progress, and I see his fingers finding a comfortable place in her hair, massaging the back of her neck, as if it is the most natural thing to do.

Her eyes are closed and she murmurs something to him, that sounds like *Saturday* in Italian, but I don't know for sure. They speak quietly for a moment, and I distinctly hear him say to her, *sei figa!* My heart thuds in my chest, as I dress for our day. Liam has plans to finish painting me in the vineyard, a project he'd started a few days ago. Somehow my hands are able to complete the task as I hear him come back inside, alone to finish cooking our eggs.

In a flash I am in the kitchen. "Was that Amelia?" I ask, the timbre in my voice too strident for my intentions. I am unsure whether I want to confront him.

"It was," he says, folding the eggs over in the pan, and handing me coffee of my own.

"Oh, she brought you coffee?" I ask, as if we are incapable of making our own, and he immediately picks up on the tension.

"Yes. And she brought me some good news as well. She arranged a commission from one of Vitale's friends, a vintner, who wants me to paint his winery. It's the fattoria just two from here, the one with the black rooster," he says, trying to make me laugh. "We pass it going toward Siena," he adds, looking at me, wondering maybe what I saw.

"Good." My voice is back to normal. I'm wondering what her share of the spoils will be, but I think I already know. It doesn't matter. We eat our breakfast quietly at the table, and in half an hour, he's driven us in the old blue vehicle (that we call a gator at home) to the crest of my favorite hill, which is particularly picturesque in this morning's sunlight. After Liam assembles his easel and paints, I spread a blanket on the ground and he arranges me on it the way he wants me to look, sitting with knees turned to one side, supporting myself with my hand, like the Little Mermaid statue in Copenhagen, with my hair blowing back over my shoulder, my blouse pulled down over it, exposing my own sun-kissed skin.

It's a hard pose to maintain, and we have to stop at intervals so I can stand and stretch; otherwise, my wrist and hand go to sleep. I try to relax, and he gazes down at me. He drops to his knees beside me and kisses me softly, stroking my hair away from my cheek in the breeze.

"*Bellissima,*" he whispers.

I try to reorient my thinking, to forget about Amelia, and to be thankful that I am here for at least another day. It is a beautiful view, the hill that descends before me, patterned with grapevines the hopeful green of spring, of new beginnings, and I hang my thoughts on my own new possibilities. The place captures me in the moment, though, and Liam's words from the other morning return to me. *We have three days. Lose yourself in them with me.* I can do this, one more day. I can pretend that this is Heaven on earth, and believe that this man loves me. I think he does. I think he loves many people, or depends on many people for his existence, which makes me sad, that he is not more than a rolling stone.

"What are you thinking?" he asks. I know he is painting my face. He will tell me to relax in a moment. I am not supposed to look so pensive. But I think it makes the better picture. What is art if it is not true?

"Just what a miracle this all is. Tuscany, Chianti…there's no place I've seen that's more beautiful. It's as close to Heaven as I've ever been…yet," I say, smiling.

"If you believe in that sort of thing."

"I do," I say, truly convinced of what I believe will happen when I die. "Don't you?"

"I don't. For me, it's all science. Wonderful, amazing…but still science."

"You don't believe in some higher power? You don't believe in God?"

"I believe in love…and art and science…and miracles."

"How can you believe in miracles and not believe in God?"

"Call it what you want, but there are exceptionalities and coincidences all around us. Things that make us marvel and cry. You're a miracle, Hope. I've never loved anyone the way I've loved you. But God? No."

I'm touched, especially by the way he says it, but I've never known anyone who loves the way he does, but actually said he didn't believe in God. It doesn't make Liam a bad person, but maybe this explains a lot of things. Like why I've never seen Liam pray, or why he has never been to church with my family. It's why he laughs when someone says *bless your heart.* Maybe it's why he feels he can love two women at the same time. I feel bitter about it, just the same.

"So if there's no God, there's no guilt."

"I'm not a sociopath, Hope," he says, chuckling. "I *do* have a conscience. Guilt is a somewhat necessary emotion. We should be responsible as human beings. I believe we all need to do our best and realize our potential. We should be ashamed if we don't do our part to help each other. But I find that those who are always saying '*Give it over to God*' are always the ones who are trying to control it all to their way of thinking, and screwing it up for everybody else. It pervades our politics…. Supporting capital punishment but not abortion, that kind of thing. People who are married and then cheat on their spouses. It's so hypocritical."

"Everybody's a hypocrite," I blurt. "That's what makes us human. We're all sinners."

"That's what makes it a cop-out. Why believe in something if you aren't going to practice it? Jesus said, '*Go and sin no more,*' but everybody does it anyway. What makes a Christian any different from me?"

"Well, you don't believe in everlasting life, so Jesus has no meaning for you. So, what are you saying your philosophy is?"

"Just...be honest. Be who you are. Say what you believe and don't try to put a label on yourself. Do your best but don't expect to be rewarded, because there might not be a reward. And don't be angry when someone changes his—or her—mind. Forgiveness, you know?"

His answer is startlingly open, the raw quality of it making my heart ache. I look up and see that he's looking at me. Who is to forgive who here?

"Is that why you don't buy into marriage? Because people change their minds?"

"Partly. Turn your head, please."

I've looked into his face, so he's had to redirect me. But he is not testy with me.

"So where do you stand?"

"Usually on the fence, only because that's where everyone wants to put me, but I think the way I think."

"I meant, where do you stand with me?"

"I've told you, Hope. I love you. But I can't give you what you want."

"So...where do you stand with Amelia?" I've broken my pose at this point, resting the hand I've been leaning on.

He is quiet a moment, wiping his brushes with a cloth. "I like her. I appreciate her. She's smart and helpful. She's beautiful."

"Do you sleep with her too?" I'm looking directly at him this time, and my courageous question doesn't seem to surprise him. But he stares at the brushes and thinks a moment before he answers, measuring his words carefully, so as not to shatter me.

"*Nicolo* sleeps with her," he says gently, his tone telling me what I'd suspected. I know he desires her...and she wants him, but Nicolo is in the way, and they won't hurt him. Cheating with Amelia would be his ticket straight back to America.

I sigh, in spite of myself. It is a pointless conversation, I realize. What he says makes sense in a strange way, and it explains everything about him, but I believe there is more to life than his way of thinking. His view of love is too loose for me to accept. Love is sacred. And as for his dismissal of God—for me, science can't explain everything. What is life without wonder? Isn't that what faith is for? What is the point of life without the ever after? How alone would we be without God by our side, or carrying us, the way He has carried me since Liam left me the first time? As foul-mouthed and undeserving as I have been, I have felt God's presence in my life. Aren't things meant to be, or are we just sitting around waiting for butterflies?

"I believe some things are meant to be; don't you?"

"Nope. I think things happen and you deal with it. Then you can't be mad at God. What's that all about anyway? Saying you love God, and giving him control, but blaming him when things don't go your way?"

"What about faith?"

"I have faith, in myself, in other people. I believe in trust and honesty, and a hard day's work, but I think that's where it ends. You die and you go to dust. That's it."

"I believe in so much more, Liam."

He nods. "I know you do," he says, replacing the paintbrushes on the easel rack. "Do you need a break?"

"Sure," I shift my weight and stand as he helps me up. I shake out my hand and walk around to look at the painting. The way he has captured the light, the colors are beautifully rich, and his impressionistic rendering of the scene is stunning, as I had expected, but on his canvas, my face seems incongruently solemn as I gaze out over the magnificent vineyard. Good. He's certainly captured the mood, and it's already a better painting.

Conundrum.

Chapter 33

CHERIE

Dave is at the coast, as he will be every Thursday, collecting this week's seafood, with orders to fill for his new repeat customers, so I've stopped in to see Toots in the hospital on my way home from school. She is in moderately good humor, except for the absence of all the visitors she thought would be coming by—visitors she'd planned to kick out after five minutes anyway—but nonetheless, she seems a little miffed at her lack of popularity. Go figure. Anyway, she's made me promise to eat my spinach. It's ironic that she has lived such a healthy life and colon cancer has hit her like a stray bullet from someone else's sick Russian roulette game, but she hasn't given up her campaign, especially on her disappointingly overweight family, so she is compelled to pass on her wisdom by reciting her mantra, "If we all *did* everything we *knew* that was good for us, we'd be practically perfect." She's right, and I do know how to take care of myself and Dave, but I will never have the self-control this woman has, even if it is driven by her unrelenting narcissism! Still, today, she acknowledges the seven-and-a-half pounds I've lost, so there is one more coup for me. Reminding me of her obvious detention in the surgical ward, she regrets not being able to attend Wesley's graduation. Surprising even me, she has written her a check, and she asks me to find a proper card that she can sign before we present it to Wesley. She asks about the girls, and then her good friend Walt, who has sent his regards, and after my five minutes (that have stretched to fifteen) are up, she dismisses me with a wave of her hand. It's fine. I have given up being offended by Toots a long time ago. It's really not personal, I've come to realize. She is the self-appointed CEO of the Johnson family, whether or not we choose to acknowledge it!

It feels odd to be alone again in my house, with only Little Miss for company. Rowdy, of course, is outside moping. I have to think of what I did before Hope moved in, when I had all that empty time on my hands. Tonight, after I've finished my spinach salad and cleaned up the kitchen to my liking, I am curled up on the couch with Little Miss snuggled up beside me, and a cup of herbal tea on the end table. I am rereading *The Shell Seekers*, which is like visiting once again with an old friend, sitting in my sweats, resisting the urge to finish off the chocolate gelato that is calling my name from the freezer. The leisurely pace of this evening is delightful, so I revel in this rare moment of self-indulgence, knowing that the upcoming graduation weekend will be a blur, starting with Hope's arrival at the airport tomorrow evening.

It is also odd that throughout all these crises in my house, I feel as though I have no control over any of the situations that go on. I merely observe the comings and goings of the people in my nest, much like the narrator in a play. I suppose that is life with adult children and unemployed spouses. Being a daughter-in-law places me in a subservient role as well, much like being the mother of the groom; *wear beige and keep your mouth shut!* Still, being on the outside looking in doesn't alleviate the stress involved in all of it. If anything, it makes it worse not having some rein on things. If something were to go wrong, I feel sure that somehow I would bear the blame, ironically. That, I am well aware, is one of the thorns of motherhood!

I close my eyes and say a quick prayer of thanks that we are all safe and healthy. Toots is out of the woods for the moment. My daughters have grown into beautiful young women, and I am happy now that hopefully their days of speeding tickets and minor brushes with the law over underage drinking are over, and that both of them can move on with their lives. Wesley is certainly on her way to a happily-ever-after life with Ren, but we have only responded with a whimper, and not the bang she deserves, but maybe that will all change soon. Her room is clean, ready, and waiting for her arrival as well, for however long we will have her with us. I am dying to know how Hope has fared with Liam on her trip, but I'm glad at least that she's had a chance to see Italy, sure that however it all turns out for her, that she has grown as a result of her experience. Dave has more than he can handle with the business, his job search, the band, and now his mother to deal with, but he thrives on being busy, and he seems more like himself, despite his worry over Toots. He has yet to open up to me about his feelings. At least they are civil to one another. And with the warm weather, those tiresome old sweatshirts have disappeared at last from Dave's wardrobe! I sigh happily and return to my favorite book; life is good today.

Chapter 34

HOPE

Whatever inferno Liam and I had going between us must have died down to warm embers after our conversation on the hilltop. When he looks at me, his face holds a distressed kind of sadness that I feel as well. We are distracted effectively from each other by my farewell dinner that Mara has prepared and served alfresco. Although we sit side by side, drinking wine under the stars, and Liam touches my hand occasionally during the conversation, I believe that something has left us, both emotionally and physically. We linger with the family late into the night, talking and joking about all the things that have happened at the fattoria since I've arrived, making me realize that they've come to include me as one of their family—the family that includes not only Vitale and Mara and their children, but Liam as well. Liam and Nicolo go back and forth in Italian about today's mishap in the winery, good-naturedly kidding each other, like brothers do, about whose fault it was. They all like the framed photograph of the family that I took at this same table. The spirit of it represents them well, laughing, hugging, goofing around. They are a vivacious bunch. Liam helped me get it framed so I could extend it as a gift of thanks for hosting me. Mara watches us fondly, seemingly unaffected by any inconsistencies in our behavior. Amelia watches too,

247

however through the perceptive eyes of a woman who knows her time is coming. Apart from her apparent realization, it is as though I am a sister, or a daughter-in-law, and that they fully expect me to return at some point to visit. I can pretend that it might happen, and so I smile serenely at them all, truly grateful to have been a part of the family, and wishing in a way that it might really be true.

After dinner is cleaned up, dishes are put away, and everyone has had their proper farewell hugs and kisses, Liam takes me on a final moonlit stroll through the vineyards. It is past eleven o'clock, and I have an early morning flight, but I have already packed, out of need for something to do earlier while Liam worked, and we both know this is the last time we'll talk at length. He holds my hand until we are well out of sight of the farmhouse and the guest houses.

"I have one more thing I want to share with you before you leave tomorrow," he says, his smile returning. "Look," he says, gesturing upward when we are in the open space, away from the houses. "It's a diamond thief's delight, isn't it?" he laughs, as we throw back our heads, taking in a million sparkles scattered across black velvet. The whole effect is thrilling, making chills race up my arms, and he holds my hand a little tighter, understanding my reaction.

"I haven't seen stars this bright since I was a little girl, at my grandmother's place on Sullivan's Island. That was back before it got so popular." It feels good to make conversation with him that isn't forced or controversial. We can both still marvel at the beauty of nature, whoever or whatever we believe created it; we've both abandoned that discussion and rediscovered our common ground. Liam's eyes are sparkling as well, pleased that we have returned to our special brand of intimacy. Only he can do this to me. Still, I think we are over, and it makes me want to cry. Under an arbor, he pulls me to his chest and kisses me tenderly, holding my face in his hand.

"This is so bittersweet, isn't it?" he says.

"Yes, it is....I won't see you again, will I?" I ask.

"Let's don't say that, Hope. I mean, who knows? I could end up back in the States next year, maybe even at my parents' house in Virginia, at least for the holidays..." he says, eyes searching mine, for a trace of evidence that I'm still in love with him, what he's always seen, even when I was hurting back in February. A melancholy breeze stirs our hair and I look away.

"This has been a wonderful gift, being here with you. Thank you for bringing me here. Mara and Vitale have been so great, and I don't even mind Amelia so much anymore." We laugh about that, and he pulls me back into his embrace, pressing his lips into my hair.

"Your Italian has gotten very good while you've been here, too. And the photographs you've taken could constitute a good show."

"And thanks to Amelia, I have some ideas about how to market my work more effectively."

"This is really not what I want to talk about," he says, stroking back my hair and kissing me again. I know we'll sleep together one more time and it will be intensely sensual. Making love has always been our anchor. In the morning, I will leave, taking sweet memories home with me, but I will be able to let go this time and move on. This is why I came. This is my sign. He should be happy that we are finally done, but Liam seems sad. Arms around each other, we wander back to the house and undress each other slowly in the dark, to love each other one more time.

I sip the last of my coffee and walk back down to Liam's house. I've forgotten my purse. He has walked up to the main house to fetch Amelia's car to drive me to the airport. I hear him talking to one of the more gregarious workers in the winery who has arrived early, and I giggle, know-

ing it may be a few moments before he returns with the car. After duck-
ing under the startling departure of one of the barn swallows, I go inside
and locate my Tory Burch, and take the extra time to browse through his
paintings one more time, to remember the beauty he has already created
here. Canvasses are stacked against the wall in the living room, a cramped
studio, with barely enough room to paint a person, but except for me,
Liam doesn't usually paint portraits. There are studies of landscapes and
the farmhouse, and as I flip the through canvasses toward the back of the
stack, a red blotch on one catches my eye. This is one I haven't noticed
before. I pull it out from the stack to see....

And gasp.

I am sitting in the plane, stoned from my Dramamine, trying to focus
so I can write the last entry of the trip in my private journal. If I decide
not to put it on paper, however, the memories will fade after time.... The
pen remains motionless in my hand as I choose to think about what I saw
one more time, to sort it all out in my mind, and then I will forget. Who
am I kidding? I'll never forget any of it. Still, it doesn't matter, nothing is
changed in my mind, so there is no reason to dwell on it.

The last picture should have been no surprise, even though seeing
it made my heart sink like a stone. It was a bed, Liam's bed, with the
red coverlet and rumpled sheets, bathed in morning light, with Amelia
sitting sideways in the sheets, one leg bent and an arm draped languid-
ly across her knee, covering part of her breast. Nude. Not just nude....
Naked. The way Liam paints, there *is* a difference. It wasn't the nudity, or
even the mussed tangle of dark hair down her back that got to me; it was
the carnal look in her eyes. Liam is an impressionist of the highest caliber,
but I also know he is a realist in the way he captures his images. He paints
the truth, and in that painting, Amelia's feelings for him were more than

obvious; they screamed off the canvas...an *orgasm* in oil paint. She is his muse now, complete with all the sexual tension he creates in his subjects. It is his game, his quest to see how far he can push the envelope before the inferno engulfs them, subject and artist. He is a master at manipulating women, so evident in the way he teased me as well, before he allowed himself to fall in love with me. But I believe his game might become his downfall at the farmhouse if he chooses to push it too far. Instead of the anger and jealousy I was expecting, though, I only feel relief, that I am finally out of the picture, flying away to what I know is real, and from now on, none of Liam's affairs are my concern.

I'd put the canvas back in its place and walked directly out of the house, closing the door solidly behind me, and joining him at the car, where he'd just closed my suitcase into the trunk. I didn't mention the painting, and it was a quiet ride to the airport, with me leaving him at the gate, the same shell-shocked expression on his face that I'm sure he'd seen on mine that day I'd left the pool house. Like me also that day, he'd had difficulty finding words to say to me when I gave him one final hug and wrapped it up tidily, my way this time.

"*Arrivederci*, Liam."

Chapter 35

CHERIE

It is after midnight on Friday and I know I should be going to bed, but it is difficult to tear myself away from my daughter. I'm sure I will finally sleep tonight, now that Hope is back safe and sound. We can hear Dave snoring from the back bedroom. It's been going on for hours. Who knew the old Hope would have stayed in Italy and this transformed, glowing young woman would return to me, full of new insights and overnight maturity? God does answer prayers! I am sitting across from her on the couch, both of us drinking our Sleepy Time herbal tea in hopes of softening her jet lag, and I am fighting my own fatigue, finding myself hanging onto every word of her story. Liam is an atheist, and she knows they will never have a future together. Now she's telling me about the half-Italian ho whom he's painted in the nude, who sleeps with her younger step-brother, but is in love with Liam. He's using the lust to his own advantage and driving this poor girl to madness while she helps him sell his paintings. Wow! And Hope is not even angry! My daughter's maturity surpasses even my own. I had no idea she was so broadminded!

Still, I've counseled her to visit her doctor. She is smart enough to be on the pill, and may not be pregnant, but who knows what other effects this man has left with her? If she is ever to have another romantic involvement, she should be realistic enough to consider not only her own health, but that of the next man in the queue, ready to sample her charms. She does not flinch when I mention this, but tells me she has already thought about it.

"I'll go, but it's not like there's anybody else in my immediate future, Mama," she says, but I've seen a look about her that makes me wonder.

"Well, there might be, even when you don't think it will happen...."

"I know, like a butterfly is going to come fluttering along and change my life," she scoffs.

"What's meant to be will be. I want you to have the love you deserve. I truly believe there is somebody wonderful out there for you, sweetheart."

She looks dubious. "I'd like to believe that, but if there isn't, I'm fine with it, Mama. I don't *need* anybody but myself.... Well, as soon as I get a *real* job, I won't need to be lodging with you and Daddy anymore. You know how much I appreciate it, right?"

"I know you do, honey. I'm really looking forward to having Wesley here with us for a little while, too. It will be good for us to be together as a family again." After looking at her slideshow of the Fiori family, I can understand how much they all seem to enjoy being together, and I wonder why I've always seen my children's return to the nest as something negative. I should remember to appreciate living in the moment, even with Toots.

"Yeah," she says wistfully, looking off, as if she's once again in Tuscany. "I can't believe Wesley's graduating tomorrow! And the school year is almost over for you, too. Are you getting excited about the summer?"

I laugh out loud. "As always! I'm dying to get back down to the beach and open up Mama's house. I've never been away this long, but with Daddy's situation, it's been hard. He'll be so tied up with the business, I may be spending most of the summer down there by myself...unless Wesley comes down. You're certainly busy enough, and now that you've had your vacation, you won't be able to get away like you did when you were teaching."

"You could ask Toots to keep you company down there!" Hope says, her eyes going large with mischief, making me swat at her.

But then I think about it, and the idea is not half-bad. "Well...that's a possibility. After all, I am on her A list right now. I've lost weight, which she thinks is because of her, and I've sent Walt Hurley her way, and that made her look really good too. And God knows, poor Martha Jane could use a break! Or, heck, she might even want to come along too."

"Oh, I love Martha Jane! That would be so much fun! But you know, Daddy would have a cow."

We stand and stretch, rearranging the sofa pillows and the blanket, finding a sleepy Little Miss underneath, whom I'd completely forgotten about.

"It would be a first for sure. Daddy is just going to have to get used to it. He's been in denial for far too long, and I'm not talking about a river in Egypt, either. Toots and Eric are all he has left, so he needs to grow a pair and get on with building a relationship with them."

"Mama!" Hope laughs, as she takes my cup and deposits it with hers in the top shelf of the dishwasher.

The University of North Carolina at Chapel Hill graduation ceremony is a phenomenon to behold, the graduates resplendent in their caps and gowns, collectively forming a sea of blue the color of the sky, almost making one think that Heaven is here on this campus. I am so proud I could burst! Dave is on one side of me, holding my hand, his good ear turned toward me so he can hear me better, and Ren is on the other, awkwardly juggling Hope's camera case since he's assisting her with changing lenses so she can zoom in on Wesley, who will appear at any moment. She's been taking pictures incessantly since we parked the car! I'm fanning myself in my light blue polka dot dress, filled with excitement as I watch Hope running through her camera roll, narrating her travel log for Ren as we wait for the nursing school graduates to enter.

"Wait, look. That's a good picture of Liam, even though he's a dick."

"No, Ren, he's not. He's just true to who he is. He knows who he is and he tells you up-front, so you shouldn't be mad at him. You were friends, after all, remember?"

"Yeah, but he's still a dick. And it's not like I'll ever see him again. He's made sure of that. You deserve so much better, anyway."

"Aw! Jeez, do you have a *brother* tucked away somewhere you haven't told me about?"

"No, but look around today; we should be able to find you *somebody* in this crowd! Better yet, come to Austin. I know about a million single computer geeks!"

I laugh, hearing them carry on, completely unconcerned that I can hear them. I feel completely at ease today after my conversation with Hope last night. Dave is happy too, and it seems as though it is not just because we are all together, but that life is falling back into place for all of us. A good place. There will be dinner tonight with Ren's family in Chapel Hill, and then he will fly back to Austin after Mother's Day brunch with all of us tomorrow at a favorite restaurant in Hillsborough, a little historic town between our two homes. His mother and I will no doubt use the time to immerse ourselves in the wedding plans. Thank goodness she was not offended when we turned down her offer of Duke Gardens as a venue for the wedding. Missy Henry has the good sense and manners I'm counting on to get us all through this whole affair, and not just because she is being the subordinate mother of the groom; she's just a nice person, and one whom I'm glad to call an in-law. Dave and I have talked about inviting them all down to the beach house after the wedding for a few days to debrief. I'll be taking several days off from school, something that would normally send me into a tailspin, but at this point in my career, I think I deserve it! This is the new me. I'm calling the shots, and starting to let go of my stress all at the same time. This is freedom. This is fun. Who needs retirement? Well...but for right now, my life is not a bad gig.

And here comes my daughter, outstanding from the sea of Carolina blue because of her height, even in flats, and the long blond curls that cascade over her shoulders. Wesley has lamented because she is four-hundredths of a point away from claiming *cum laude* status, but it doesn't matter to any of us. Right now it doesn't seem to matter to her either; she looks like I feel, and we watch her laugh as Dave and Ren whistle and call her name, waving like maniacs. Soon she finds us in the bleachers, waving unapologetically, pointing us all out to the friend behind her. Her gig is not bad either, I think, as I share a hug with Ren, who is pulsing with excitement for her. He has already cracked his tie, and his blue buttoned-down shirt is soaked through with sweat, making me glad I'm not the only one about to expire in this heat. Ren is a solid and exuberant young man, with his clean cut looks and mischievous eyes, who can barely see eye-to-eye with Wesley, but doesn't care. I love it that he shouts his devotion to his tall girl from the mountaintops, and I believe that she'll be not only adored but well-cared for. I know how that feels, and I couldn't be happier for both of them. She will have a good job, an exciting new home, and a man who loves her, not to mention a sailing trip to die for, following their wedding, when Ren takes her to Tortola. Always a sailor, it was his dream trip, and his passion for the sea has rubbed off on Wesley as well. They will spend their honeymoon on a twenty-foot sloop in the British Virgin Islands, and go island hopping to their hearts' delight for a week. I find myself once again living vicariously through my child's experiences. For right now, my mother's beach house will do nicely, and I'm looking forward to going there to sit in the sea breeze and do next to nothing, when the time comes.

We listen to all the speeches and cheer our hearts out as Wesley walks across the stage when her name is called and a picture of her with her name is flashed on the big screen. She stops in front of our place in the bleachers and raises her diploma folder for Hope to take a photo. Then, tassels are turned, the class is pronounced commenced, and hundreds of sky blue caps are tossed into the air, as tears pour down my face. Dave smiles at me and offers his handkerchief, reminding me of something his dad would do, and then he kisses me solidly, offering his hand in the air for a high-five. Hope reaches behind Ren to give our hands a squeeze, and then we have to do the group hug thing with Ren. I look back into the crowd of graduates and watch Wesley grinning and holding up her diploma for Hope, for one more picture. Our girl is on her way!

Chapter 36

HOPE

Jessica is enjoying a well-deserved night off on Monday, sitting at the bar with Taylor. They are catching a late dinner after the last movie matinee of the day. I'm telling my story for the third time, once for Mama, who relayed it to Daddy, and then the second time for Wesley and Ren. I'm getting the same awed reaction to the part about the painting that I've received so far from everyone else. When I get to the airport part of the story, they all cheer for me. Amelia is the villain/victim in this story, but they all seem to want to sink Liam in a lake somewhere with concrete shoes! Taylor is riveted to every word I've said, as usual, but tonight he's especially intrigued with my love life.

"Do you *swear* you didn't cry when you saw that painting?" he says, taking a bite of Natty's homemade chips which are the absolute bomb. "Because I'd have cried my eyes out."

"Me too. What a total *douche bag*!" says Jess, as only she can.

Yes. Everybody on the planet thinks Liam Ferguson is a dick, except me. But I'm not going there anymore, because they don't understand him like I do, and it's over between us, so it seems like a waste of energy to take up for him. I can't explain it to any of them. Strangely enough, my mother is the only one who gets it at all.

"No, I didn't cry. By then I knew we were done. If he did or didn't sleep with her, it doesn't really matter. I could have asked him, but what good would it have done?"

"You think he would have told you the truth?" asks Taylor.

I'm still wondering about that one. "He might have lied to me to spare my feelings. That's why I didn't ask. But I think he did tell me the truth, without really coming out and saying it. Painting women is all a tease to him. It's the way it works for him. I actually think it's an addiction. He was so honest about everything else, and he *did* buy my plane ticket, and we *did* hang out with Amelia every day. I mean, why would he mess up his thing there? The Fioris are providing his lodging and everything. He loves them. He's a lot of things, but he's not stupid."

"So it's really over? And you're okay?" asks Jessica, refolding her napkin and watching me for any indication that I'm preparing to melt down.

"Yes."

"Good for you."

"You go, girl!" says Taylor, raising his fist to bump knuckles with me.

"It was a great trip. I don't have a single regret," I say and they scrutinize me with a guarded sense of understanding, as if I've passed a test, or as if they *think* I might have passed.

"I know; it's a conundrum, but it's over and I'm ready to move along. Oh, and I have an interview next week. I just found out today. Wake County Schools."

"Good job!" Taylor says. "Do you have letters of recommendation?"

"Yep. I'm all set."

"Well, speaking of school, I've got an early call in the morning," says Taylor, and I bring him the check. It's nice to see him and Jess hanging out. They leave together and things quiet down to just a few people at the tables and a pair of businessmen at the other end of the bar.

I'm humming along to a song and restocking clean beer glasses for closing when John emerges from the kitchen. It's the first I've seen of him all evening, aside from an occasional glimpse through the window. He's playing it cool since this is my first night back at work. I feel badly about the way we left things after he kissed me the night of the band rehearsal. When we got the news about Toots, he'd asked me if I'd wanted company and I'd said that I'd be okay. I think he took it as a brush-off, but I didn't mean it like that. I was just a little rattled and didn't know what to do. Nonetheless, he'd backed off at work, and I thought it might have to do with my going to visit Liam. So here we are.

"Hey," he says, removing his apron and taking a seat at the bar. He looks sweaty in his T-shirt and stretches his arms across the bar.

"Hey," I smile at him, and he looks uncertainly at me.

"You came back."

"I did. I said I would, remember?"

"Yep, you did. Can I get a Buckshot?"

I nod and go to the tap to pour his draught.

"How was your trip?" he asks, warily.

I chuckle at his expression, as if he thinks I'm going to announce that I'm married.

"It was great actually. I took a zillion pictures and saw some really beautiful places. The family at the vineyard was wonderful."

"And your guy, Liam? Are you guys back on?"

"Uh, no, we're off. It's totally...*off*."

"Oh, I'm sorry."

"No, it's totally fine." Jeez! I keep saying *totally*, but I'm nervous around John for some reason. He just looks as though he's going to keel over at any moment. Breathe! Please breathe! I want to tell him. "We weren't meant to be, I guess. I think I knew that before I went over there, but it was something I needed to figure out. I mean, if that's what you were wondering."

"Oh, yeah. Good. I mean, that's good, right?" He shakes his head and looks sideways. "Wow! This is going really badly. I sound like I'm thirteen," he says, chuckling and rubbing the tip of his thumb across his lower lip. I've seen him do that before and it's endearing for some reason.

"No, it's...fine. It was a great trip and a good opportunity. Maybe a once in a lifetime kind of thing."

"Nah, not for you. I'm sure you'll have lots of chances to travel and see the world. It's awesome."

"So how are you?"

"Good. Tired but good," he says rubbing his forearms. "How's your grandmother?"

"Oh, she's doing well. She had surgery but she's doing better. It was colon cancer," I explain, washing up drink glasses in the sink.

"Oh...that sucks."

"Your dad had cancer, right?"

"Yeah. It was pancreatic cancer. Not good. Colon cancer's rough too."

"Yes, but they caught it early. Stage one. She's really healthy otherwise, so it was kind of ironic."

"Huh." He takes a long drink of his beer, making me wish I had one, too. Sometimes being a bartender is so hard! He rubs his arms and looks tired.

"Was Jess here earlier?"

Ah, he was expecting the *masseuse!* "Yes, she and Taylor went to a movie and stopped in for dinner."

"Oh, that's nice. A date..."

"Well, yeah, I guess. They're friends." I shrug, wondering whether Taylor likes to be seen with women to throw people off, but then dismiss that thought. He is much more genuine than that.

"We could do that....But I was really hoping for one of her killer massages tonight."

"Well, I guess you're out of luck, unless...." I shrug, as the men at the bar leave and I notice the tables have emptied out too.

"Got any lotion back there?"

"Nope. Why don't you go get some olive oil?" I ask, going to the end of the bar to retrieve the empties.

And with that, he shoots me a look, that glint in his eye, like *now we're talkin'*, and he struts back to the kitchen, returning after a minute, rubbing his hands together. He reseats himself and rubs the oil on his arms, extending them across the bar to me. Man's arms. I finish with the glasses and dry my hands on the bar towel. I'm going to massage a man's arms. A man I've kissed in the moonlight in someone's backyard. John does not give me the same vibe I'm used to with Liam. It's different, sensual in a way that doesn't make me feel as if I'm being manipulated, and it catches me off-guard. *Why am I not prepared for this?* I've thought about John, and that kiss, but my fantasies always come to a dead end. It's too soon.

He cocks an eyebrow at me as I begin rubbing my hands up his forearms. "Relax...friends, right?" he says lightly, and we both take a deep breath as I stroke down. His skin is hot, and underneath my hands, his arms are well-muscled and covered with light hair. He closes his eyes and groans with exaggerated pleasure, making me giggle in spite of myself. He is making me relax.

"*Oh, God!* That feels so good. We should *definitely* do this more often. Where have you been all my life?"

I go back and forth a time or two, discovering I'm really getting into the feel of his arms under my hands, going all the way to his sleeves this time, and he peeks at me, glancing side to side, checking for other employees. "We should, you know, do something sometime."

"You mean like a movie?"

"Yeah, we could do that."

"When are you off next?"

"Next Wednesday, but I've got a job interview in the afternoon in Raleigh."

He looks nonplussed, so I counter with another date. "How about the next day? I'm not working that Thursday."

"I am."

We go back and forth with this. I have Cayenne's engagement session to photograph in Wilmington. Then he's in Atlanta visiting friends. Before I know it, he's pulling his arms back from my hands and we've gotten nothing nailed down.

"Thank you," he says, his hands brushing mine as I release him, just as our manager appears at the end of the bar.

Caitlyn comes to collect my cash drawer and informs me I can sign out, so I wipe the oil off my hands and locate my purse, fishing out my car keys.

"Wait, I'll walk out with you," John says, finishing his beer. I wash his glass quickly while he waits and we walk out to the parking lot together. We've done this together for safety reasons at least thirty times before; at times, it's a whole gang of us leaving work late at night, but tonight I'm feeling a thick consciousness between the two of us as we walk across the street, his hand at the small of my back. We pass his truck in the lot and are standing in front of my car under a streetlight. It's a warm muggy evening and there is no breeze. I point my remote at my Civic and it beeps once.

I start to speak, but John beats me to it.

"Listen, Hope...I'm trying not to rush this. Maybe we can just do something on the spur of the moment, I don't know, like go for a walk around the parking lot or something?" We are only free in the early mornings when we are usually sleeping, but he shrugs. "Breakfast?"

Breakfast sounds amazingly intimate and I feel my face burning. He goes on, "I just like being with you. And I'm glad you're done with your guy in Italy," he says, and the sincerity in his voice gets to me. It's in his eyes too, and then he leans forward, and takes my arm in his warm hand, and pulls me closer. He has that smell I like. Then he kisses me. It's soft at first, like the last time, and then he presses his mouth harder on mine, slipping a hand up in my hair. I'm kissing him back, and it's so different. *Wanton and wet.* I didn't expect this at all. I'm afraid it's too soon for me. But I like it. I like John and I don't want to discourage him again. He releases my head and looks into my eyes with that look that means there will be more of this, much more. "You seem happy, Hope. I'm glad. I didn't like seeing you so hurt before, you know?"

"You've been...watching me?"

"Everybody watches you, Hope. Yeah, I've had my eye on you for quite some time, now. I'll see you tomorrow, okay?"

"Okay," I respond, and it sounds even dumber than I feel right now. He's still holding my arm and gives it a little squeeze.

"You drive carefully going home now."

"Thanks. You too."

He kisses me one more time. "Bye now."

He watches me back out of my parking space before getting in his truck. I am shaking. I'm praying I don't hit someone's car in my current agitated state.

I think I need to make a doctor's appointment!

Chapter 37

CHERIE

Something is up with Hope. She is so helpful and present that I don't know what to think. Even Wesley has noticed it. Hope cooks dinner, meat sauce, a *ragu* that she's learned to make from Mara. Hope takes out the trash. Hope does dishes. Hope pours wine or coffee, and sits and talks to me in the kitchen when I am cooking. I have taken over the kitchen again, since Dave has been working, but it seems to be the four of us together most evenings, more like a group of friends gathered around in someone's kitchen, rather than parents and children.

Having Wesley at home seems to make everything complete, although I realize how much smaller the house is with all of us in it, and an extra dog in the mix. Wesley spends most of her time holed up somewhere, studying for her nursing boards, or texting with Ren with Little Miss under her wing. She and Dave have been working on integrating our dogs under one roof, so that when we go to the beach, they can coexist without wrecking the beach house. When I'm out of school for the summer, she and I will tackle the remainder of the wedding plans.

The four of us gather in the kitchen at different points of the day and talk about everything; Wesley's wedding, their job interviews, Hope's photography, her progress on eliminating her debt. The girl has not bought an article of clothing in five months, and I have watched her cut up her credit cards. She makes phone calls to Toots, who is convalescing happily at home, telling her that she and Wesley have taken up yoga. There has not been one word spoken about Liam since she told us the whole crazy story when she got back from Italy.

It is June. I have one more week of exams and then school will be over. I will miss Walt and Audrey, but I have a feeling I will see more of Taylor since he and Hope have become friends. I won't miss my job, though, because this has been an especially taxing year, with the new curriculum, and the screeching halt that came to my retirement planning, so I am extra ready for this break to rejuvenate myself and regroup. We are planning our beach trip over dinner tonight—drunken chicken, made by turning a chicken neck down, impaling it over an opened can of beer, and left to roast in a pan on the grill. After patting it down with olive oil and salt and pepper, I've plunged a long sprig of rosemary down inside the cavity, making the whole thing look like a pagan sacrifice. It's creepy, but delicious, and Dave's favorite meal.

Tonight, we're dining alfresco on our screened porch, something I always look forward to in the spring and summer before the weather is unbearably hot. At Wesley's request, we're pretending we're in Italy, so Hope is playing Italian arias to accompany our meal. Wesley has brought white wine and pours it into our glasses as we sit down to dinner, listening to the crickets and cicadas singing our evening song from the woods behind our house. It is so pleasant here. Dave points out that the hummingbirds are back, and we watch the ruby-throated one and the green one take turns buzzing the feeder. We call them Buzz and Ruby. They are the only two we ever see, and they probably aren't the same ones every time, but we have a penchant for our pets, so of course, we have to name them.

The conversation turns to the beach trip. Dave has been stressed about it because of his new job, and specifically because he works from Thursday through Saturday and sometimes on Sunday if the weather keeps customers away on Fridays and Saturdays. He's wondering how we will get everyone down there and fretting that he'll have to haul the trailer on the back of his truck, but I've reminded him that we can pack our groceries in the empty coolers. Hope will drive separately so she can return early and go back to work.

"I can stay down there indefinitely if you want to come and go," I offer, watching him tuck into his chicken and mull it over. "All of you can just come and go when you can, and bring friends if you'd like. Rowdy can stay with me and keep me company."

Hope looks up and glances at Wesley, as though bringing friends might be a possibility. It's at that moment I decide to drop my bomb.

"I'd like to include Toots if she's feeling up to it."

Dave stops chewing and regards me as if I've lost my mind. He lays his fork carefully on the side of his plate and blinks at me.

"For a few days..." I add.

"Why?" he asks, shrugging.

"Why not? I think it would be nice to have her. It seems as if she's had a change of heart about a lot of things, and I think it would be a good thing."

He stares at me. "She won't come, even if you invite her."

It's my turn to shrug. "Okay, then there's nothing to worry about."

"Don't even go to the trouble. And we don't even know what her schedule will be, with her doctor appointments. Someone needs to be around to take her to those."

Hope takes a sip of her wine. "I don't know, Daddy. She might be willing to take us up on it." I'm relieved that she's on my side. Wesley is watching and staying out of it.

Dave thinks about it for a moment, but I can see he's ill about the whole idea. "Fine. Ask her."

"And I thought about inviting Martha Jane, if she'd like to come, but she might prefer the break."

He waves a hand in defeat. "Then let's make it a house party," he says, voice dripping with sarcasm. Dave loves a party more than any of us, but a party with Toots is not his idea of a day at the beach. And we're also talking about a house full of women. Poor Dave! I'm treading on thin ice here.

"You'll be fishing and swimming and playing your guitar, so what difference will it make if she comes? I'll be entertaining her."

"That's not really what you have in mind. I know what you're trying to do. If I go down there, it's going to be to relax and not have to watch what I say around her. She makes everyone uncomfortable."

"Dave, this is childish. You and your mom need time to mend things."

"Nothing's broken, Cherie. I don't need to fix anything. We have it just like we like it."

"Estranged? That's acceptable?"

"Whatever. If you want my mother around, feel free to invite her. Have your little hen party. I probably won't be there anyway."

Tonight, Dave goes to sleep on his side of the bed in a huff, without kissing me goodnight. I know he thinks I'm meddling, but it's time to get this relationship rolling so he won't have regrets once Toots is gone. By yet another incomprehensible twist of fate, she may outlive us all, but if she doesn't, I don't want it on my conscience that I didn't try to set things right. Boy, are they two peas in a pod! Loving my parents the way I did, it's hard for me to understand the disinterest that exists between Dave and Toots. I miss my parents tremendously, and being an only child, I can give him all the perspective he needs about being alone, if he were inclined to listen. I sigh and roll over on my side, missing him tonight, wrapping my arms around myself and hoping his mood will pass as his moods usually do.

Chapter 38

HOPE

I can hardly stand to go to work at the boutique anymore. The clothes are as beautiful as ever, but they've somehow lost their appeal. The customers have little interest for me as well—self-indulged women spending money on impulse buying the way I used to do. It's called retail therapy. At Mama's urging, I've gone through my closet to clean out all my unworn items to donate to charity. Daddy told me it would be a good tax write-off, and I'm glad someone can use the old clothes I haven't worn in a year or two. I can't imagine trying to lug all those clothes around to a new place when it comes time to move out.

I find myself champing at the bit to get to Natty Greene's at night, to witness John strutting around and singing in the kitchen, making us laugh with his witty little quips. I wonder what he'd be like in another kind of job, wearing business clothes or working outdoors. I try to imagine him in a hard hat, pouring over plans at a table with other engineers; it's hard to picture, but not impossible. He intrigues me more than ever, and it's irritating not to be able to pursue him outside of work. He's been to Atlanta twice to visit friends so we haven't had a proper date—just walks to the parking lot, with the usual chaperones. His sister, Molly, comes in from time to time with friends, straight from work, and I hardly recognize her; she is the epitome of the confident young businesswoman, not at all whom I remember from that night in John's old bedroom. If she'd wear some makeup, she'd be a freaking knockout.

It's somewhat frustrating that of all the stellar job interviews I've had, I've gotten no follow-up. It's June, for Pete's sake, and school will be starting in two months. Mama laughs at me, reminding me that school is not over yet, and that they are having workdays, finishing up the previous year. She says it's to be expected that right now all the in-house transfers are all being settled, and that I, along with the other new hires, probably won't hear anything until the end of *July! Or even August.* How is a person supposed to prepare? She worries that I won't like teaching, with the unruly students I may have at the needy schools that can't keep teachers, and that things are going backward in the educational system. Our state's pay is at a standstill, compared with the rest of the country, as the cost of living goes up, but still, Daddy reminds me, it is one job that still offers a pension. For now. I have a Roth IRA set up just in case all this falls through, and I have to resort to Plan B, whatever that is. Life is such a crapshoot.

I, however, am still excited about my future, and I have way too much going on to worry about it much. I've been to Wilmington to photograph Cayenne and Jonathan, her fiancé, and even cute little Lena was in the pictures. It was so much fun and went so well that they booked my services for their September wedding. It will be a small affair, in the Airlie Gardens, under the historic Airlie Oak, so I should be able to handle it without an assistant. It will be good practice before Wesley's wedding in October.

I'm the last in to report to the bar this evening, meaning I'll be closing up again. I'm too keyed up to imagine I'll be tired. John is there, working away in his usual spot when I arrive, and he shoots me a wink while he talks to one of the other cooks. He doesn't often wink, just gives me that earnest look that makes me think he wants to know how I'm doing, like he's concerned or something, so I smile back and get to work at the upstairs bar, a little sad that I won't get to steal glances at him through the kitchen window. Jessica is downstairs tonight, and I feel a small stab of envy that she, not I, will be going to work on him with the EVOO tonight. The other bartenders aren't as much fun, either. It's a busy night and the time goes by quickly, but I realize I'm dragging by the end of the night. Mark and Jason are done with their clean-up and have vanished before I have finished washing glasses, and I wonder who is left in the kitchen downstairs as Caitlyn unlocks my cash drawer and takes it with her.

John is waiting for me at the downstairs bar, looking over the screen of his cell phone.

"Want to walk?" he asks, as we head out the door with another one of the cooks, the one he calls Justin Bieber.

"Sure," I say as the three of us go out in the muggy evening air, and a hot breeze hits my face, making me lift my hair to cool off. We bid Justin goodnight as he spots his car in the parking lot, and then we are alone. *At last.* It's so corny, but I laugh, thinking of the old Etta James gem with the violin runs and her sultry dark voice, singing what I want to say to someone....

"Are you tired?" he asks, eyes angling me from the side the way he does.

"Not really," I lie, and he grins, seeing right through me.

"Why don't you come home with me for a little while? Do you think your parents would mind?"

"No," I say quickly, knowing I'll text Mama, and knowing she'll lie awake until I'm in, but this is a big step for us.

We smile at each other and he ushers me into my car. I follow his truck to his house, where he parks in front this time, and I send my quick message before he is at my door, opening it and extending a hand out to me.

"Where's Molly?" I ask, knowing as soon as we enter the front door, that no one is there.

"She's at the beach with some of her girlfriends," he says, crossing the living room and tossing his keys into a basket in the hall. He turns and extends his hands. "Make yourself at home. I'm going to change this shirt." I use the bathroom, wishing I weren't wearing my tank top from the bar, but there is nothing that can be done about it now. "I have a surprise for you," he says, coming out of his room and leading me into the kitchen. He selects a bottle of wine from a metal wine rack on the counter, and he opens the refrigerator, pulling out a platter with prosciutto and mozzarella. I set my small purse and keys on the counter where there is a phone and a notepad, and a stack of mail. Then he goes to work, slicing a loaf of crusty bread and setting it in a basket.

"What is all this?" I say, running fingers through my hair.

"I thought it was cool the way your family pretends to be in Italy sometimes, so I thought you might enjoy going there with me, too. Do you mind grabbing those glasses and the wine? We'll go out on the front porch."

I shake my head and follow his instructions, and we go out onto the dark porch where there is an old metal glider with tables on each side and a coffee table in front of it. John sets his tray of food on the coffee table and begins to light candles. He takes the bottle of wine, which I've noticed is a Chianti Classico, and begins extracting the cork.

"This is so...thoughtful, and unexpected. You planned this?"

"Well, things weren't falling into place like I wanted, so I thought I'd take charge. I hope you're not too tired."

"No!" I lie again, and we sit on the red glider together. "I haven't seen one of these in a long time. This is a classic," I say, running a hand over the checkerboard pattern of the glider as he pours my wine.

"My dad collected antiques. We used to sit out here on summer nights all the time, and eat watermelon, and he'd teach me and Molly to play the guitar."

"You must have been close to your dad."

"Yeah.... He was determined we'd have a normal life even though my mom left. He made sure we went to Sunday school and swimming lessons...took us fishing and stuff. He wanted us to learn music and read all the right books. When Molly and I were in high school, he helped out some with our church youth group, and he'd go on mission trips with us to do home repairs after some of the hurricanes, for people who couldn't help themselves rebuild. I hope I'm a good dad like he was."

"He never remarried?"

"No. It was hard to date with two little kids, I guess."

"That's a shame. Do you think he was lonely?" I ask, as he spreads mozzarella on a piece of bread and hands it to me with some of the prosciutto. I realize I'm starving.

"I'm sure he was, but he never complained. There were plenty of church ladies who fussed over him, but they were just looking out for him. I guess he stayed busy enough with our stuff so that he didn't have time to let it get him down."

"What did he do?"

"He was a chimney sweep," he says, grinning, taking a sip of his wine. "The only one in town, so he had a corner on the market."

I let the image of their lives settle in my mind. I don't want to be lonely. And time isn't standing still. John is moving the glider gently with his foot, lulling me into peacefulness in the candlelight.

"How'd I do?" he asks, offering me more bread and prosciutto.

"You did damn good. Where did you get all this?"

"There's an Italian market near the military park. I've been going in there for their meats. They have the best in town. And the wine, well, I did a little research. I'm learning. I'm more of a beer guy, myself."

"I'd say you nailed it. All we need is a little tenor trio and we'd have it made."

He laughs. "Hang on…. There's an app for that…" he says, fingering the screen on his phone, and in a moment, we are listening to Andrea Bocelli singing "Time to Say Goodbye." I laugh, wondering if it's a little jab at Liam and our situation. But he doesn't go there. "So, how's your job search going?"

I sigh. "I'm discovering why patience is a virtue. I haven't heard anything yet. The jobs I want aren't here," I say, watching his brow knit.

"Where are you looking?"

"Raleigh, Charlotte, Wilmington, even Winston-Salem and Asheville."

"Oh…so you're looking to make a city change?"

"Yeah. I think I need to make a move. I want to be on my own, but…I don't want to be lonely, either," I say, catching his eye in the candle glow.

He nods. "I know. I should tell you…I'm thinking of changing towns too."

I feel panic. "Really?"

"Yeah, that's why I've been going to Atlanta. I've been interviewing for a job down there. Plan A, anyway."

We are quiet as we sway gently back and forth and he rubs his lip again.

"What kind of job?"

"It's a land surveyor position. I'd be working for a company that deals with property development—doing surveys for phone lines, cable, electric, water and sewer, that kind of thing."

I'm seeing him standing on the side of the road, looking through one of those yellow things. That's as much as I know about it. A thought comes to me.

Raking my fingers casually through my hair, I ask, as nonchalantly as I can manage, "Who do you stay with down there?"

"A buddy of mine from school, Mike. He's getting ready to start up a sushi bar. That could be Plan B, by the way," he says, taking a bite of bread and prosciutto.

"Oh..." I say, wondering if he can hear my sigh of relief.

"My interviews have gone well. But I probably won't get the job. I don't have as much experience as the other guys out there, looking for the same jobs."

"Well, you never know.... My dad's on the other side of that coin, worrying about guys like you. So there you go. I'd say you have as good a chance as anybody. What about Molly? Are you okay with leaving her?"

He snorts. "She *wants* me to go. She's already lined up two roommates. Think about it. She wouldn't have a house payment because this house is paid for, and she could bank the money she'd make off the roommates in addition to her salary and her 401k. The girl's got it made."

We laugh about it and sip our wine.

"When will you hear?" I ask.

"I don't know. It could be as early as next week."

We are both thinking about it now. We could each end up in another city, another state, and suddenly my bright and exciting future seems to be shaking and blurring, as if the film on the reel is about to snap. John is sitting with his knee turned in toward mine, with his elbow propped on the glider, his head resting on the palm of his hand. Bocelli sings, the candles flicker, and the wine is making my face warm. This new serious John is not the person I know at work, the witty, slightly cocky goofball that I'm used to. He's gazing at me thoughtfully.

"Was that what happened with you and Liam? The distance did you in?"

"No, not really. The distance didn't help, but no, that wasn't it. We had too many differences."

"Do you still love him?"

I'm surprised at his candor. No one has asked me this question, so I haven't had to say the words out loud.

"In a way, yeah. It doesn't go away, but I'm over him. We were never gonna work out."

He nods. "That's nice to hear...in a way."

"Really?"

"Real love doesn't go away. That says a lot about you, Hope. I think that's one reason my dad didn't remarry after my mother left. He still loved her."

"But you don't see her anymore?"

"No."

"What happened to her?"

"She had addiction issues. We don't know where she is," he says, looking directly at me.

"I'm sorry. That must have been so difficult for all of you. But, just so you know, I don't feel the way your father did...I mean, about Liam. I'm ready to move on."

"You are?"

He is looking at me with a new intensity. I've never seen John this serious before.

"Yes. I deserve better than that." The wine has made me bold, but I believe it as soon as I've said it.

"Yes, you do. I'm sure they need teachers in Georgia," he says, barely audibly.

I don't know what to say to that. I think he's kidding. I want him to kiss me, but he doesn't move. I take his wine glass and set it with mine on the table and inch closer to him. I've never touched his hair. My fingers stroke through it and he closes his eyes, letting me explore for a moment, and then his hand is around mine, pulling me close to him, and we are locked into a passionate kiss, his hands grasping my head and plunging his fingers through my hair. I want to touch him everywhere, and he seems to move right with me, answering every sensation I'm having, a thoroughly mutual make-out session, in which I could dangerously lose myself, and I feel my inner voice telling me to stop before this train speeds completely out of control. Pulling back, I look at him as he opens his eyes, wondering what I'm doing. He seems confused at first, but checks himself immediately, sensing we're way over the line.

"Wow!" he whispers. "I'm sorry..." he begins to apologize.

"No, don't apologize. I'm definitely there with you. I just...probably need to go home."

He studies me a moment. "Okay. Can you make it? If you're too tired to drive...I mean, I'd love to have you stay over, and if you want to, I promise I won't touch you."

I laugh and place my hands on top of my knees. "Well...I can't promise I won't touch *you*, so I'd better go."

"Next time we could go to your house," he offers, combing fingers through his hair since I've pretty much destroyed it.

"Right," I murmur, remembering those high school dates, trying to figure out all the mysteries I so richly understand now, on the couch outside my parents' bedroom.

"What's next week like for you?" he asks, sounding desperate, but I don't care.

"I'm going to the beach with my family from Sunday through Tuesday, but I'm coming back to work the rest of the week."

"Are they coming back too?"

"No," I say, suddenly surprised that I'd overlooked this small window of opportunity. "My dad will be back with his fish on Thursday, but that leaves Wednesday free and clear. Would you like to come out after work on Wednesday?"

I can't believe I've just invited him, or maybe I can, but at least I have a few days to think about it. Time isn't dragging its feet. I feel as though I need to learn as much about John as I can, especially if he's going to leave soon. Why is it that the good ones always go up in smoke? And then I think about *breakfast*....And my doctor *has* cleared me for active duty. But oh, this is so soon! Am I really ready for this? What kind of girl *am* I? "*An old girl*," the old John answers in my head, and it's weird that I'm already starting to think like him.

He's talking to me as we're walking to my car. "So, Wednesday then?"

"Uh, yeah. Thanks for taking me to Italy tonight. It was fun."

"Probably not quite like the real thing, but hopefully the company was okay."

"The company was great," I say, grinning, hoping he believes me.

Then he kisses me before helping me into my car, and he lets his hand rest on the door before I start it up, giving me that tender quick look again that says, *I hope you get home okay.*

"Text me when you're home, okay?"

A month ago, I would've rolled my eyes and said, *Yes, Mother,* in my most sarcastic tone, but after talking to him tonight, I know he really means it. Pulling away from the curb, I feel a little flutter and have a sudden thought that makes me chuckle. Maybe John is my butterfly.

Chapter 39

CHERIE

This was such a bad idea! I'm thinking as Toots and I are driving down Interstate 85 South as thunder crashes around us and lightning flashes right on top of my car. There is so much rain I can hardly see out the windshield, and all of the drivers have resorted to using their hazard lights and cutting their speed in half, but I still feel the car hydroplaning. Karma was *not* invited on this trip, and here she has the nerve to show up before we've even left High Point! The bitch!

Toots sits rigidly in the seat beside me, no doubt wishing she'd declined our invitation, but she has the sense not to speak since it's taking every bit of concentration I have to see the road ahead of me. She's brought a stack of magazines in a fashionable tote bag with which to entertain herself for the drive down, and for the rest of the time she's there, in case she cannot tolerate our family's mundane conversation. I have got to stop thinking this way if I want this trip to succeed.

"Well...?" I say. "I'm sure that once we get down there the weather will improve. Today was the only chance of showers. Hopefully, it won't do this for the next five hours!"

I feel her wince in the seat beside me. Maybe she will take one of her pain pills and knock herself out for the remainder of the trip, but knowing her, she is off the drugs completely. Her surgery was weeks ago, and she is doing well, but her energy level is definitely not up to her usual speed.

"I'm so glad the dogs aren't in the car," she says, and so am I.

"Me too! Rowdy loves to ride in the car, but he would definitely be in your lap, or breathing in your face, so it's best that he's riding down with Dave. And I don't think Little Miss handles traveling very well, so it's a good thing Wesley can hold her while Hope drives in this mess. We *are* the lucky ones." I smile at her, but she winces again, probably imagining the week.

As I had feared, the weather does not let up one iota, and when we all arrive exhausted but miraculously in one piece, we drag in our luggage and our pets, in rain that has now dwindled to simply a steady shower. Toots stands around awkwardly like the guest without a purpose as we open up bedrooms, deposit suitcases, and retrieve clean linens to make up beds and equip bathrooms with fresh towels. Dave dries off Rowdy and corrals him on the back screened porch while we get settled, and then Toots heads upstairs with a sandwich for a private lunch and a nap. I can't blame her. The rest of us sit in the kitchen, shaking off the treacherous drive with cups of hot tea and chicken salad sandwiches. Dave finds his golf tournament on TV and switches to beer from one of his coolers he's brought up, and the rest of us follow suit. The girls clean up the dishes and disappear upstairs to settle into their bedrooms, taking Little Miss with them. They've talked for hours, but they are still ensconced in their conversation, which seems to be about men from what I can hear. I need to call my Aunt Sophie who lives in my grandmother's house nearby in Mount Pleasant to let her know we are here, but there is plenty of time for that. Dave and I take the opportunity to invite Rowdy into the house, letting him snooze at our feet on the rough wood floor while we snuggle on the couch, waiting for the skies to clear.

Dave kisses the top of my head and yawns. "I'm ready to say hello to the ocean, aren't you?"

"Absolutely. I think the sun is trying to peek out. Maybe there'll be a rainbow," I reply, drowsing beside him on the comfy old couch, pulling a yellow blanket across our legs. A rattan ceiling fan ticks merrily above us. The house still has that welcoming feeling, as if a big old granddaddy was holding his arms open for us, giving us a place on his lap to nestle into and nap for a while. The walls in every room are a stark white, and the upholstery and pillows are done in cheerful colors—the cool blues, greens, corals, and yellows of the beach. Shells and dried starfish sit in glass bowls on tables and decorate shelves, and perch upon every windowsill, and hurricane lamps sit ready on every table. The only artwork in the house is original—framed watercolors done by my grandmother, from whom Hope got her talent. Less delightful but much loved drawings and paintings by my mother and me, as well as my children, in simple colorful frames decorate the walls. There are oil paintings and pottery from an occasional artist Grandmere knew. My favorite part of the house is its bookshelves, filled with destinations and people I won't want to leave after I turn the last page. It is a happy place. I am transported from my inland life when I walk through these doors and leave the rest of the world behind. For me, entering this house every June magically starts summer, as if I were Dorothy, stepping onto the Yellow Brick Road and into Technicolor. It's a time when I automatically revert to shorts, flip-flops, and bathing suits. Nothing else matters. Nothing can ruin it.

Dave watches Phil Mickelson sink a dramatic putt, as I fill the large pickle jar with water and tea bags to make sun tea. We leave it on the table on the porch and take Rowdy with us across the boardwalk to the beach. Dave holds my hand with the leash in his pocket since no other dogs or people are out just yet. The sand is wet and cool on our bare feet as the crickets start up and the sun bursts triumphantly from the clouds.

The ocean is a deep jade, ravaged with sand from the storm, and it crashes angrily onto the beach as we come in view of it. We take deep breaths, filling our souls with the sea air and letting the sun caress our faces as if we are refugees emerging from months of darkness. I feel my husband physically relax as he grins at me and wraps an arm around my shoulders. Maybe I am forgiven at last.

We have filled our days with fishing and swimming and lazing under our cabana. Toots spends the hours in her on-trend swimwear and cover-ups under the tent reading magazines in her sunglasses, slathered to ghostly whiteness in her SPF 50 sunscreen. Her sense of style and dedication to her appearance amazes me for a woman of eighty! She walks on the beach with us for short distances, returning to wade knee-high in the water, watching Dave and the girls reeling in croakers and spots, and the occasional sand shark. She looks nostalgically on the scene, as if she remembers the same sport with her boys and Philip. I wonder whether she did the same thing then, observing their interactions from afar, while not participating. Toots makes me sad, and I understand why she's filled her life with her nutrition studies and her practice. It was a way to keep busy at something she was obviously good at, and indulge her vanity at the same time. She spends time here on the phone with her many clients, giving them advice, and sending them emails, referencing articles and recipes so they can be like her. She wants to feel needed by someone.

Toots has loosened up by the second day, after our visit with Aunt Sophie, someone whom she's found interesting, and joins us in the kitchen in the evenings while we drink our cocktails and prepare the evening meal together. Naturally social, she can play the game with us, and she seems to be enjoying herself, especially with the girls, when the talk turns to clothes and decorating, and the wedding planning.

"Do let me throw you a shower, and at least the bridesmaids luncheon. If the weather is nice, we can have it out on the terrace. It would be lovely!"

Wesley glances at Dave and me, and Dave gives a shrug and a nod, so Wesley agrees. I'm so relieved that Toots wants to participate and that Dave is letting her.

"So what colors are you planning on using?" she asks, suddenly invested, and I hold my breath, hoping she won't squash Wesley's enthusiasm with one of those horrified looks or judgments.

Hope gets out her laptop and the girls put their heads together over the screen as Hope searches through her photo gallery. "I saw the most amazing wild orchids in Tuscany while I was there," she says, turning the screen to Toots. "We thought with the lavender sash on Wesley's gown, that this purple would complement it nicely," she explains, as Toots croons with approval.

"Oh, yes, that's lovely!" Toots says, putting on her readers to get a better look. She sips her one allotted glass of white wine. "And have you decided on the bridesmaids dresses?"

Hope scrolls through the pictures, nodding. "This is what I'll be wearing, and Wesley's roommate. And this is for Mama," she says, showing long purple dresses for the girls and the lavender one for me. "The guys will wear orchid boutonnieres and we'll carry stargazer lilies and Wesley will have white lilies with lighter purple orchids."

"Oh! That's going to be stunning! And something old, something new; something borrowed, something blue?" Toots is into it now, and the girls are beaming in her attention. *It's about dang time!*

"I'm going to use Grandmere's old silver cuff to wrap around my bouquet," says Wesley, referring to my mother's bracelet. "My dress is new. Mama is giving me her blue embroidered handkerchief to carry because we *all* know I'm going to cry!" she laughs, and we join her.

"So you need something borrowed...." Toots thinks aloud, making us all wonder what little treasure she might come up with. "Hmmm. I have some lovely diamond drop earrings that I might let you borrow if you'll promise to be *very* careful!" she says, smiling her broadest, most sincere smile.

"Oh!" Wesley says, her hand going to her mouth. Dave smiles. I know the earrings. It's not too much and a really lovely gesture. "That would be great!"

"Well, let's see your engagement pictures!" Toots exclaims, so Wesley produces the book Hope has made, a masterful collection of shots of Wesley and Ren in their cowboy boots, playing in the snow in front of an old red barn; kissing in silhouette at sunset; images of their feet, in boots, walking across a rickety bridge; jumping off an old stone wall; with a few obligatory shots thrown in of Wesley's hand on Ren's shoulder, displaying The Ring.

I watch Dave, watching them, the same nostalgic look on his face that I saw on Toots's earlier at the beach today. How can he fit in? This wild man in a sea of women; with one he regards as respectfully as he would a copperhead, ready to strike at any moment. There is so much healing to be done here.

It's Tuesday and we were out on the beach early, planning our farewell dinner for early in the evening at Dunleavy's, our favorite pub on Sullivan's Island. Hope is taking Toots back home tomorrow, which will be interesting, considering that Toots will be in charge of Little Miss in the car for the five-hour trip. God love Little Miss and all of her charms. She has won the heart of Toots, who can't quite see the attraction of Rowdy. It will be nice to have Rowdy to ourselves without having to worry if he's too stimulating for our little Papillon, but they have gotten along so much better than I would have thought, no doubt because there have been so many of us to entertain them.

The girls have taken turns in the bathroom, after Toots has showered; they graciously defer to her each day, as if she is the queen, and I suppose she is. I hope I get that kind of treatment when I'm eighty! I walk up the stairs to replace the used towels with fresh ones when I catch a glimpse of the girls in their bedroom, their faces the color of light mint, as they've smeared themselves in mint mask, indulging in some home beauty treatments.

"Welcome, Earthling," Hope says to me, a quip appropriate for the surprised look on my face.

"Wow! Look at you guys!"

"This is nothing. You should see Toots," says Wesley, gesturing toward the bathroom. I peek around the corner where I find her in a white toweling bathrobe and her hair wrapped in a turban, thick white cream covering her face, and holding an appliance to it that whirs as she moves it in a circular fashion around her face. It's quite frightening!

"What is this?" I ask, my mouth agape.

She grins and holds out her appliance that continues to whir as I see that there is a small circular brush doing the spinning. "Oh, this. It's micro-dermabrasion. I'm exfoliating. You should try it. It makes your skin feel amazing!"

Now I am fascinated and shrug into the doorway, watching her go at it.

"How long do you do it?"

"About three to five minutes. I do it two or three times a week," she says, and I feel myself getting sucked into her equivalent of an infomercial. "Do you want to try? It will smooth out all your wrinkles."

"Oh, *hell* yeah!" I say, wrapping my hair into a twist and pulling over the stool so she can go to work on me. I watch as she rinses her face and washes out the circular brush. Hope and Wesley come in too, taking turns at the sink, rinsing green mask off their faces, as Toots takes charge of my face, first wiping a rough wet pad over my skin, and then slathering on the white cream. Before I know it, she's holding the brush to my face and it whirs away as she moves it in circular patterns over my fine French bone structure.

"This will make you look *fabulous* if you do it at least once a week. Once a week to start with and then you can work your way into two and three times a week," she says as the girls watched, transfixed.

"Dad *so* needs this," says Hope, who goes to the top of the stairs, shouting for Dave to join us.

He is here as Toots is finishing with me, and he stands safely at the doorway, watching with dubious interest.

"What's that?" he asks, as Toots is once again removing the round brush and washing it off under the faucet in the bathroom that is much too small for all of us.

"It's my micro-dermabrasion brush," she explains and he laughs.

"It looks like my old Norelco!" he chuckles.

"What's a Norelco?" asks Wesley.

"It's an electric shaver," says Dave. "I had one when I was old enough to shave. It was shaped exactly like that, and it had three heads on it that rotated around. It sounded just like this too, but mine had a cord," he says, and I notice that he is fresh from his shower and cleanly shaven. His hair is still damp.

Toots laughs. "I remember when Dad and I gave you that for your seventeenth birthday! The next morning, you were making fun of it at breakfast. Do you remember that?"

Dave laughs, "Yeah, with the blueberry muffins?"

"Yes!" she looks at us to explain. "He took—" she begins, but laughter takes over. "I'd made blueberry muffins for breakfast and he took one and put it in his mouth—" she laughs again, "and then he took two more and held them at his eyes and made his head go around and around, just like the *Norelco!* We all laughed and laughed! I thought Eric would pee his pants, he laughed so hard!" she says and we are all laughing. It is such a Dave kind of move, and we can all imagine it.

"Come on, Daddy; you need to try this," says Hope, pulling Dave by the hand into the crowded bathroom, and I relinquish my seat on the stool to him. Before he can protest, Toots has slathered him with the grainy pad, and added a healthy dollop of the cream to his face, and is smearing it all around. Uncharacteristically cooperative, he lets her massage his face with the new tool, and Hope gets another idea. She starts the bathwater, tossing a bath salt tablet into the warm water as I'm rinsing my face at the sink.

"Next, you're getting a pedicure," she says, grinning as Toots wipes his face with a warm washcloth and agrees, with a hearty laugh.

"Great idea! Spa day for Dave," Toots says. She helps him stand up and turns him around so he can immerse his feet into the warm bathwater. Dave groans, but so far, he is being a good sport.

"And while you're doing that, I'll do your manicure," says Wesley, collecting nail clippers and warming another washcloth to hold over his hands.

Dave looks warily at me from his stool, as Hope is guiding his feet into the water. "And what are *you* planning to do to me?"

"Hmmm, let's see...." I say, feeling the delightful smoothness of my newly exfoliated face. "*A massage maybe*...later...after dinner."

Dave grins. I think my husband has discovered the joys of being holed up with a houseful of women.

Chapter 40

HOPE

I have deposited Toots at her house, thankful that she rode with me, because she was a godsend in getting Little Miss home without my strangling her. I thought dogs liked riding in the car, but we all think that Little Miss may be part cat. If I'd been alone, I would have let her lick one of my Dramamine pills to knock her out. Toots surprised everyone this week, including herself, I think, with how well we all got along. I'm glad to see that she and my dad are done with their bickering. It was really getting old! When she visited the Catch of the Day tent that time, she'd been impressed that he was explaining how to cook scallops to one of his customers. She asked so many questions about his new business and wanted to take all the credit for the excellent recipes that we'd printed up on cards with my logo. I guess it was Toots who taught Daddy to cook, but all this time, I thought it was Mama. And then, she must not realize that he *is* in business with the best seafood restaurateur in town. It's amazing how some people want to think that it's all about them! Anyway, she seems newly fascinated with my father, and it makes me happy.

Now, two hours after I've dropped her off, I'm rushing around the house, straightening up, hiding the pile of mail, thawing shrimp in the sink, and icing down John's favorite beer. I have a load of laundry in the dryer, fresh towels in the bathroom, and I've made sure there's toilet paper in each one, and a brand new toothbrush in its package by my sink upstairs, so he won't have to ask, and I'm frantically wondering what to wear. It's *John,* he says to me in my mind, and I know he won't care what the hell I'm wearing, but I answer back, Yes, John, it's *me*, and I *do* care what I look like—especially tonight, and especially since it's you.

I have tried on five different outfits, and I finally settle on my white shorts, which show off my tan, and a pale blue print top that looks sexy and feminine and sets off my blue eyes. My mouth is dry, I am so nervous. I don't understand it. I am never nervous over a date. I never acted this way with Liam, whom I swear I am not going to think about tonight. It has been less than a month since I slept with Liam in Italy and liked it. I always thought you should give a failed relationship at least a month before moving to the next person, but John has stepped up in record time, and I was *not* ready for any of this.

And I know he is coming out here, fully expecting to sleep with me tonight, so I am feeling a large dose of pressure that is so unnecessary. I have bacon and eggs for breakfast, and I've already set the coffee to come on at 8:00 in the morning. I have to work at 11:00, so I hope to have him out of here by 9:30 so I can get ready. Oh, *God!* What am I doing? I just told Mama that I didn't need anybody but myself, and I really do believe that. So what is going on with me? I shouldn't let him come in here and call all the shots. If I don't want to sleep with him, then I'm not going to sleep with him. The trouble is, I think I *do* want to sleep with him. Which makes me a ho. Am I a *sex addict?* I think the answer is yes, and I am not happy about it. Whatever the case, John is a *really* good kisser. Oh, how shallow does that make me?

I have put the shrimp in a pot to steam in beer and old bay, and set out plates and plenty of napkins. I am lighting candles at 10:30 when I hear his truck in the driveway, and Little Miss barks at the sound. As I open the door, she shoots out in the dark before I can catch her. There is no sign of John at the door, and then I see him walking up the driveway, holding her in his hand, as if she were a small sack of sugar.

"Hey! Is this yours?" he asks, grinning, and I know he's changed into a fresh shirt, and upon sniffing him as he passes through the doorway, I think he's had a shower too. He hesitates before coming in, waiting to be invited, and I gesture for him to enter.

"Hi. Yes, she's mine. This is Little Miss," I say, and he hands her to me, as she is scrambling in his arms the minute she sees me. I expect him to kiss me, but he doesn't and hangs back, sending me his look, as if he's holding his breath. I catch his eye, hoping he'll relax, and give him an easy smile.

"What were you doing out there?"

"I was just checking out the stars. It's darker out here than it is in town. You're almost off the grid out here."

"Yeah. Welcome to the country."

"It's nice out here. Quiet. But I wasn't expecting a neighborhood. You look great!" he says, eyes going up and down over me, noticing my tan.

"Thank you. How was work?"

"Kind of slow. People are starting to leave town, going on vacation, you know." He passes through the doorway, and I rest my hand on his arm, making him look at me again.

He leans in slowly and kisses me. *His* kiss. There is no perfunctory peck on the cheek from this man, not yet at least.

"So, how was your beach trip?"

"It was really good. I was kind of dreading it because my grandmother can be kinda domineering, and sometimes really abrasive, but I have to say it was great! Aside from the stormy ride down there, the beach was beautiful. Would you like a beer?" I ask, realizing that I'm not nervous, now that he is here.

"Sure," he says, looking around. "What a great house," he says, immediately gravitating to the photos on the wall. Our whole house is a photo gallery of the Johnson family, and the Johnson Furniture Company showroom, circa 2000. He notices my father's baseball collection in the family room.

"Wow! These are autographed. John Smoltz, Chipper Jones; is that one Greg Maddux? This is unbelievable. Did your dad ever take you to Braves games?"

"I went once. Mostly, that was something he did with the guys—and his dad."

He sees my photograph of the collection in the *I Spy* format and asks, "Did you take this? It's awesome."

"Yeah. Thanks," I hand him a beer in a bottle and take one for myself.

"So what country are we visiting tonight?" he asks, and I feel slack for not being more creative.

"I—I think it's plain old North Carolina back porch. I'm sorry. I guess we could pretend we're at Sullivan's Island. Are you hungry?"

John eyes the shrimp, chilling over a bowl of ice on the island beside a smaller bowl of cocktail sauce.

"Yes. My favorite," he says, assisting me as I serve shrimp on our plates and lead him out to our back porch, where I've lit candles, and suddenly, I feel like a copycat.

"Perfect," he sighs, making me feel better. Little Miss comes to join us and sits at my feet while we peel our shrimp and talk about the week. He has so many questions! How long have I had Little Miss? Who went to the beach? Did we catch any fish? Where is my mother's place? He wants to know the history about Grandmere Porcher who left us the house and why I don't go live there and work in Charleston or Mt. Pleasant.

"You ask really good questions," I say, having not even considered the possibility of living in the beach house, as if Mama would ever offer it up as an option. I'm stuffed from the shrimp, but John continues to peel them, tossing the shells in a bowl and dipping them in the red sauce.

"Sorry, I didn't realize how hungry I was."

I smile at him, realizing I haven't asked him anything.

"Have you heard from your job interviews?"

"Yeah," he says, finishing his shrimp and wiping his hands on the napkin. "They hired me. I got the contract yesterday."

My face falls, and he gives me a sympathetic look.

"Oh! I'm happy for you. I really am. When do you start?" I hear myself asking, unable to process all of this.

"The first of August. I'll have a month to give my notice at work and then get moved in somewhere. I'll be going down to look for a place to live," he says, but his voice is devoid of the excitement I'd expected. He knows this is a shock. I should have been ready. I shouldn't have gotten so excited about him. I've jumped the gun in a big way. We look at each other in the candlelight, and I don't know what to say. I wish I hadn't thought to ask. He might have saved telling me until later....

"Here, I'll help you clean this up. Do you want to go out and sit in the driveway and look at those stars?"

"Sure," I say. One more hopeless situation, one more evening filled with stargazing with a guy I can't have. So much for butterflies. We get up from the table and carry everything inside with Little Miss at my heels. After the dishes are put inside the dishwasher, we squeeze lemon on our hands to kill the smell and I pull the quilt off the back of one of the sofas. He carries two beers and Little Miss, and he lets me lead out to the driveway where we sit in the middle of it, watching the sky.

He watches me, struggling with my thoughts, and then asks, "How is your sister doing with her fiancé out in Texas?"

"They're fine. She'll be going out there to live with him after she passes her nursing boards in a couple of weeks. Then she'll find a job out there... and they'll live happily ever after."

"So it's workin'...the long distance relationship thing?" he says, I think trying to give me hope.

I shrug.

"What's wrong?"

I sigh, frustrated. "I seem to be the queen of failed relationships."

"Well, if you're the queen, then I'm the prince of failed relationships."

"What? The prince?"

"Would I really be here with you if I hadn't failed at all of *my* relationships?"

"Oh, I guess not," I laugh.

"See, I *am* here with you. I'm hoping this one doesn't fail. Maybe you're the one who's going to change my luck. If you've kissed a lot of frogs, well...maybe I'm your frog prince." He looks sideways at me and gives me a smile. I wonder how lonely he's been, especially after going through his father's decline, and eventually his death. Still, he's going away.

"But. You're leaving...."

"Just because I'm going away doesn't mean it won't work with us. And again, I'm not trying to rush it, but I have a feeling about you...."

"You don't know about my failed relationships," I say, swatting a mosquito at my ankle.

"What's to know? It didn't work, you started over."

"I was engaged."

"Oh," he says and swats a bug on his arm. "To Liam?"

"No, to a guy named Matt, in Raleigh, right out of college. We couldn't stand each other by the time we called it off." I am gauging his reaction when I smack another mosquito on my neck.

"Are you getting eaten up? We could go in..."

I nod, and we pick up the quilt and go back inside. We pick a couch and sit down together. The beers are empty, but neither of us gets another. I pull out my laptop and show him all my pictures from Italy. I tell him about Mara and Vitale. Things start spilling out of me, and I can't seem to stop; it's much like projectile vomiting! I tell him all about my jobs. I tell him how much money I owe on my consolidated credit card debt, and his eyebrows pop up. I tell him I think I could be a sex addict and he grins. I tell him the whole story about Liam, and discovering that he was an atheist, and Amelia and Nicolo, and feeling old, and feeling frustrated, and out of control, and soon his arms are around me, and he's soothing me.

He takes his turn, telling me about his ex-girlfriend, the one who counted enough to discuss. They'd dated for three years and then she broke his heart, dumping him for his best friend. It took him two years to get over her.

"It was Mike, by the way."

"The guy you know in Atlanta."

"Yeah," he chuckles.

"And you're still friends?"

"Yeah. They lasted about three months and he dumped her. He's still busting my balls about why I hung in there with her for so long."

I shake my head and laugh. Then I glance up at him and see that he's watching me.

"Don't try to scare me away from you, Hope. It's not working. I know you. You're like me. You can be quiet, but you're busy inside. I like that about you. You're nice to people. Everybody likes you. I like you. A lot. Can we just forget I'm moving...for a little while, okay?"

It sounds too much like *lose yourself with me for the next three days*, but I smile at him anyway and let him kiss me. I kiss him back, and there is still that chemistry. John is sexy, without calling me baby or sweetheart or winking at me or looking lascivious, thank God. I feel myself reciprocating, liking the way he touches me. He laces his fingers with mine and kisses my hand. I feel him stifle a yawn above my head and I know he's tired. We've talked for hours.

"Where's your bedroom?" he asks, giving my insides a stir. He stands and takes my hand, helping me blow out all the candles. We let Little Miss out one more time and then I lock the door. As I start to go upstairs, he pulls me back and kisses me, that urgent kind of down-your-throat kiss that lets me know exactly where this is going, and I'm fine with it, giving it right back so he knows. He lifts me in his arms and I stifle a giggle, but then it erupts again as he tries to navigate the stairs with me. It isn't working. He's stronger than I thought, considering he's not much taller than I am, but he realizes what he's doing isn't safe. He chuckles and puts me down, picks up Little Miss, and follows me upstairs. My room is dark, with barely enough light to determine the outline of my bed. He lifts me again and sets me on it. He toes off his shoes and slides onto the bed beside me, taking me in his arms while Little Miss finds her place somewhere around my knees. John strokes her head and she moves over to him. She makes that noise that sounds like purring. She is such an odd little dog.

"She likes you," I murmur against his mouth.

"Is she going to watch us?" he whispers.

"I don't know. I didn't have her when..."

"Oh. I'm not used to having pets watch. That could be creepy," he says, kissing my forehead.

"Have you ever had a pet?" I ask him sleepily.

"Molly has a cat."

"I never saw a cat at your house," I say, giving in to a yawn of my own.

"That's because she hides when new people come around. It would take her a few days to warm up to you...but I still don't think she'd watch. Cats have more dignity than dogs, I think."

I giggle and yawn again as he strokes my cheek, sliding his fingers into my hair. I snuggle into his chest and sigh. John is delightful.

I hear the coffeepot gurgle and sputter before I open my eyes. It is 8:00. John's arms are still around me as I look around, trying not to move my head, waking him. Shamefully, I'm thinking about all that I've revealed to him last night, and I find myself a bit surprised that he didn't slink away during the night. He had the chance to escape, but he's still here. Little Miss is circling the bed, so I know I've got to get up and take her out. Gingerly, I manage to move out of his embrace and off the bed without disturbing him. Still fully clothed, I realize that we have been out cold since we hit the bed at around 3 a.m. John has not moved, and I listen just a moment to check if he's still breathing. I see his chest rise and fall, and I smile, relieved that he's not dead. And he doesn't snore.

When Little Miss has done her business, I am back in the kitchen, pouring a cup of coffee, and arranging bacon on a plate for the microwave, when I hear his footsteps on the stairs. He walks stiffly into the kitchen and shakes his head, hair flattened in the back of his head where he slept.

"Good morning," he says, coming over and giving me a tender kiss on the side of my head. I sense that he has brushed his teeth.

"Buongiorno."

"What can I do?" he asks, smiling at my Italian greeting.

"Want to do the eggs?" I offer, setting the carton of eggs and a bowl in front of him at the sink.

"Sure. Is there more of that coffee?"

"Yes there is. How do you like yours?"

"Black is fine," he says, cracking the eggs with one hand and tossing the shells in the sink. "I slept like a log. How about you?"

"Me too. Neither of us moved."

"Sorry about that."

"No, it was fine."

"I wasn't sure...you know...that you were ready," he says, leaning his hands on the counter and meeting my eyes.

"I was...I think we were both just too tired."

"Well, I'm okay with it if you are," he says, going to the stove and spraying cooking spray into the pan I've started heating. He whips the eggs with a fork and pours them in while I pop two English muffins into the toaster and take the bacon out of the microwave. I feel as comfortable with him as my parents seem to be when they go through their morning ritual together. "I'm not trying to push you through your vetting process, you know."

His choice of words makes me smile. I don't feel pushed at all this morning. He's definitely playing his cards right. He's brave still to be here! Especially after all the extra innings our conversation went into. I touch his arm, and suddenly I'm wrapped in it, and he's cradling my head in his hand. There is no doubt in my mind that making love with John would be amazing. Whenever it happens, I know it will be worth the wait. He kisses me, a dizzying, proper morning kiss, not too crazy, but with just enough feeling to make me feel cherished. *Cherished.* There's a word I haven't thought of in a while.

"I'd say you're pretty close to being vetted, seeing as how you didn't escape during the night after all the junk I dumped on you," I say, making him laugh, but I have to continue. "I wonder about the timing of all this myself, you know? You seem really sure..."

"Yeah, Hope, I am. Don't forget, I'm older than you are. Time isn't standing still for me, either. And I figure when you know, you know. Do you feel that way, too? I don't think God put you in my path so I could walk around you."

Chills go up both arms when he puts it like that. I blink at him and go to the cabinet for plates and forks. He helps me serve the plates and carries the butter and fig preserves to the table. He looks at the jar.

"Mara made these from their figs. I brought them back from Chianti."

"Mmm." He opens the jar and spreads the preserves on his muffin. We eat in companionable silence for a moment, and then he speaks.

"You know, if you wanted to come to Atlanta, Mike is going to need bartenders for the sushi bar. It's opening in August, and I know he hasn't hired all the help he needs."

A rush of emotion makes me tremble and he notices when I set down my fork.

"Too fast?"

"No. It's just...I—I think I have a hard time with change. I can definitely see myself going. And maybe that's the problem. I've never been very spontaneous."

"Me neither, but I'd like to be," he says, taking a bite of his bacon. "I like having a well drawn out plan, and I usually stick to it." He chews, looking at a spot on the table, and he rubs the old wood a moment, as if he's admiring the antique. "I also know that you're fighting for your independence, and I wouldn't want you to think I'm trying to take over or anything." He's politely telling me that he knows I'm a control freak.

And I am done with being manipulated. He knows this, too, after my rant last night.

"So, I'd have my own place." It's a statement. I'm not moving in with a guy again. Even John. Right now.

"Of course. I could help you look for something. You could look for a teaching job in the meantime while you work at the bar. I just know that when I go down there, I'll miss you. A lot. Especially if this is headed where I hope it is."

The sincerity is in his eyes again, and I like the new John. Who knew? I look away, concentrating on his spot on the table, eating eggs and drinking my coffee. I'd never see him, if he worked days and I worked nights. My head is swimming and I think that this could actually work, but I can't say it out loud. I nod instead. *What if I ruin it and he doesn't like me once he gets to know me better?*

He's trying to figure out my dilemma. "It's a lot to think about. But at least you know you have more options. I know you're frustrated, trying to make something happen. There's a lot to do in Atlanta. Maybe it's worth embracing."

He gazes at me across the table. I feel a sudden urge to introduce him formally to my parents, at a proper dinner or a Sunday brunch. I smile at him.

There is a lot worth embracing.

Chapter 41

CHERIE

It's funny how things turn out—first Wesley and Ren are getting married, and then out of nowhere, Hope has found John, I think, gazing at Wesley fastening Toots's diamond earrings while Hope snaps pictures of me watching her. We're by the window, in front of the full view mirror in one of Toots's glamorous bedrooms, and it's hard to believe my younger daughter is really getting married. Her friend, bridesmaid Kelly, is finishing her hair and posing for Hope.

"Those are lovely!" says Toots, checking the earrings and clasping her hands as Hope takes a shot of her with Wesley. As if quite comfortable in front of a camera, Toots says, "Time for the veil" and reaches for it. She has taken over most of this wedding, and I'm glad to let her, but at the moment, she is handing me the veil so I can have the honors. Hope takes pictures of me fastening the sheer veil to the back of Wesley's hair that's been caught up in a loose bun.

"That's going to move nicely in the breeze," Hope says, squinting slightly, imagining another shot for later. It's the first crisp fall day we've had, so we went with Plan A, which was having the wedding on Toots's lawn under the pergola. We could have easily moved it inside with the dramatic effect of having Wesley descend the grand staircase, but the garden is infinitely more beautiful.

Wesley is ready, so lovely in her princess dress, and Hope takes a few more shots of us—Wesley and me, Wesley and Toots—and then I take the camera for a picture of Wesley and Hope, then a couple with Kelly. Toots excuses herself to check on the guests who are arriving downstairs. Hope takes Kelly and goes to snap photos of the men's preparations before the whole show gets underway. I have butterflies again as Wesley and I stand together at the window, gazing out into the garden where the white-dressed chairs are set up facing the pergola, and beyond it, the fourteenth fairway of the Sedgefield Country Club golf course.

"Are you nervous?" I ask Wesley, alone with her for the last time as my single daughter.

"No, Mama. I've been waiting a long time for this, so no, I'm not nervous. Neither is Ren. It's going to be great."

I nod, listening as the string quartet starts its music, and we watch the people in the yard milling around and greeting one another.

"Daddy and Toots are okay with each other, aren't they?"

"Yes, finally. I'm so glad he agreed to let her host the wedding. She's been the perfect wedding planner. You couldn't have done any better." And it was true. Toots had taken care of it all, since she had all the best connections, from arranging the string quartet, to the caterer, to the florist, who'd flown in the most breathtaking orchids for the occasion.

"Daddy said she'd even had the course officials suspend play for an hour so we won't have errant golf balls flying into the ceremony!"

"I know! Isn't she a hoot?" We both laugh and I hug her.

"I'm so happy for you! You have a great guy, and a *job*, and you're going to have such a wonderful life…so *far away from here*!" I say, tearing up again.

"Oh, Mama, it will be fine. You and Daddy are expected to come and visit. You'll love Austin."

"I know; it's just that with Hope in Atlanta now, I really miss you all again."

"You're an empty-nester again," she giggles, squeezing my hand.

"*I know!* I wanted the house all to myself, and now that we're back to that, I'm going to be so lonely!"

Hope is back without her camera or Kelly. "Time to head downstairs, Mama."

"Where's the camera?"

"John's got it. He's taking over until the ceremony is over. He's downstairs taking pictures of Aunt Sophie and Ren's family and Toots, and they need you, so off you go."

Hope is gorgeous in her wild orchid dress, with her hair pulled back and orchids pinned in place. Who would have thought she'd have taken off like a rocket the way she has? The excitement suits her. She's never seemed happier or more vibrant.

I kiss Wesley and squeeze her hands before I leave. Holding up the skirt of my dress, somehow I make it downstairs in my dyed-to-match lavender silk shoes without killing myself. Dave and the other groomsmen are having a celebratory shot by the French doors, and I notice a tray of crudités on the coffee table where the ladies are having small glasses of white wine to calm their nerves before the ceremony. I grab one without hesitation. The guests are beginning to fill the chairs as the golden afternoon sunlight slants across the lawn, touching the grass with autumn magic.

Aunt Sophie and Uncle Ross are standing by the fireplace, looking like lost souls, so I make my way to them and give them welcoming hugs. They were unable to get in for the rehearsal dinner so I am happy to see them.

"Hellooo! You made it! How was your trip?"

"Hi, darling! It was fine," says Aunt Sophie, patting my arm. She is younger than Toots, but not as well-preserved, of course. Who is? Still, she looks great in her pink dress with the obligatory southern pearls and a hefty dose of Shalimar.

"Have you met everyone?" I ask, looking around the room at the wedding party and Ren's family. Uncle Ross nods, gazing at the guys and the shots, evidently wishing he were on the other end of the room. Sophie wants the scoop, as I knew she would.

"Well, yes. Toots has introduced us all around. Now, tell me about this *John*. Is he Hope's young man?"

We glance over, and John is snapping photos of Dave, Ren's father and brother, the other men in the wedding party.

"Yes! They worked together when she was at the restaurant here. He's wonderful!"

"She said she was living in Atlanta. When did that happen? I don't remember hearing a thing about that when you all were down in the summer!"

"I *know!* It was all very sudden. She'd been applying for teaching jobs all over the state, and the next thing you know, there's an art museum in Atlanta wanting her to come interview. She took a job there as an educational coordinator for children's programs, and she is just loving it. She started in August, about the same time that John took a job down there, too. He's a land surveyor."

"Oh!"

"Yes, we've been doing a lot of moving lately."

"Are they living together?"

"Oh, gosh, *no!* Hope is being very careful this time. She's not jumping into anything before she's good and ready. John is quite smitten with her, and she with him, but she's playing it on the down-low as they say."

"Once bitten, twice shy."

"Mm-hmm."

Uncle Ross is finally able to get a word in. "What's Wesley doing?"

"She got a job working in an oral surgeon's office. She likes it better than the hospital jobs because she won't ever have to work nights. It's secure, and she and Ren are home at the same times."

Toots takes the floor with her commanding voice, looking regal in her aubergine gown. "It's time, everyone!"

"We'll take our cue and get seated. By the way, you look gorgeous! See you later, sweetie," says Aunt Sophie as Uncle Ross whisks her away through the French doors and Dave is instantly by my side. John is shooting the camera at the staircase behind me, and when I turn around, our girls and Kelly are floating down the stairs.

"Oh, my God," I murmur. Dave gives me a quick kiss and tells me it's time for me to process in. Toots has already gone.

Missy Henry and I stand at the doors, waiting for our groomsmen to usher us down the aisle. It's already a blur, but I want to remember it all. I turn and watch the bridesmaids in line behind me, and Wesley, looking like a dream in her white veil on Dave's arm. He looks so proud and vulnerable at once. I know he's wishing his father were here. I am wishing my parents could see it too, and maybe they are. Wesley lifts her bouquet, showing me my mother's silver cuff wrapped around the lilies and orchids.

Ren's brother Will is there as I turn, offering his arm, and we make our way down the aisle to the tune of Schubert's "Ave Maria." Friends are everywhere, watching me from their seats, as I cling to Will's arm, trying not to aerate Toots's yard too badly with my kitten heels as I make it to my chair.

The music changes and I wink at Missy across the aisle as handsome Ren and his father, the best man, take their places under the pergola beside Father Roger. Will processes in next, followed by Kelly and then Hope. Another change in the music, now "The Wedding March," is my cue to stand, and the guests follow suit. As we turn, Dave and Wesley glide slowly down the aisle so he can properly show her off, and sure enough, the breeze catches her veil, making it billow out behind her. The sunlight catches her face, making her eyes sparkle along with the diamonds. Then Dave is passing her to Ren, and he takes his place beside me, as I wipe a tear from my left eye.

I will never forget the view, as I sit beside Dave, holding hands in our chairs in his mother's garden, looking past Wesley and Ren under the pergola, to the willows that sway in the breeze and kiss the ground as Wesley and Ren become husband and wife.

Chapter 42

CHERIE

A mockingbird sings through his repertoire in our maple tree that is now tinged with flame-colored leaves. As I breathe in the woodsy smell and look out over the woods from our back porch, it pleases me that the view is a riot of fall color. Autumn is my favorite time of year; peaceful, with shorter days and early-to-beds that suggest it is time to slow down and reflect. Dave and I are back from the beach, having finally recuperated from Wesley's wedding. Rowdy and I have had our walk, the laundry is done, and I am taking a respite before the next event. It's almost evening on an October Saturday. Dave will return soon from the shrimp tent, and I need to get dressed. We have plans to join Audrey and her husband for a late dinner at Walt's house. He has a new significant other we've only met at Wesley's wedding, the cellist from her string quartet. He talks about her from time to time at school when we ask, but otherwise he is tight-lipped. Even Taylor doesn't get much out of him. Walt has never been one to kiss and tell, and it's been a long time since he's had a lady in his life. He met Carla, one of Toots's symphony acquaintances, at the black tie gala last spring. Despite all the drama that night, and quite possibly because of it, his ballroom experience with Toots paid off in a way that I never could have matched.

Wesley and Ren's wedding day was perfectly beautiful, I reminisce, as I sit on the porch snuggled into my sweater, glad that cooler weather is finally upon us. I'm looking over honeymoon photos on my laptop that Ren has posted on their Facebook page. They look so happy, in pictures that they've had other tourists take of them in Tortola; Wesley, laughing in Ren's arms at a seaside cafe, her wild blond curls wafting in the sea breeze. It could have been me, thirty years ago. Their sailboat looks sleek and serene as it lies at anchor in the harbor, and she sends us texts about what they do, exploring a different island each day, snorkeling, and eating fried conch, having lots of drinks with limes, it seems, while assuring me they have not gotten sunburned. I'll bet. They've had other preoccupations to keep them out of the sun!

So many pictures run through my mind from the wedding; Hope's shots of the rehearsal, the bridal preparations, the ceremony, and all the revelry with Dave's band that followed were so expressive. Our family has never been happier. Having the wedding at Toots's house made it much more affordable for us. She took care of it all. Thinking back on it all, I am amazed at what she did. Having the golf course staff suspend play for the time that it took for the ceremony, showed so much thoughtfulness on her part, and *nerve!* It would be nice to have that kind of clout.

Hope and John pulled off the wedding photography with aplomb. He was so cute helping her manage her lenses and the tripod. She has a new confidence since she's made the move to Atlanta. John is patiently biding his time with her, but I think she is ready to take the matrimonial plunge with him, and Dave and I both hope she'll give in soon so he can become part of our family. She tells me she loves him deeply, and that she's finally ready, but she wants him to be sure they're making the right move. As if she ever had to convince *him*, but it's her way of making sure. From what John tells Dave, they have been looking at old houses to renovate, so maybe it won't be long. I'm happy for Dave. It's nice that he finally has male companionship again—first with Ren, and now with John, who's an avid Braves fan and a musician as well. And all of them like to cook. What lucky ladies we are!

With Wesley in Austin, and Hope in Atlanta, I have an empty nest once again. It is an adjustment I'm having to make all over again. I miss them all, and even Little Miss, although Rowdy is quite content to be top dog again, as he has assumed his rightful place in our house once more. He's snuggled at my feet right now. I don't mind working, and I feel blessed to have a job, but this year is going to be it for me. I have told no one, because I really do not care again to entertain Karma, the bitch, so I have kept my retirement plans secret from everyone apart from Dave. He's happy for me. He's also happy to play in the band, and sell his shrimp by the roadside, and even has plans to expand to a second location, and in the long-term scheme, he'd like to have a permanent location where he could have orders cooked on site, to be taken home, or eaten on site in a cafe setting. Big dreams for my Dave, but I know he can make it happen.

I can sit for hours mulling it all over in my mind. Without all of them around, I find I have so much time on my hands, even with yoga in the evenings and on weekends when Dave is working, so what else am I going to do with myself to stay out of trouble?

A thought comes to mind, as I open up a new document on the laptop. Do I have the nerve to do this? They'd all probably kill me, so I will have to twist and convolute my story and change all the names to protect the innocent. I rub my fingers together and take a deep breath, and then begin to type.

It's Valentine's Day, I remember thinking....

CHERIE

EIGHTEEN MONTHS LATER

I'm stretching my legs, enjoying the extra space, thankful for Dave's forethought that we should get bulkhead seats on the plane—unlike Toots, whom he's gone to check on in first class. I'm talking on the phone with Jennifer, my agent, letting her know we are running on schedule and we'll meet her at her office in New York when we land. Jennifer tells me that my timely story has resonated with her publishers, so much so that our original deal is going to be big, a lot bigger than she thought, and I don't know what that means. A movie? I get chills thinking about that.

Toots was dying to go to New York with us this time, and she offered to hire us a car. She also got tickets for a Broadway show while we're there. Hope and John are flying up tomorrow for my TV talk show, and they will go to the theater with us tomorrow night. I wish Wesley and Ren could have made it, too, but they are busy working, after just returning from their vacation. I fan the back of my neck with my magazine, feeling a wave of nausea with all this major attention centered on me, thinking of all the exciting things we have to do, and hoping I can hang with them all.

Dave returns and sits beside me, patting my knee and giving me an eye. He likes my new dress.

"How is she?"

"Holding court in first class. She was the first passenger to get her Bloody Mary," he laughs.

"Of course she was. She couldn't wrangle us an upgrade? Not that I'm complaining," I say, gesturing to the expanse of space before me.

"No, but I think since she cut her hair and let it go back to her natural color, she's had people eating out of her hand."

"I know! Before, when she looked so amazing, I think people just resented her out of jealousy. I think the white hair suits her. And she still looks amazing."

"Will you excuse me a minute? I'm going to the head before we take off."

"Sure," I smile at Dave, and return to my magazine. People are still coming aboard, and I look around. Flying out of Charlotte is always busy, especially with people boarding from connecting flights. It's then that I see him.

Of course, he is taller than most of the passengers. His long hair and enigmatic soft brown eyes meld into the good looks that have captivated others' attention as well as mine. He looks tired, but fit, in his sweater and jeans, as he searches the aisles for his seat. He will forever remind me of the J. R. R. Tolkien quote, *"Not all who wander are lost."* But is he lost? Glancing up, he catches my gaze. He looks surprised, caught off-guard for a moment, but then his face breaks into a wistful smile. He finds his seat and deposits his carry-on bag into his seat and walks the extra steps to speak to me, as I watch the various nuances of emotion pass across his face. No telling what he sees on my face. As many times as I've wanted to strangle this man in the past, I feel only affection for him now. It is as Hope has said, *Real love doesn't go away.*

"Hi, Cherie," Liam says gently, meeting my gaze full on, and I stand to extend my hand to him.

"Hi, Liam! How are you?" I ask, and our intended handshake turns into an embrace.

"I'm good. How are you?"

"Very well, thanks."

"Hey, I read about your book on Facebook. Congratulations!"

My face goes even redder than it was, wondering whether he'll read it, and wondering whether he'll recognize the character that's like him. I'm surprised he's kept up with us.

"Thank you. Sales have been surprisingly good. Dave and I are on our way to New York to kick off my book tour."

"Oh, that's fantastic! Was that *Toots* I saw in first class?" he asks, gesturing with his thumb toward the front of the plane. "She has different hair, but I heard her voice and thought it had to be her."

"Yes! Hope is joining us as well tomorrow."

He breaks eye contact for an instant at the mention of her name. His face looks as if it might fall apart, but then he recovers.

"So...she's happy? I heard she got married," he says, making me realize they really haven't kept in touch, and it's sort of sad; understandable but sad. If he's seen my news, I'm sure it was because he was checking on her.

"Yes, she's very happy. She surprised us with the wedding."

"She eloped?"

"Something like that," I say, not wanting to get into it. Why rub it in? "And *you?* When did you return to the States?"

"A couple of months ago. I've been in the Florida Keys visiting some friends. I'm on my way to New York too, for a gallery showing of some of my work I did when I was in Italy."

"Oh, that's wonderful, Liam! Congratulations." *No visit to the psychotherapist while you're here?* I still can't help myself. I'll always be a mother.

"Friends in high places," he shrugs. "Thank you," he says, and I feel the conversation winding down as people try to squeeze by his tall figure to stow their baggage in the overhead compartments. He glances around for Dave, who is slipping in among the other passengers. I am dreading this moment, but Dave is gracious and makes a show of greeting Liam, slapping him on the shoulder and shaking hands enthusiastically, making Liam grin with relief.

"Hi, Dave!"

"Hey, Liam! What a surprise!" They talk briefly, getting up to speed as the other passengers look irritated. Dave is explaining that he has expanded his business and that he has five guys working for him in the two locations, and that he's playing in the band again. They are aware that they're in the way and try to wrap it up. Liam looks at me again.

"It's great to see you both! Please tell Hope...send her my best wishes," he says, taking my hand and giving it a lingering squeeze.

"We will. Goodbye, Liam." We share a last look together, and I exhale as soon as he turns away.

Dave and I sit down together wordlessly, as he cocks his eyebrow subtly. I lean back in my seat and close my eyes, listening to the flight attendant beginning her safety speech. My thoughts go back to that lovely June evening in South Carolina....

We'd been invited to another party at my Aunt Sophie's house, the third one celebrating my retirement while we were staying at Sullivan's Island, and I remembered thinking it was overkill, but Sophie had insisted and told us to dress up for an evening picnic under her live oak tree in the backyard. There is no place on earth more beautiful than my grandmother's home place, where Sophie and Uncle Ross live now—a traditional low country home built in the center of a grove of live oaks, with a double-ended staircase leading up to the proper front porch. They'd had to rebuild after Hurricane Hugo leveled the original home and many of the trees back in 1989, but now, it looks much the same as I remember. The old iron dinner bell from our ancestors' plantation still stands beside the cistern, the only two original structures left. The back-yard is especially magical, as it recedes to the creek and the marsh beyond it, and when the twilight gives way to the summer moon, it is a sight to behold. Never have I felt closer to Heaven than when we are sitting as a family under those trees with the cicadas making evening music amid the humid marsh breeze that cools our skin.

As soon as we'd arrived, with Toots in tow, I'd wondered what was going on. Hope and John were planning to meet us there after having spent the day in Charleston by themselves, shopping for lighting fixtures for the house he'd bought, and I saw his car among others. There were Grandmere's pretty white lawn chairs set in a semi-circle under the big-gest tree, where there's a table built around it for serving food on the lawn, and food was already set out, covered, and waiting. Fairy lights hung from the trees, and other family members and a few others I didn't know were already there; a young woman with pretty blond hair, *was it John's sister?* And why was she there? Wesley and Ren, of course, were there, and even Eric, whom I was shocked to see, was chatting with Aunt Sophie and drinking a beer under the canopy of live oak and Spanish moss. And this was all for *me?* It seemed somewhat confusing, absurd, and a bit redundant, but I'd decided to abide it humbly.

Toots took the lead as soon as we were out of our car, going to give Eric a hug, and pulling Sophie off to the side, making me wonder what other little surprises she'd had up her sleeve. I saw a priest among the guests and my heart did a little flip, as Dave and I locked eyes, and it dawned on us what this was.

"Everyone, could I please have your attention?" Toots said, tapping a fork on the glass of white wine she'd just been handed. She was smiling that broad, classy smile of hers, her genuine smile that night, and there was mischief in her eyes. An unusually cool breeze for June blew about us as we looked around in confusion. We were all standing in rapt attention as she placed her arm around Aunt Sophie and continued.

"We are almost all together. Hope and John will be joining us in just a moment, so I need to tell you what we have in store for you this evening. They've been busy putting together a little surprise for some of you. And Cherie, you'll be glad to know this is *not* another retirement party for you, although we're all still thrilled for you! This is...*a wedding*. A surprise wedding. Hope and John have planned it as a surprise for...well, *some* of you. They wanted to do it their way, simply, without making any of you feel stressed, and with Sophie's help, and the few things I did, I think we pulled it off! Are you surprised?" Everyone hooted with laughter, and looked around at one another in wonder. "Well, good! If you will all take your seats, we'll get started!"

Toots came to Dave, wrapping her hand inside his elbow, and beckoned for Wesley to come over. "Would you mind meeting your daughter at the front door?" He shook his head and chuckled, kissing me on the cheek before doing as he was told. Then Toots asked Wesley to follow Dave. She looked so lovely in her filmy party dress that she'd bought on King Street with Hope's help the day before. She gave me a little shrug and a wink, and then a wan smile, giving me chills all over as she followed Dave across the lawn to ascend the porch steps. *She knew about this.*

We were seated and I saved a seat for Dave, as music started from a speaker somewhere, Hope's favorite, Pachelbel's "Canon in D," played by a string quintet. John emerged from the back porch, wearing a flax-colored linen suit and a huge grin, and strutted across the backyard, joining the priest underneath the tree. He found my eyes and winked at me, his grin growing impossibly larger. Soon, a good-looking fellow in a matching suit that I thought must be John's friend, Mike, came happily down the stairs and walked across the lawn to join John and the priest under the tree. Then Wesley followed, smiling broadly, holding a bouquet of the palest pink peonies, walking slowly in her sandals to stand opposite Mike. The music stopped and the priest looked at me and smiled, motioning for me to stand. Everyone else stood as well and we turned to the porch as the music changed. It was Rascal Flatts's "Bless the Broken Road," and I began to cry, right on cue, as Dave and Hope made their way gingerly down the stairs. She was wearing her Vera Wang that no one knew about except for Wesley and me, and it looked stunning on her in the fading light. But what I noticed more than her gown was the radiant and joyous smile on her beautiful face. She paused to give me a hug and kiss, handing me a creamy peony from her bouquet. "Don't faint, Mama. I don't want you to miss a thing!" she whispered in my ear. Dave winked at me as he led her past me, and then he placed her hand in John's.

The End

THREE GIFTS

"There is a Celtic saying that heaven and earth are only three feet apart, but in the thin places, the distance is even smaller."

"Throughout Three Gifts, *you will be rooting for Chelsea and Kyle, young marrieds so appealing, yet real that you'll wish you could clone them. They settle in the mountains, near Boone, North Carolina, and when they are faced with tragedies, they handle them with courage and grace. Even those oh-so-human doubts and fears that threaten occasionally to swamp them are banished through humor and the abiding love that sustains them. This is a journey of hope, faith, and love that you'll want to share with them."*

**- Nancy Gotter Gates, author of
the *Tommi Poag* and *Emma Daniel* mysteries,
and women's fiction *Sand Castles* and *Life Studies***

A FOREVER MAN

"There are friends and there are lovers; sometimes the line between is thinly drawn."

"Just when I thought I would never see Kyle and Chelsea Davis again, Mary Flinn brings them back in A Forever Man; *they returned like old friends you feel comfortable with no matter how much time has passed, only this time with eight-year-old twin boys, and a new set of life-complications to work through. In this novel, Flinn provides a deft look at marriage when potential infidelity threatens it.* A Forever Man *is Flinn's masterpiece to date, and no reader will be disappointed."*

**~ Tyler R. Tichelaar, Ph.D., award-winning author of *Spirit of
the North: a paranormal romance* and *The Best Place***

A native of North Carolina, award-winning author Mary Flinn long ago fell in love with her state's mountains and its coast, creating the backdrops for her series of novels, *The One*, *Second Time's a Charm*, *Three Gifts*, and *A Forever Man*. With degrees from both the University of North Carolina at Greensboro and East Carolina University, Flinn has retired from her first career as a speech pathologist in the NC public schools that began in 1981. Writing a novel had always been a dream for Flinn, who began crafting the pages of *The One*, when her younger daughter left for college at Appalachian State University in 2009. The characters in this book continued to call to her, wanting more of their story told, which bred the next three books in the series.

Flinn has recently been the recipient of the Reader Views Literary Awards 2012 Reviewers' Choice honorable mention in the romance category for *A Forever Man*. First Place Award for Romance Novel in the Reader Views 2011 Literary Book Awards, as well as the Pacific Book Review Best Romance Novel of 2011 went to *Three Gifts*. *Second Time's a Charm*, also released in 2011, won an Honorable Mention in the Reader Views Literary Awards.

Mary Flinn lives in Summerfield, North Carolina with her husband, and near her two adult daughters.

The Nest is her fifth novel.

www.TheOneNovel.com

www.ingramcontent.com/pod-product-compliance
Lightning Source LLC
Chambersburg PA
CBHW031320210726
48287CB00005B/1631